THE KINGS OF HELL
COLE

By Alexis Maree

THE KINGS OF HELL
COLE

Cover by Alexis Maree | Edits by Fluffy Fox Publishing | Proofreading done by Adrianne Normanton
© 2022 by Alexis Maree

CONTENT WARNING

This book contains scenes of dark natures that may trigger some readers – e.g; torture, graphic sexual scenes, and coarse language. Not all possible triggers have been mentioned. By reading further, you, as the reader, are continuing with the understanding that this book has darker tones and that not all possible triggers may have been mentioned. The author and any who contributed to this work cannot and will not be held accountable for a reader's actions, reactions, or state of mind after reading this book.

OTHER BOOKS BY ME

Did you know I write under three different names?
Alexis Maree, T. Maree, and Luna Maree.

ALEXIS MAREE
THE KINGS OF HELL SERIES:
The Kings of Hell - Cole

T. MAREE
THE LEAH REYNOLDS SERIES:
Sins in the Silence
Sins of a Daughter
Sins of the Past
Sins of the Enemy
Sins of the Forbidden
Sins of the Blood

STANDALONES
Falling for the Mountain Man
Colorful

LUNA MAREE

L'Amour Island
Her Sir & Sire

This book is dedicated to my best friends,
Katie & Jemma.
I couldn't have asked for two better people to survive this world with.
Love you both!

~

I'd like to thank Quell T. Fox at *Fluffy Fox Publishing* for giving me a chance in many regards. You've been so helpful and thoughtful, and I love getting my manuscripts back from you and reading your hilarious commentary.

As always, thank you to my family for understanding my need to write and for not making me feel bad about the time I spend sitting at my laptop talking to make-believe characters. I couldn't do this without you.

THE KINGS OF HELL
COLE

ALEXIS MAREE

THE PROPHECY OF THE NINE

From the first to the last, the Brothers Nine will fall...

The first will face death and prevail,
The second shall follow her blood trail.

The third will endure his deal of time,
The fourth need only await his sign.

The fifth will betray his woman of binding,
The sixth will save she he must be finding.

The seventh will take her to keep her safe,
The eighth will have to rely on Faith.

The ninth alone is left to find,
She who was taken, now hidden by design.

From first to the last, the Brothers Nine must fall,
Or chaos reigns, and they will destroy it all.

THE KINGS OF HELL
COLE

Bound to the First

THE KINGS OF HELL
COLE

CHAPTER ONE
COLE

The first time I saw her, I almost killed her. I almost wiped her from the face of the earth with little more than a wave of my hand.

I could have.

I should have.

But I didn't.

Call it a moment of fate or destiny. Call it anything you fucking like. At the end of the day, I didn't realize I was looking at my salvation—or my destruction. I didn't realize that by letting her live, I was setting in motion a chain of events that would forever change my life as I knew it.

I'm gonna back up and explain things a little better here. Let's rewind a few hours.

"Where's the fire?" I called out as my brother, Donovan, or Nova as we called him, stormed past. He threw an exasperated look over his shoulder and I chuckled, having made the same fire joke for centuries. Because you know, we were in Hell.

Hell. Fire.

You get it.

"Got a situation on the surface," Nova replied and continued his storming.

"Okay... so, why the rage?" I demanded, keeping pace easily. A 'situation' on the surface would be a welcome bloody relief to me right now. I was going out of my mind with the tedium and repetitiveness of eternity.

Nova was one of my eight brothers; he ruled the sixth circle of hell. There wasn't a lot of difference between the nine of us.

Well, except for Devlin and Corvin. Devlin was brother number eight, and he had a bit of a temper and tended to make humans nervous just by being around them. But *all* of us were a little unnerved around Corvin, brother number nine. We each had a way of dealing with our eternity ruling over a hell dimension, and we each had a way of keeping tabs on the outside world so that we stayed informed. Not just on what the humans were doing, but to keep an eye on the fucking winged dick-bag Angels. The Hollier-than-thou feathered fucks were so righteous and pretentious, I wanted to strangle each and every one of them with their goddamn halos… if they actually wore the things. Which they didn't.

No, that was another detail humans got wrong. They didn't wear white robes, either I'd never seen one of them playing a harp, and none of them wore halos. Unfortunately for us, they were actually pretty fucking deadly, and were not lacking in the combat department. Of course, that was part of the reason this never-ending war waging between us Demons and the Angels was, well… never ending. We were too evenly matched, so lately we'd been going through a bit of a stalemate.

Anyway, Corvin was the oldest brother and dealt with some pretty messed up souls. It had been over two hundred years since he'd set foot on the surface, and to say we were all a little worried about him was an understatement. And we were Kings of Hell—not a lot disturbed us. But where Corvin was concerned, we each felt like we were sitting on a volcano that was almost ready to erupt, and no one would survive the fall-out.

"Hello?" I prompted Nova when he continued walking without comment.

"I have an overflow of souls at the moment and the fucking Demons in charge of punishing them aren't doing their jobs well enough. Now one of my Knights has thrown out an SOS, and I need to go up there and handle it," Nova explained.

"What kind of SOS?" I asked with a frown. Each of us Kings had a group of Demons we called Knights. They were Demons who rose up the ranks and whose power and ability in a fight were almost unmatched. They had literally been forged in the fires of Hell, put through the worst tortures imaginable and then mastered dolling out those tortures themselves. They were lethal.

We entrusted each Knight with a band of Demons, and any time an Angel was up there causing havoc by spreading around their bullshit about *living closer to the Lord* or *being a servant of the Lord*, we sent up a Knight and a group of Demons to send them scampering.

Like I said, those fuckers were pretentious.

So, for a Knight to be sending out an SOS was pretty serious, which explained my brother's concern.

"I don't know what the problem is, but it sounds like they're outnumbered," Nova explained.

"I'll go," I volunteered. Nova stopped walking and turned to face me; his dark blue eyes confused.

"Why?"

I shrugged. "I'm bored. I swear to Luci, if I don't get some action soon, some near-death experience… if nothing interesting happens, I'm going to toss myself into The Pit and let all those fuckers torture me just to see some variety around here," I told Nova, meaning it. The Pit was where we kept all new souls who were being divided up and tortured.

Awe now, don't be like that. Those shitheads deserved it. We dealt with the dregs of humanity here. Rapists, child molesters, murders, those fuckers who did ten under the speed limit and then sped up in the overtaking lanes so you can't get past them. You know, the real monsters of the world. So don't go getting all sensitive about the torture.

Nova laughed at my statement, but I meant it. I was seriously considering letting the newbies torture me for a little training just so I could do something different.

"Seriously," I added. He shook his head.

"Oh, I believe you. I was laughing at you calling good ole' dad, Luci," he explained. Oh, right. But the guy was retired and had buggered off to parts unknown, so I wasn't worried about a reprimand from Him.

"Okay," Nova added with a shrug.

"Awesome, where are they?" I cheered.

Nova gave me the address to a warehouse in Seattle and I grinned. I loved the warehouse fights; they were usually full-on and bloody.

"Who is your Knight?" I asked.

"Krae. He's one of my better Knights, so if he's calling for help, be prepared," Nova warned. I nodded.

"Thanks, brother. I'll let you know how it goes," I assured. Nova nodded and then waved as he turned around and headed back to his other issue. I let a grin spread across my face as I thought about the fight to come, and the blood in my veins began to hum. Nothing like a little Angel bloodshed to change things up.

I started back down the hallway. To some people who pictured Hell, they probably didn't imagine it looked like this. This wasn't exactly Hell, though. This was more like the visitors' waiting room. We had polished black marble floors and walls in a long hallway. Along the hallway were four red doors on either side and one right at the end. Each door led to a circle of Hell. Each door would only open for the King whose quarters it guarded. I strode through mine which led me to my personal quarters. I hurried to where I stored my weapons. Now I know most people would expect me to have a room *full* of weapons, but I didn't. It just wasn't necessary. I had a bow with a quiver that never ran out of arrows—arrows that were tipped with the same metal used for a Demon Blade which was the only thing capable of killing an Angel. I had two rows of blades, different sizes and shapes depending on what I needed them for, an axe that I had spent hundreds of hours using hellfire to carve intricate designs into, then I had three swords, again, different ones for different needs. But otherwise, that ended my weapons cache.

Grabbing two blades and my axe, I started back out the door, ready for the fight to come.

In hindsight, I probably should have heeded my brother's warning to be prepared a little more closely. But I was bored, and unless I was stupid enough to get stabbed with an Angel Blade, I didn't have a whole hell of a lot to fear from the fight ahead.

Turns out—I got fucking stabbed.

Angel Blades have the same effect on Demons that Demon Blades have on Angels. They not only hurt like a mother fucker, but they take their time killing you. Once upon a time, there were Witches capable of healing this kind of wound, but someone got wise at some point and decided to start collecting Witches as their own personal healing army, so then both sides went on a literal Witch Hunt, each scouring the earth to gather more Witches than the other side. Fools that we all were, we hunted them into extinction. Our view on time was vastly different to humans. A hundred years to us was a long weekend, and we sometimes forgot there was a large discrepancy between us and them. Witches were human, they lived normal human lifespans. So, while we were all so busy collecting them and hiding them away, they were all dying off and not reproducing. Now there were no more Witches.

The only other thing that could cure a wound from an Angel Blade, was the blood of the Angel it belonged to. Since I wasn't holding my breath for the Angel in question to suddenly grow a heart and lend me a little O-neg, I was sitting in the dank, now blessedly silent warehouse, contemplating my end.

It had never really occurred to me to do so before. As you could imagine, as a King of Hell, I'd never really had a reason to suffer from an existential crisis. But it was kinda nice to know there were still some firsts for me after all these years. Or in this case, a first and unfortunately one of the last things I'd ever do.

Still, the thought of dying didn't bother me as much as I thought it would. I'd lived eons; longer than I cared to remember. I'd been witness to things humans would never dream of seeing. I'd watched Kingdom's form and crumble, watched the ages of humanity take over the lands and destroy everything they should have valued, and I watched their greed and violence taint what was supposed to be pure.

No, I wasn't suddenly reconsidering the way I lived my life. I was born and bred for one purpose, and one purpose only, and that was to lead legions in Hell, torture the damned, and create Demons strong enough to keep the balance between us and Angels. Sure, my brothers might notice my absence and perhaps might even regret my death, but there wasn't a lot left here that would suffer without me. Someone else would take my place as King—I think—or maybe that circle of hell would simply close up and all the souls would be spread out amongst my brothers, my Demons and Knights divided among them. I wasn't exactly sure as none of my brothers, no King of Hell, had ever died before.

"Fuck," I hissed as I pressed my hand harder into my side where the blade had sunk. The fucker had twisted it as he removed it, going for maximum damage. I was in pain, yes, but I knew none of it showed on my face. I couldn't remember the last time I'd allowed such a display to occur. Hell wasn't a place you wanted to have a weakness, and so one learned quickly to hide any and all vulnerabilities and weak spots. Up until this moment, I hadn't thought there was a single thing left that could cause me pain. That was of course because I'd never been stuck by a fucking Angel Blade before. Oh look, another first! I'd been alive this long, waged many-a-war with the fluffy fairies, and had never had to deal with this.

I glanced over the death and carnage spread out before me and sighed.

Humans were not allowed to know of us, and this was one rule both sides seemed to whole-heartedly agree on. You see, the Demons I created, the lower-level Angels that were made, all came from Human souls depending on how they lived their lives. If humans knew for sure about the existence of Angels, they'd strive to be better and give that side a higher advantage, and those who couldn't be fucked or didn't wanna spend eternity floating around like a pretentious douche-bag, would act up as badly as possible in order to work their way up the ranks of Demon as quickly as possible.

I hadn't even seen the dick who stabbed me. How fucked was

that?

There I'd been, swimming into the fray of Demons and Angels, blades swinging and blood spurting. The shithead must have snuck up behind me. Typical Angel—stabbed me while my back was turned. From what I could see, none of Nova's Demons had made it out alive, and only the Angel who had stabbed me was likely to have escaped.

I sighed. I wondered how long it would take to die. What happened after I died? For humans, their souls went to either Heaven or Hell based on what their final score was. Where else was a King of Hell's soul meant to go? As far up the food chain as I was, I still wasn't privy to the grand plans of The Big Guy. I didn't know what the meaning of life was or why we were all ultimately here. I was pretty sure He was just bored one day and started playing with his toys and then forgot to pack them up. But other than that, I wasn't sure what was going to happen.

Pain leached further into my bones, and I shuffled down onto the abandoned crates, wondering what I should do. I could call out to my brothers; we all had a connection in our minds we could use. But what would be the point? They'd all feel it when I died, I was almost certain of it. What would calling them here to me now do? Judging by the increasing amount of pain I was in, it wouldn't be long before I was a goner. So, it wasn't like they could do anything to help, like track down the Angel responsible. Calling them here to watch me die didn't sit so well with me. I mean, we weren't exactly the most touchy-feely of families, but we were all each other had over the centuries. There was a bond that could not be broken.

Besides, what was there to say? Sorry I'm dying, have fun taking on my workload? Nah—it was better this way.

I closed my eyes as pain burned through me again, and it was then that I felt a presence.

A human.

I cloaked myself in the surrounding shadows and waited as I felt her approach. I knew it was a woman; men and women carried a different signature with their presence. I frowned as I paid attention to her. There was something else to this woman, something *more*.

I could hear her now—her shuffled and timid footsteps. She was cautious, which led me to believe that she knew what she was walking into, or at least had an idea. Still and silent, I watched as her shadow appeared first in the doorway. I heard her sharp intake of breath before she appeared. Tiny, a waif of a thing, she couldn't have been more than five-foot-two.

"Angels," she whispered, and I could hear the regret and sadness in her voice as she crouched down to touch the nearest one. She closed her eyes and I frowned. How the Hell did she even know about us? She was human. Despite the something *more* I could feel, she was totally and utterly human. I raised my hand, dragging in a breath and preparing for her death. It wasn't exactly a loss, but I took note of the fact that killing this woman for knowing more than she ought to was going to be one of my final acts on this Earth.

Her head snapped up and she looked in my direction and I froze. I was wrapped in shadows, there was no way she could see me. "Oh," she uttered in surprise and stood up, her wide eyes—a stunning, vibrant green—narrowed on me. Not a single muscle in my body moved. And my pain, as all-consuming as it had been only seconds ago, was suddenly forgotten.

How could she see me?

"Are you okay? I-I didn't see you there," she called out, her voice wavering slightly. I kept my eyes on the human before me and spread my other senses out far and wide, suspicion weighing heavily on me. Was this a ploy? Had Angels gotten to her and brought her here to distract me so that they could finish the job? Or perhaps they were going to heal me and attempt to keep me prisoner? They had tried such a thing with Nova over a hundred years ago. Or maybe it was another Demon? Just because I was a King of Hell didn't mean there weren't those who tried to take my throne. We were Demons—none of us were to be trusted.

"Do you need help?" she asked again, carefully sidestepping celestial innards. I frowned. I could sense no other being nearby. Humans were several blocks away, the odd animal here and there, but nothing to be concerned about. So, what the hell was going on?

"My name is Mika. Well, Tomika, but everyone calls me Mika," she explained.

"How can you see me?" I asked, forcing a command into my voice. She froze for a moment, her large eyes wide. I watched as she visibly swallowed hard, and her shoulders straightened as if she were steeling herself.

"I-I've always been able to see your kind. Angels and Demons, I mean. I've never met anyone else who could, but I've always seen," she answered and stepped closer. How? I was concealing myself from human eyes, there was no possible way she could have seen me or sensed me. I narrowed my senses in on her, trying to ferret out what that other quality I'd sensed in her had been.

"Are you hurt? I mean, I know you're hurt. I could feel your pain from outside, but you're not showing any signs that you're in pain," the woman who called herself Mika asked as she edged closer, now clear from the blood and gore near the entrance. I kept my mouth shut as she shuffled nearer, her large eyes skimming over me, looking for injuries.

I took a harder look at her, trying to see past her human features. She was attractive in that respect, if not a little odd looking. Her eyes were too large for her heart-shaped face, bright and green, but they were framed with long, thick lashes. Her skin was sun-kissed, as if she often spent a lot of time in the sun. From what I could tell, her hair was raven-black, shimmers of blue shining in the pale moonlight and fanned out around her face and rested about her shoulder blades. She was tiny, everything about her was small and petite, and yet she was slightly curvy.

I dug deeper, trying to learn what I could as she stepped ever closer, but I was still only picking up signs that she was human. "How?" I asked. She froze and frowned. "How could you feel my pain?" I rephrased. Understanding cleared her features and she gave a small shrug before coming to stand properly in front of me.

"It's a gift I've had all my life... among a few others. Will you let me look at your injuries? I might be able to help," she offered. Frowning again, I decided to let her closer. Hey, if she was there to finish the job the Angel Blade was eventually going to do anyway, who was I to deny her hastening the process? And if she was there to lure me into a trap, there was no torture the Angels could perform that would break me and allow for them to gain any useful information. But if she *was* there to trap me for the Angels, I would take great pleasure in ripping her heart from her chest before they did. No one could ever accuse me of being one to lay down and take whatever anyone else dished out.

Slowly, she reached out with small hands and tugged my jacket aside, her gaze intense and focused as if she already knew where my worst injury was.

She gasped and dropped her hand for a moment, as if the wound had burned her.

"How can you be so calm when you're in so much pain?" she gaped, her green eyes shimmering with tears. An uncomfortable knot formed in my stomach at those tears, along with a whole hell of a lot of questions. Who the hell was this woman? Why did her tears affect me? When was the last time anyone had shown any real concern for me, much less this level of concern for my pain? I wasn't sure anyone had ever cried for me.

"I can ignore it," I found myself answering. Her wide eyes squeezed shut for a moment and before I could stop myself, I reached out to capture the small tear drop that had fallen from her eyes. She gasped at my contact and my chest restricted almost painfully at the feel of her warm, smooth skin, at the fire that lanced through me at that merest touch.

I slowly brought my hand back and closed my fingers over the shimmering teardrop. Closing my eyes, I focused my energy on my palm, and when I opened it again, a small, shimmering diamond was in my hand. She made a sound of surprise, and I watched as she shook her head, a small smile tilting the corners of her lips.

"I've never seen one of you do that before," she said, her eyes jumping back to my face.

"It's unique to my kind," I explained, referring to me and my brothers. I wondered if she knew of the hierarchy of Demons or the different breeds. Her smile grew slightly, and she shook her head and looked back to my side.

"Will you let me help you?" she asked. I cocked an eyebrow and slipped the diamond into my pocket.

"How?"

"I… I have a gift. I promise it won't hurt. But I can take away your pain. Will you let me?" she asked.

Curious as to what she meant, I neither agreed nor disagreed. I sat still as she shuffled closer again and she lifted my shirt from my side that was now soaked with blood. I watched her face intensely, caught her small grimace and I found myself eager to puzzle her out.

Nothing and no one had surprised me in a *long* time. And when I say a long time, I mean it was back when man had figured out how to make fire.

Her eyes ran over my body again, and I watched as she zeroed in on every little injury. Although, how she knew they were there, I could not tell. My shirt was still on, and yet I felt her gaze on every wound like a brand.

"Just… don't freak out. And don't tell anyone you saw me do this, okay?" she asked. "I really don't want to end up on some doctor's table being poked and prodded for experiments," she muttered, almost to herself.

Again, I gave no indication either way, and she heaved a sigh before she closed her eyes and slid her hand across my ribs to where the knife-wound was.

And then it happened.

Light and searing heat radiated from her hand to my body, and I jolted in surprise. She didn't move though, and I gaped down at her, stunned.

A Witch.

She was an honest to Lucifer, living, breathing, Witch. She frowned, her face full of concentration as her other hand slid to the other side of my torso and she began healing the more minor wounds with that hand.

How? How the fuck was this woman here? How did no one know about her? How was she walking around free? Why was she so willing to out herself to me? She knew what I was, that much was obvious. So, how did she not know that by revealing herself to me, she was effectively signing away her freedom? Because there was not a chance in hell that I was letting her go now.

Mine.

The word rose up in my mind like a tsunami, an overwhelming urge inside me roaring to the point that I was unable to ignore it. I didn't understand it or what it meant, only that I had to do *something*.

Acting on nothing but pure instinct, an instinct as old as time, I reached into her mind, surprised momentarily by her natural resistance but forced my way further in. Once there, I found her thoughts and impressions of me. She'd noticed my looks; she thought me attractive and had even had a powerful physical response. I could use that—I *had* to use that. Whatever this feeling was, it wasn't going away, and I needed all the help I could get. Because no matter what happened next, this woman, this Witch, was mine. I would make sure of that in any way I had to in order to keep her with me. I fed that part of her that found me alluring, enticed her to keep thinking that way, to build up the need to see me, to feel me, to want me. I fanned the flames of desire, feeling not the least bit of guilt. The base emotions and responses were already there, I was just capitalizing on it.

"What are you doing?" she whispered, but there was a small pant in her voice now. I watched her as her cheeks pinkened, and her chest rose and fell more rapidly as her body reacted to me. I didn't answer and slowly withdrew from her mind. That was enough.

I could feel the pain in my own body receding, and to my utter astonishment, I was almost entirely healed once more. There was no more contamination from the Angel Blade, no more pain. And just like that, the wound was healed.

Her eyes fluttered open, and before she could do more than part her lips to speak, I acted on instinct. Gripping her by the back of the neck as my palm suddenly burned white-hot, I hauled her forward between my legs and brought my lips crashing down on hers.

CHAPTER TWO
MIKA

How did I get myself into these situations?

I'd been out looking for the culprit responsible for the number of ritualistic killings over the last several months. All the victims had been children or young women who did nothing but give and sacrifice for the good of others. No, I wasn't a cop, and no, I wasn't a PI. To the government, I was a freelance journalist. But being born with supernatural abilities and a gift to see beings no other humans seemed to be able to see, I took my job seriously to help find the culprits to murders and disappearances the regular human police would never be able to solve. I knew there was more out there, creatures who went bump in the night, beings like Angels and Demons. But no one else seemed to know, and if they did, they were doing a piss-poor job of taking care of the problem.

I'd wandered over this way, following my internal alarm that got louder and louder the closer I got to the warehouse. The burning in my very soul told me someone was in pain, and it had been impossible to ignore as it always was when it came to these celestial beings and their eternal enemies. I'd been close enough to hear the ruckus and had chosen to stay back until it quieted down. I was gifted, yes, but I'd seen Angels and Demons fight before, and no way in hell did I stand a chance of surviving a fight with either of those beings.

After the noise had stopped, I could still feel that pain emanating from within the building, and knew I had to do something. One of them still had to be alive, so I had a chance to save them if I hurried.

What I hadn't expected was to see the eyes of a Demon, burning at me intensely from the other side of the warehouse, or feel a compulsion unlike any other to heal him and save him. He was a Demon—the world could probably do with a lot less of them— but I also knew from experience that ignoring the call to heal would leave me in pain until I'd done my duty, or the being died. Now here I was, pressed against the dark and seductive Demon I'd healed, his hot hands on my body and his soft lips devouring mine. And did I put up even a small fight? To my own disappointment… no, I did not.

A sharp blade of ice seemed to pierce the back of my neck as he kissed me, using his hand there to drag me closer to him. This was quickly followed by a firestorm of heat that relentlessly lashed through every part of my body. Every cell inside me reacted to the kiss, dormant parts of me woke up and screamed with a vengeance to get closer, to feel more. His tongue slipped between my lips, and I moaned, allowing him access when on some level, I knew this was wrong. He was a Demon, and one would think that between Angels and Demons, I'd have the state of mind to stay clear away from his kind. But that wasn't how this *gift* worked. I felt pain, I had to do something about it. The pull to heal wasn't as strong for regular humans, but for Angels and Demons, it was like my soul was on fire unless I acted and did something about it. It didn't seem to matter for which side, only that I healed who I could.

I was being dragged under in a tide of desire and heat. I'd known I was in trouble the second I saw him. I'd never met a Demon with eyes that literally glowed with the fires of Hell. But when I blinked, the fire was gone, and I was left staring at eyes so dark they were practically black. And oh boy, I hadn't realized Demons were allowed to be so sinfully sexy. His voice was a dark seduction, whispering of pleasures and temptations I would never experience anywhere else.

His hands gripped my hips and hauled me against him so that I could feel the long, hard length of him pressing against me, and I'll admit, my knees trembled a little. I mean, if kissing him could reduce me to a puddle of need and want, what would *more* do? I ran my hands up his impressively built biceps, my lower abdomen flipping wildly at how defined they were. This girl had a thing for biceps—it was a weakness of mine.

His kiss became more demanding, more needy and I accepted every bit of it, batting back the sane part of my mind that tried to remind me that I needed to get away from him *now*. I didn't want to. I'd never experienced a kiss so heady, so enticing and alluring, and I was desperate for more. Every part of me was aching now, and it took a moment for my mind to register that it wasn't just aching with pleasure. One of his hands brushed my side and I tore away from him with a cry of pain, reality crashing back down on me.

"Tomika?" he asked, and I wanted to smile at how foreign my name sounded in his voice, but the pain that was suddenly racking my body crashed over me again, dropping me to my knees. He was there in an instant, his hands surprisingly gentle as he laid me back on the ground to look me over. I watched his eyes drift over me and freeze at my waist. I could feel the thick stickiness there, so I could only imagine that he'd seen the blood. He yanked my shirt back to reveal the knife wound I'd absorbed from him.

"What the fuck?" he growled, and those flames were back in his eyes. "Tomika, what the fuck?"

"I-I take the injuries of others onto myself. It's how I heal them," I explained as another wave of pain crashed over me and my back arched, a scream working its way up my throat. How the hell had he managed to sit there so quietly and seemingly unhurt if this was what he'd been experiencing? It was like nothing I'd ever felt before, a powerful, ripping sensation through my abdomen was working its way up my body, as if each wave tore a deeper and larger hole inside me.

"You took the fucking wound of an Angel Blade onto yourself? You're human, you'll die," he snapped. A trickle of fear worked its way down my spine at hearing that, but it was soon washed away as another bone aching pain tore through me. My body stiffened and contorted on its own, my scream burning its way up my throat and almost deafening me. Tears tracked uselessly from my eyes and down my temples, and I began to honestly fear for my life. No matter the injury I'd taken on before, it had never killed me, not even when it would have killed the person I was healing. But this time... I wasn't sure I'd be so lucky.

"Fuck!" he roared, and then I was being lifted into his arms. I braced, expecting more pain at being moved, but nothing came. My body seemed to be at its limit to the kind of pain it could experience, and I didn't feel anything as he pulled me close to his chest.

"I-I'll heal," I stammered, sudden exhaustion trying to drag me under.

"How?" he demanded. My eyes fluttered and I struggled to stay awake.

"I always do. I take on the injuries of those around me, and then I sleep, and my body heals," I explained. The effort it took to do so was astounding. He stopped and I forced my eyes open to look at him. He was watching me with wide, almost panicked eyes. I didn't realize Demons could look like that or even experience panic. And this one... there was something more to this one, and I had a nagging suspicion he didn't care much for anyone but himself. So why was he looking at me like that?

"How do you know this won't kill you?" he demanded, his breathing labored. But I knew it wasn't from carrying me, Demons were ridiculously strong and there was no way he was tired yet.

"It never has before," I answered and worked my mouth to try and wet it as darkness tried to take me again.

"Just take me home. I'll sleep and live. You'll see," I murmured.

"Tomika," he growled, but I could feel that wave building inside me again. I clutched his shirt and my eyes opened wide, panic flooding me. I really didn't want to feel this anymore.

"Just take me home. Please... I'll be okay. Home," I begged, and I felt more tears track down my cheeks as that wave built and built inside me. The pain was no longer a feeling, but a living breathing entity that encompassed every part of me.

I *was* pain.

Tomika Johnson no longer existed, just this blinding, blistering, never-ending pain that now possessed my body.

I could hear the Demon calling my name, I knew we were moving, but then pain took me and there was nothing but darkness.

~

Awareness pricked at my consciousness, and I tried to slip back into sleep. But I couldn't. Along with my gift to heal, was my gift of being able to sense others. And I was most definitely *not* alone. The presence in the room with me was so powerful, so all-encompassing that I knew before I even opened my eyes who—or rather what—it was.

The Demon.

He was still here. But where was here? And how long had I been out for? I tried to feel around me without opening my eyes or moving. I was somewhere soft, and there was the sound of wind chimes I knew only too well.

I was home, in my own bed. Somehow, he'd managed to find where I lived and brought me back here, just as I'd asked. I did an internal check, trying to feel where I still hurt. But other than a lingering ache that always seemed to be present after I healed someone with such grave injuries, I was as good as new.

"I have things to do, so if you would stop pretending to sleep, that would be great," a deep voice rumbled.

Asshole.

Frowning, I gently opened my eyes, waiting to see if a blinding pain would accompany it, but relaxed when nothing else happened. I slowly raised my arms and checked myself over. I knew the worst injury had been his stab wound, but there had been several other cuts and slices he'd sustained which I had taken on as well. But my skin was as smooth and soft as always, not a single blemish left over from his injuries.

"What the hell was that the other night?" he demanded.

"The other night?" I asked, my eyes opening wider. "How long have I been out for?"

I'd never needed more than twelve hours to recover.

He didn't answer, so I slowly pulled myself up into a sitting position. The blanket fell from me, and I gasped and yanked it back up, realizing I was in nothing but my bra and panties.

"You undressed me?" I demanded in shock.

He smirked, and I'm ashamed to admit that it did something to me. The guy wore sex and sin like it was a second skin. He was sitting in a seat against my far wall, his long legs stretched out in front of him, and his thick, tattooed arms crossed over his impressive chest. His dark eyes no longer held any hellish flames, but they were intense and smoldering, and staring at me with an intensity that made me antsy.

"I needed to see if your wound was healing," he justified. I glared.

"You couldn't have done that by lifting my shirt when you wanted to check?" I argued.

He shrugged a shoulder, unrepentant.

"How long have I been out for?"

His dark eyes regarded me intently, but I refused to squirm.

"Two days."

"*Two days?*" I repeated in shock.

"What the hell were you thinking?" he snapped suddenly. "If you knew that healing me would mean taking those injuries onto yourself, why the fuck did you do it?"

I clenched my jaw at the reprimand, gripping the blanket tighter in my hands.

"I don't need to justify myself or my actions to you. A simple *thank you* for saving your life would suffice," I retorted hotly.

"Since I had to carry your unconscious ass back home to make sure you weren't left alone in a warehouse full of Demon and Angel remains, I think I deserve an explanation," he replied somewhat calmly, but I wasn't fooled by his attempt at civility.

"I should have realized I'd get nothing but trouble by healing a Demon. I should have kept walking, but no, I had to go and let your pain influence my decision," I grumbled, crossing my arms over my stomach while I glared at him. Slowly, he leaned forward to rest his forearms on his knees, and damn, if that one graceful move of rippling muscles wasn't sexy as hell.

"Do you have any idea what you are?" he asked in a much quieter voice, but I had the sudden impression that he was a rather large jungle cat, and I was his prey trapped in a corner. He was just playing with me first. I swallowed hard as the feeling increased, and I wondered how I could escape my room before he could get me. He was fast, he was powerful, but I had a few tricks up my sleeve I was sure he didn't know about. Danger seemed to press down on me, and the feeling there was a noose around my neck slowly tightening had me steeling myself for an attack.

"I'm a human," I answered, but in the back of my mind I was gathering power and planning my escape. I had no idea where I'd go or how I could hide for long, but like hell I was going to let whatever was about to happen, happen without kicking up one heck of a fight.

"You're not technically wrong, but that's not all you are. Do you know?" he asked.

I frowned. I was human, I knew that. I also knew I could do things other humans couldn't and had learned early on *not* to let people know about my abilities. But I'd never once been told I was something more.

"You're a Witch," he stated blandly.

I froze. The idea had occurred to me, but I'd never found any legitimate Witches before. The ones I'd found were all New Age Witches without a lick of *actual* power, just a bunch of crystals and incense. I'd never found a spell in one of those books to actually work, never found "moon water" to be anything more than plain old water.

"Witches aren't real," I responded finally. He shook his head and smiled.

"Until last night, I, along with every other Angel and Demon, knew Witches to be extinct," he explained. I didn't move, hardly dared to breathe. Because despite what I'd found, or rather lack thereof, I always knew I was more than just a human with special abilities. And to have a name for myself was a soothing balm on an ache I'd always lived with.

"Why?" I barely managed to whisper, trying not to hope but it was too late. "Why were we thought to be extinct?"

"Witches are healers. You are of the Earth. Angels and Demons have been at war since the very beginning. Your kind were put here to even the playing field, to heal us and others," he answered.

"Then why are my kind extinct?" I repeated. He didn't look like he was going to answer me, and I glowered. His lips twitched as if he found it funny, but thankfully he continued.

"Some time ago, someone got wise and started collecting Witches as their personal healer army and to prevent as many Witches as possible from healing the opposite side. A literal Witch-Hunt began. Witches are powerful, yes, but still mortal. Somewhere along the line, you stopped producing the next generation of Witches—or so we thought."

"So, you and the Angels are to blame for me never knowing who or what I was? You're to blame for me never knowing another person who is like me?" I demanded.

His face was impossible to read, and I found myself wanting to throw something at it.

"I guess you could put it like that," he finally answered.

Tossing back my covers, I moved quickly to my dresser where I pulled on a pair of soft cotton shorts and a tank top before I whirled around to face him. His eyes were raking over my body slowly, and I squelched the part of me that noted the heat in his eyes. Demons were bad—and this one had just admitted that he and his kind were responsible for my life being so utterly lonely and desolate. Anxiety pricked my mind when I realized he'd mentioned Demons and Angels had actively *hunted* my kind before. I wasn't going to forget that point anytime soon.

"You need to leave," I decided suddenly, crossing my arms over my stomach.

He smirked again and cocked an eyebrow.

"Oh?" But even as he said it, he settled back in his seat, amusement alight in his eyes.

"Yes. Thank you for bringing me back home. I saved your life, you saved me from…well, waking up somewhere gross. So, let's call it even," I suggested.

"If only it were that simple." He exhaled heavily, but he didn't look in the least displeased.

"Why wouldn't it be so simple?" I asked.

"Because you're a Witch," he answered plainly. I waited for him to elaborate, and when he didn't, I huffed and threw my arms up in exasperation.

"So?"

"So, you're an endangered species. It's a miracle you haven't been discovered before now, but it will only be a matter of time before someone else finds out what you are and they steal you away. I'm not letting the Halo Huggers get their hands on you, so you're stuck with me," he answered.

Halo Huggers?

"How would they find me?" I demanded, ignoring his insult to the Angels.

"Because a Witch cannot help but heal. So, in the next fight, you're going to go out and do your thing because you can't help it, and healing others soothes that burning in your soul that *demands* you heal. When you go out and do your thing, you're going to be revealing what you are, and those guys will swoop down and take you away before you can blink," he assured. I squinted at him in disbelief, and he shrugged.

"Look, I appreciate your concern, but this war between you and them has nothing to do with me. I'm not a pawn in anyone's game, and I refuse to be a collector's item. I'm not something you own; I'm not something you claim. I am a person, pure and simple. So, thanks for your 'concern,'" I began, making sarcastic quotation marks with my fingers, "but I'll take care of myself from here on out."

The Demon slowly got to his feet, and I felt my eyes widen. Sitting down, I could tell that he was tall, but I hadn't been able to see just *how* tall until he was towering over me, taking up far too much room, like he was now. My bedroom had never felt small until this moment. The guy was a veritable giant.

"That's where you're wrong," he argued, his voice deep and smooth and I felt my skin prickle. He stepped closer and I backed up but found myself hitting the wall. He stalked closer; those dark eyes narrowed on me. I didn't scare easily, but damn did this guy make me worried.

"H-How?" I stammered.

The corners of his lips turned up again, and he glided closer until he was leaning down towards me, coming so close that his nose brushed the edges of my jaw. He slowly slid his hands over my hips, and I inwardly screamed at myself to move, to push him away, to do *something!* But I was useless, struck dumb by the sheer sensuality he wielded like a weapon. Every move he made was fluid and graceful, precise. But there was a deadly quality to every movement that reminded me I was dealing with something a whole hell of a lot more powerful than me.

"I've already claimed you," he whispered, his breath warm on my neck.

My eyes rolled back, and I tilted my head back, helpless. Damn, I wanted to feel his lips on mine again. Desire and need flooded through me, my skin was tight and uncomfortable, and my clothes were super itchy against my suddenly sensitive skin. I opened my eyes halfway, my heart thudding harder as he brushed his lips across my jaw, aligning his body with mine.

"You're mine, little witch. And I protect what is mine," he murmured, his voice almost a growl in my ear. Sense and reason tried to push into my mind, and I struggled for a moment, knowing I needed to listen to them, but it was so hard when my body felt heavy and in need of something only this Devil in disguise could give me.

"You're coming with me," he added. The desire I'd been feeling only seconds ago halted with a brain-jarring screech.

"Uh, what?"

He pulled back slightly to look down at me. "You are coming with me. You're mine now," he answered as if it were that simple.

"No, I'm not," I replied, sliding my hands up to his chest so that I could push him away.

Nothing. He didn't even rock slightly.

"I have claimed you as mine. I'm not leaving you around for someone else to pick up and play with you. You're coming back to my dimension with me," he explained.

"You can go back to Hell all on your own, buddy. I'm not going anywhere," I snapped, shoving him harder. He took a slow step back, and I was annoyed when it was obvious that he did it as a courtesy and not because my strength had forced him backwards. "I am *not* a toy!" I shouted, outraged. "I am not a tool or a weapon for you to use. I am a person," I argued.

"A person who is now the property of a King of Hell," he added. I stilled, a sudden chill washing over me at his words. A King of... woah.

Nuh-uh.

No way.

Had I really healed a King of Hell?

"I'm sorry, you're a what?" I asked with a hiss, genuinely hoping for the first time in my life that I was going insane and hearing things incorrectly.

"I am a King of Hell. I have staked my claim on you, so you will accompany me back to my realm where I can keep you hidden and safe from others," he continued, looking bored now.

"You can go fuck yourself and your claims!" I denied, beginning to panic now. His glittering obsidian eyes narrowed on me and he stepped in close again, the air around us taking on a sudden menacing feeling.

"You do not know me, so you won't know this yet, but I do not make a habit of explaining or repeating myself. I have been lenient on both counts, I will not continue to argue a moot point," he replied, his voice a whip of command, his features darkening with impatience. I opened my mouth to argue some more and tell him what the hell he could do with his demands, when he made a sound of impatience and yanked me hard against him. I inhaled sharply as he kept me pressed tightly to his chest, and then darkness enveloped us. I could feel wind rushing around me, tugging at my hair and clothes, yanking the oxygen from my lungs. My eyes watered slightly, and I felt dizzier than I'd ever been before.

And then suddenly it all stopped.

I gasped, trying to pull air back into my lungs. I closed my stinging eyes and staggered away from him when he released me, trying to get my head to stop spinning.

"The first time you travel by shadow can be disorienting. It'll wear off quickly," he explained. I opened my eyes, glad to see that the room had stopped spinning, and glared.

"And where the heck are we?"

He smirked. "Hell, of course."

CHAPTER THREE
COLE

My little Witch had fire.

That was good to know, and it also made things a lot more interesting. The last thing I wanted to do was deal with a weepy, frightened mess of a woman. It was nice to know she'd bite back and arc up whenever she felt unjustly done by. Not that it would do her any good when it came to me, but if it kept the tears and the pleading away, I was all for it.

I watched, half amused, half bored as Mika ran her hands over the smooth surfaces of the room we were in. She was desperately looking for a door, a way out. There wasn't one, and I'd told her as much, but she wasn't about to listen to me, so I just leaned back against the polished marble wall, crossed my arms over my chest, and watched her.

She had a fierce frown on her face, her intensely bright green eyes searching every crevice and mark in the hopes that it was an opening. This room was completely sealed, and the only options were to travel by shadow, which she could not do, or to walk through one of the nine doors that lead to each circle of Hell. And she couldn't enter any of those either unless she was escorted by whom it belonged to.

Since she wasn't about to accept any invitation of mine to enter into my realm, I was giving her a little time to come to grips with her new situation. Honestly, I was getting bored, but she was amusing to watch, and hearing her whispered curses under her breath and the creative way she paired insults about me with those words had me biting back a grin. I hadn't met a human in… well… I wasn't sure I'd ever met a human who made me want to smile like she did.

She was such a little firecracker.

She was of a smaller build, but her hips curved deliciously, giving emphasis to the dip of her tucked in waist and roundness of her breasts. Her legs were short, but gave the impression of length due to how shapely they were. And that ass? I'd always thought of myself as a breast man, but this woman had a serious ass that my hands itched to palm.

Mika glowered over her shoulder at me for the umpteenth time, as if she could read my thoughts. That was impossible, but she was a Witch, which meant she could probably pick up on my emotions. Although, there was that new mind-link I had discovered between us this morning which could make things a little more interesting...

"Are you done looking yet?" I asked.

"There has to be a way out," she snapped, bending over to run her hands along the length of the floor. I tipped my head sideways as it gave me a perfect view of that delectable ass.

"You're free to keep looking," I murmured and was so far in my fantasy land of bending her over a table that I didn't realize she's straightened and was glaring daggers at me. "What?"

"Stop staring at my ass. It's not going to happen, Hell Boy," she lashed out.

I grinned.

"Never say never, my little Witch," I returned.

"Mika—I have a name. Stop calling me yours," she argued, crossing her arms under her breasts, unintentionally pushing them up. My gaze dipped and I swallowed when I felt my mouth water. What the *fuck*? Since when was I ever as physically affected by someone as I was with her?

Stalking forward, I brought my attention back to her face and watched as trepidation flickered in her stunning eyes.

"You *are* mine, little Witch. I found you; I get to keep you," I explained, stepping close, crowding her.

"I don't belong to *anyone*," she hissed, her eyes darkening with anger. A thrill shot down my spine at the fire she was capable of, and I smirked.

"It will make your life a lot easier if you simply accept the fact rather than fighting against it. But if it makes you feel better— fight. I like all that fire," I explained. Her eyes widened slightly, and I didn't have to be as close as I was to see her swallow hard, and her breath hitch slightly. Fuck, she wanted me.

"*Fuck you*," she snarled, and the amount of energy she threw behind her words hit me hard in the chest.

"You're welcome to. Anytime," I replied, leaning forward, edging into her space and backing her against the wall, allowing my desire for her to show. I braced a hand beside her head and slid the other to her hip. I could hear her heart pounding hard in her chest. I could taste the sweet hint of desire from her body, and I wanted nothing more than to devour her on the spot. Brushing her mind gently, I caught glimpses of what she was thinking and groaned audibly. Scenes where I took her hard against the polished wall slid into my head, my teeth on her shoulder, my fingers tangled hard in her hair, my hand at her throat, and my body sliding in and out of hers, hard and fast.

"Admit it," I demanded in a low voice, struggling to get my raging body back under control. "You want me."

And I wanted her. I had no idea why, or why this much. I couldn't even explain what that intense need had been back in the warehouse to make her mine. After dragging her in for a kiss to rock both our worlds, my palm had burned hot, and it hadn't been until I'd pulled it away that it had lessened to an irritable itch that only seemed to arc up when I was thinking lusty thoughts about her. Which had been often.

Whatever this was between us, it was potent, it was spreading like wildfire, and it was undeniable. I leaned in closer, her scent messing with my head, her warmth pulling me nearer.

I was an inch from kissing her when her eyes shot fully open, burning emerald at me. I had a moment to brace when her palms came up and hit me square in the chest, power rushing from her hands to slam hard into me. The force sent me backwards, skidding along the smooth marble floors until my back hit the opposite wall. I was back on my feet in a second, glaring, striding toward her. She was standing tall, refusing to shrink back even when I lowered my guards enough that I knew she could feel the force of my anger hammering down on her.

"What is going on here?" an amused voice drawled. I stopped mid-stride and watched as she spun to face the voice, her eyes widening. She backed up slightly to keep us both within her line of sight.

"Fuck off, Nova," I snarled, my eyes still on the Witch.

"Not likely. Where the hell have you been? You went up to the surface to handle a minor Angel problem, and then there was nothing but radio silence. All my Demons are dead, except for my Knight, but he's MIA," Nova insisted.

"I thought they were all dead; I didn't notice your Knight missing," I replied quickly as he strode down the hallway towards me.

"How? Did you even look?" Nova demanded, looking pissed.

"I was a little preoccupied."

Nova cocked an eyebrow at me and then let his gaze slide to Mika behind me.

"Why is there a human here?" he inquired as he considered Mika, his eyes curious. And then he froze, and realization dawned. There was enough of her power still in the air that he could not fail to notice it. His blue eyes swung towards me in utter confusion and amazement.

"How?"

I dragged in a deep breath and put a lid on my anger. I loved my brothers, but I wasn't about to let any of them near Mika. She was *mine!*

"Found her on the surface," I ground out, striding forward to cut off my brother's approach. He pulled up short and looked from Mika to me and back again.

"She's a Witch," he stated unnecessarily.

"Yes. She healed me."

"When?"

"I got stabbed with an Angel Blade during that fight. Mika was drawn to the fight because of my pain, and she found me and healed me," I answered, not at all happy to have to explain myself to my brother. None of us were considered on a higher level of a hierarchy than each other, and I detested that he demanded answers right now.

His face screwed up in concentration for a moment as he studied Mika closely.

"I'm fine, by the way," I muttered, trying to draw his attention from her.

"You look familiar," he murmured, almost absentmindedly, not bothering to answer me. I watched, confused, and then Nova's expression cleared, and he looked almost pale as he staggered back several steps.

"Is your last name Wardwell?" he whispered with barely suppressed expectation and hope, and I stilled, knowing only one other Witch by that name.

"No, it's Johnson," Mika answered softly.

"Are you sure?" Nova pressed, stepping closer. I inserted myself between the two. Whatever Nova's problem was, he wasn't getting any closer to my Witch.

"I think I know my own last name," she argued, and I relaxed a little at hearing some of that fire back in her voice.

"You just... you look so much like her," Nova answered, his expression full of confusion and a little wistfulness.

"They killed Tabitha, Nova. And her entire family," I reminded my brother gently. Nova stepped back quickly and ran a hand over his head, frowning.

"I don't think you know who you are," Nova pushed, ignoring me and speaking to Mika instead.

"Well, if a Demon says so, then I must be wrong," Mika snapped. Nova, to my complete and utter surprise, grinned.

"She had fire too. I can taste your magic in the air, I can feel it. It's hers—it's exactly like hers," Nova explained, his entire being radiating excitement.

"Who?" Mika asked, bewildered.

"Tabitha. She was a Witch from over two hundred years ago. I... she was my... friend," Nova answered, struggling to get the words out.

The truth was, and I'm sure I wasn't surprising anyone with this bombshell, Demons didn't really have friends. It was a weakness none of us could afford, but Tabitha hadn't just been any Witch. She'd been strong, feisty and hard-headed. She had taken to Nova for reasons none of us ever understood, and Nova had in turn developed feelings for her. Not the romantic kind. She was a best friend, almost a sister. When the Angels had discovered this, a massive group of them had cornered Nova and captured him. Thinking they'd had him completely apprehended and at their mercy, they'd then forced him to watch as they trapped Tabitha and her family inside their home and burned it to the ground. Her entire bloodline was wiped out in one fell swoop. This was, of course, before Witches had become an endangered species. Nova had laid waste to all but one Angel on the battlefield that day. Almost none had stood a chance, not even me or my brothers had intervened. Since then, Nova had been very careful not to allow himself such a vulnerability again.

"You're her kin; I can feel it," Nova added in wonder.

"Nova," I started, caution in my voice.

"It's her!" he shouted at me.

I watched him carefully, and there was nothing but pure certainty coming from him. That, and wonder. Witches tended to have a baseline in their magic which would point to what lineage they came from. I didn't have intimate enough knowledge of Tabitha, she'd never healed me, so I couldn't say one way or another if he was correct when he said that Mika and Tabitha were related.

"How do you explain then, that until this morning, she didn't even know what she was?" I asked.

Nova frowned and peered behind me at Mika. I reluctantly stepped aside to see Mika chewing on her lower lip, her eyes darting between me and Nova like she was trying to make up her mind about something.

"What is it, Little Witch?" I whispered in her mind. Mika jumped and turned to look at me with fear and shock.

"What the hell was that?" she shrieked. I shrugged.

"I found the path from your mind to my own when you woke up this morning. It is as much a surprise to me as it is to you, since before now, I

have only ever been able to converse with my brothers this way," I explained.

It *had* been a shock, but a welcome one. Any way to get closer to her was a score in my book. For whatever reason, the thought of letting this woman out of my sight had me in knots, and the thought of anyone else trying to lay claim to her tempted me to unleash a well of fury at them.

"Well, stop it. I don't want your voice in my head."

"You can speak in her mind?" Nova gaped, not looking at all happy.

"Apparently so," I mused. "What were you trying to decide before?"

"I…" she broke off, holding back. Dragging in a deep breath, Mika threw her shoulders back and I repressed the urge to smile at the way she lifted her chin stubbornly and braced herself.

"I was adopted. I don't know who my family is," she admitted. Silence descended and Nova released a long breath, his face clearing and brightening with something like joy. It was an odd expression to see on his face, and I didn't appreciate that it was *my* Witch that brought it out in him.

"You are of her blood. I can tell. This is… this is incredible," Nova murmured, looking almost overjoyed.

"How? How can I be related to this Tabitha woman if she and all her family died hundreds of years ago?" Mika asked. Nova thought for a moment and then stepped towards her quickly. I cut him off.

"I need to show her something," Nova spat, his expression darkening.

"You can do it without touching her," I snarled.

Nova stiffened and he squared his shoulders. I could feel him gearing up for a confrontation and I did the same. No one was touching her, no one but me. I didn't understand this possessiveness I felt over her, and quite frankly, I didn't give a fuck. I had no time to delve into it and examine it more closely.

"Step aside," Nova warned.

"Back off."

"Boys, back in your corners," Mika sighed heavily behind me. I didn't budge, and I didn't blink. Nova needed to get it through his head.

Right. Fucking. Now.

I didn't care if Mika was some long lost descendent of Tabitha Wardwell. Tomika Johnson was mine, and no one was going to take her from me, not even my brother. Nova must have gotten that impression loud and clear, because he finally spoke.

"Your arm," he said without looking away from me. After another tense moment, he backed off slowly and looked at Mika. "Your right arm. Do you have a birthmark there that looks almost like a star?"

"H-how... how did you know that?" Mika gawked. I bit back a groan of annoyance and turned to look at her as she traced the small, pale birthmark on her inner arm just above her elbow.

Yeah, I was definitely a bastard for not wanting it to be true. From what I'd gleaned of her after going through her house as she slept, she didn't have any family and there were no pictures in her house showing friends and colleagues. She seemed to be a loner with no real connection to anyone. She really didn't know anything of her past. And here I was, silently cursing my brother for handing her something I could never give her. A connection. Someone to speak to who had known someone in her family. They would have a bond now, one I was not a part of, and it pissed me off. Yep—I was definitely worthy of the title, *King of Hell*, because only a fucking heartless asshole like me would resent his brother for giving her a piece of family to hold onto.

"Every Witch in Tabitha's family had that mark," Nova explained. Mika gazed down at the mark, tracing it almost reverently.

"Can you... can you tell me more about her? More about any of them?" Mika asked, her eyes suddenly alight with excitement.

"I'd be happy to," Nova answered with a smile, and I didn't miss the way his eyes traveled over her body appreciatively.

"Another time," I stepped in.

"What?" Mika hissed, the light in her eyes dimming.

"Not now, we have things to do," I interrupted, not liking the bond these two already seemed to have. She was mine, dammit. I found her; I claimed her. This was how it worked. I wasn't about to let my fucking brother come in and sweep her away from me. "I think I should look after her, brother. Afterall, I swore to look after Tabitha and her family. I failed that task over two-hundred years ago. This is my chance to make things right," Nova continued. I glared at him, and he frowned.

"No."

He opened his mouth to argue, and I backed towards Mika. "I said no, brother. I found her. I have claimed her. She is mine," I added, pushing the command into my voice so that he couldn't possibly miss it.

"Cole, just—"

"No," I snapped and grabbed Mika's hand.

"I am not arguing this point with you, Little Witch. You will come with me now or you will regret disobeying me," I snarled into her mind, pressing into her how much I meant it. Without waiting for her to fight or for my brother to push the issue, I tugged her towards the hall lined with doors.

"Stupid, arrogant, bossy, dominating asshole," she muttered mutinously under her breath as she yanked her arm out of my grasp. To my complete and utter surprise, she marched ahead of me, her fists clenched. But what stopped me in my tracks was that she walked right up to *my* door without me having to tell her which one was mine. And what was more… *it opened for her.* Glancing over my shoulder at Nova in complete and utter shock, I was comforted to see the same look on his face. How? The doors only opened for the one it belonged to…

After a few seconds, Nova shook his head, annoyance and frustration flashing over him.

"Protect her," he muttered angrily, and I could tell our argument was not over.

"I intend to," I answered.

"Yo, Hell Boy! Are you coming? Or are you going to be the kind of kidnapper that lets me have some freedoms? Cause, I gotta say, I like that last option," Mika called from inside my realm.

I grinned at her words, unable to fight the humor that lit me from within.

Yep. My Little Witch was temptation and sin, wrapped in sass and attitude.

And she was *mine*.

CHAPTER FOUR
MIKA

Cole.

So, the Demon had a name. It suited him, really. His eyes were as black as the rock-hard substance, and he had been created in the fires of Hell.

He was tall, almost ginormous. He was tattooed—oh yeah, I'd caught sight of those delicious designs winding up one arm to disappear beneath his shirt earlier. His hair was black, his jaw covered in a perpetual stubble that did *everything* to enhance how gorgeous he was. Full lips often flashing at me in a sexy way that had my lady parts waking up and paying attention. And he was built like a god-damn walking lady boner. The man was a veritable dream come to life.

Too bad he was a total asshole.

Yep, all that sinful sexiness was totally wasted every time the arrogant dipshit opened his mouth.

After he'd issued his little *telepathic command*—and make no mistake, we were going to delve into that *real* soon—I'd known without a doubt that he was done playing cat and mouse. And while I was usually one for stubbornly fighting my way out of any situation, I was also smart enough to know when I was outnumbered and powerfully disadvantaged. While I think I would have preferred to have gone with Nova over Cole, something deep down inside had refused. I was *meant* to go with Cole. Despite how often in the very short time I'd known him I found myself wanting to stab him in the chest with one of his own knives, I'd never ignored my base instincts before, and they'd never led me astray.

I had even followed those instincts when they'd told me which door was Cole's. I don't know how I knew, I just did, it felt right. I hadn't missed the look of pure shock on his face when the door had opened of its own accord either. I didn't know how things worked down here, but I was betting that door didn't open for just anyone. That thought made my stomach knot.

Why then, had it opened for me?

So, there I found myself, sitting on a stupidly comfortable couch in what appeared to be a library, watching Cole clean and replace every weapon on him.

Who knew Hell came with a library?

Yes, I'd been kidnapped. Yes, I was now trapped not only with a Demon, but with a goddamn King of Hell. I had no way out, no allies, no plan... and yet I wasn't panicked. I frowned at myself. Why wasn't I panicking? Was I in a state of shock? Hmm... no, that didn't seem to fit. It was odd. While I was annoyed beyond belief at the audacity of the Demon before me, pissed that he'd taken me here against my will, and still fully determined to find my way home and away from him... I didn't feel threatened. The man was scary, he was powerful, and he was obviously as interested in getting into my pants, as I was into his. But I didn't feel like he was a danger to me.

Maybe I was going insane? I mean, what kind of sane woman felt *safe* with a King of Hell?

Me—I'm the crazy lady who feels that way.

Silently sighing, I looked around me, somewhat in awe. This wasn't what I expected Hell to look like. I was in something of a giant cave, but it wasn't dark or dingy, it wasn't scary or cold or infested with bats, spiders, or other creepy crawlies. It was actually rather nice. Lush rugs were laid out all over the place, giving it a warmer feeling. The library was massive and extensive. To my right was a gigantic bed. I mean, California king beds had *nothing* on the four-poster platform in the corner. There was an *enormous* raging fireplace behind the couch I was sitting on, the stone that built it appeared especially old. Further down from the bed towards the back of the room was what I assumed was a bathroom. It had a giant sunken tub that looked like it was a natural hot spring. Heck, it probably was.

All in all, the place was gorgeous. There were even several plants growing along the walls and in corners. Although, how they managed to survive down here with no actual sunlight was a mystery to me. Then again, this guy was a King of Hell, so what did I know?

"What is concerning you, Little Witch?" his voice brushed across my mind, and I had to refrain from shivering. It was like a whispered seduction every time he spoke to me in such an intimate way.

"I am right here, you can use your mouth," I snarled, immediately regretting the words as soon as I said them. There was a rush of wind and I looked up to see him standing over me, that cocky half-smirk on his face.

"I'd happily use my mouth if it would please you," he began before he leaned forward, bracing his arms on either side of my chair. "And I can promise you… I know how to please you," he continued, that simmering heat back in his eyes.

"I didn't mean it like that, and you know it," I returned, but even I could hear the small note of need in my voice. What the hell was going on? I'd never responded to another person like this in my entire life! It was utterly ridiculous the way just being in a room with this Demon could make my body react in such a way. Cole grinned slowly, his eyes dipping to my mouth.

"Are you sure?" he offered, leaning closer. "It could be fun," he added, and I swallowed, leaning back into my chair until there was nowhere else I could go.

"Cole." I said his name softly, pleadingly, and I hated myself for it. But I needed him to stop because I was helpless to make him stop. He was so close, and I watched as his eyes closed and he seemed to struggle with himself for a moment. Dragging in a steadying breath, he moved upwards to brush his lips across my forehead in a curiously intimate gesture before pushing away from my chair.

"Let me show you to your room."

"I have my own room?" I gaped.

"Unless you want to share my bed?" he offered, raising a daring eyebrow at me. I glowered.

"My own room would be better, thank you," I replied dryly.

Cole chuckled and shrugged as if to say it was my loss and strode away from me. The thing was, I was pretty sure it *was* my loss not to share a bed with him, because if there was one thing I was almost certain of, it was that Cole knew how to give a woman unparalleled pleasure. He could certainly get my engine revved just with a sexy smirk, and that kiss we'd shared? Day-am. Kissing had damn near had me on the brink of orgasm. Cole no doubt knew his way around a woman's body.

"So… why do you have a guest room? I didn't figure you for the type to have guests."

"I don't usually have this room. Since I was sure trying to convince you to share my bed would end with me being gutted with my own blade, I created this room when we came in," he explained. I was in the middle of smirking at his insight into me when I finally realized what he'd said.

"Wait, you built a whole room?" I asked as I cleared the doorless archway into what had to be one of the most stunning rooms I'd ever seen. Another four-poster behemoth of a bed was in the center against a stone wall. The timber of the bed looked like it was a living tree, the posts were rooted into the floor, gnarled and twisted branches that wove together along the top, and a curtain of vines and jasmine flowers fell across one side. It wasn't as big as his bed, but still enough that I could get lost in it. The far wall looked like it was an entrance to another world, trees and ferns and a small waterfall that poured into another natural spring had me frozen in place. Nature was one of my biggest needs; I'd always been called to it. And seeing the lush forest and the dark soil ahead of me made my soul sing.

There was a bag sitting on the bed, and I recognized it as one of mine. When did he have the time to pack a bag of my belongings and bring it here?

"H-how did you make this?" I gaped. Cole shrugged.

"I can make my domain anything I want. At the moment it's a cave, but I can make this wing have an exit into a forest," he concluded, as if creating a whole other room—*complete with rainforest and waterfall!*—wasn't something amazing.

"I-I..." I trailed off, at a loss for words.

"I know you do not like how things are," Cole began, and I tore my gaze from the scene in front of me to his black eyes. "But I want to make your stay here comfortable. If there is anything else you need, you only have to ask," he added. I frowned.

"I'm not staying here forever," I snapped.

"But you are," he countered as if that was all there was to it.

"I have a life."

"Really? From what I could make of your "life", you have no friends or family on the surface. You live a life in the shadows, much like myself. You don't have connections up there, so what on Earth could you miss?" he asked.

"My freedom!" I shouted. "No, you're right. I don't have friends because who can afford the risk when you might have to run off at a moments notice because a stupid Demon or an Angel is in pain? And we've already established why I don't have a family— thanks again to you assholes," I reminded angrily, happy to have my anger back. I'd been momentarily swept away with the grandeur of the room before me and his thoughtfulness in the details that I forgot I was dealing with a King of Hell who had kidnapped me and was refusing me my rights.

"You will have a target on your back if you go up there. If you're not with me, then another Demon or an Angel will pick you up, and I almost guarantee they won't care a single bit about you or your life and only what you can do for them."

"Oh, and you expect me to believe that you don't want me here as your own personal healer? You kidnapped me for the same reasons they would," I reminded.

"Perhaps." He shrugged, uncaring. "But you are mine, and there's no turning back now."

"Like hell there isn't," I snapped, whirling to face him as he stepped around me to walk out of my room. I know violence is not the answer... but damn it, it would make me feel better right about now!

"Tomika... you're here now. You might as well make the most of it." He let out a long breath, almost as if he were exhausted from dealing with a troublesome child.

"I'd agree with you, but then we'd both be wrong," I retorted, imagining several scenarios in which I could hurt him and have him drop to his knees in pain.

"And you sound better with your mouth shut," Cole returned, his lips twisted into that sexy smirk.

"I'm completely ready to go back to the surface whenever running my mouth is too much for you to handle."

Cole grinned and leaned in closer, brushing my mind with heat and desire.

"I can think of a number of things I'd do with your mouth before I ever got tired of it," he murmured.

My lower abdomen flipped, and instead of replying, I pulled from my magic within and allowed the thorn bush beside the door to grow rapidly, creating a door of thorns between us, effectively leaving me alone in my room.

His deep chuckle of amusement rang out and I glared.

Asshole!

I ran my hands through my hair and down the back of my neck and hissed at the pain that hit me. What the...?

I looked around and found a mirror and half-turned so that I could see the back of my neck. Twisting my hair in my hand, I lifted it and froze. What appeared to be a small tattoo was on the back of my neck, up high so that it was covered by my hair. I ran for the bag on my bed and shuffled through it, hoping to find my phone. Sighing in relief when I found it, I twisted it up and over my head and took several photos of my neck.

When I pulled the photos up on the phone, I could see a tattoo, clear as day. It appeared to be a large, blank circle with nine evenly spaced, smaller circles dotted inside around the edge of it.

The circle at the top was shaded in, and looked like it was an almost full moon. The other eight remained empty. There was a small series of symbols along the base of the circle, and I suspected it was a phrase of some kind, even though I did not understand the writing.

How the hell did I have a tattoo?

I frowned. When the hell had that happened? And then it hit me. I thought back to the warehouse when Cole had kissed me, his hand at the back of my neck and the ice-cold pain I'd felt.

"That son of a bitch!" I shouted, spinning on my heel and marching towards the door. At the same time, I waved my hand and the door of thorns shrunk back. I had been having the kiss of my life, and he'd been fucking *branding* me?

"Miss me already?" Cole smirked with his back to me.

"What the hell did you do to me?" I snarled; my fury so heated it was amazing he wasn't burning where he stood. Then again, he was a King of Hell. What was a little fire to him?

"You'll have to be more specific," he replied, turning to face me.

"This!" I spun around, lifting my hair so that he could see. There was silence, and I turned my head to see him staring at my neck with a look of pure shock. I stilled, trying to discern whether the expression was legitimate or not. I watched as he blinked and then slowly looked down at his hand, a small frown marring his face. Dropping my hair, I turned to face him and waited. He'd withdrawn inwards, his thoughts masked by a granite expression.

"Well?" I prompted impatiently, beginning to panic.

"I'm sure it's nothing," he muttered, his gaze slowly moving to the massive wall of books.

"Nothing? I have a fucking *brand* on my neck! It wasn't enough that you kidnapped me, but then you branded me too?" I cried. Cole's attention shot back to my face, and he shrugged, back to his normal self.

"Does it really matter? I told you that you are mine. I meant it. Now you have a reason to believe it too," he muttered. I gaped, and I was positive I was doing a perfect imitation of a goldfish.

"Remove it," I seethed, feeling heat and fire burn hot within me.

"No," he answered simply, stepping past me to look at the books.

"*No?*"

"No. I will not remove it," he replied, but his attention wasn't even on me anymore.

Furious that he would do this, pissed that he was barely paying me any attention as if I were nothing but a minor nuisance, I released my hold on my magic. Throwing my hands out in front of me, I threw my magic at him. Cole, unprepared for such an attack, was thrown forward several feet. He turned mid-air and landed hard on his back but did an impressive flip and was back on his feet in no time, his glittering black eyes filled with anger.

"Did you dare use your magic against me again?" he snarled.

"Sucks, doesn't it?" I returned heatedly, preparing to defend myself.

"Little Witch, you have no comprehension of the kind of power I wield. I will give you this warning once, and once only. Do not test me," he growled. I know I should have listened. I know I should have heeded the warning. The hairs on my arms were standing on end, the ice-cold shiver down my spine was a hell of a red flag—but I'd never been someone to start something and not finish it. And quite frankly? I felt that allowing this man to get used to me kowtowing to his every order was a bad precedent to start.

"Fuck you," I hissed and threw more of my magic at him, intending to hold him to the ground. But he was fast, faster than I ever could have anticipated, and he was on me in a second. I gasped and he gripped my wrists punishingly in one hand and shoved me roughly against the wall behind me. I panted hard, looking up at his face that could have been carved from stone. Pure, dark hunger glittered back at me, and I was disgusted to say that its effect on me was devastating.

Before I could try to retaliate, Cole brought his lips crashing down on mine. I opened my mouth—to argue, obviously—when he slipped his tongue into my mouth, and I groaned. Before I knew it, I was kissing him back, desperate to taste more of him. His hips pushed into me, and I could feel the *long*, hard length of him pressing into my stomach. I shifted slightly, widening my legs and he slid his knee between my thighs. I rocked against it, needing the friction it created. Keeping my hands pinned above my head with one hand, Cole gripped my hips and pulled me further onto his thigh, grinding himself against me. I moaned into his mouth, and he moved to kiss down my jaw to my neck. He nipped and bit hard enough for me to yelp in pain before he soothed it away with a swipe of his tongue.

"C-Cole," panted, half out of my mind with need.

"Get there, Little Witch," he ground out, his voice harsh and thick with heat. He firmed his grip on my hip and brought me harder over his thigh, helping me to chase that high that was just out of reach. I rocked faster against him and threw my head back when he dipped lower and suckled one nipple straight through the fabric of my shirt.

So close, so close, so close!

"Come for me, Little Witch," Cole whispered in my mind, and I hadn't realized until that moment that I'd said the words to him in my mind. His voice was dark velvet against my skin, enticing and drugging. I rocked faster, my breathing ragged and sharp.

"Cole," I whimpered again, knowing on some level that I shouldn't be letting this happen, but the rest of me just didn't care. I'd never felt this kind of chemistry with anyone before in my life and I was unprepared for the sheer power of it.

"You're almost there, I can feel you. Come for me," he groaned, his breathing as erratic as my own, his voice deep and gravelly. He rocked against me some more, his hand diving under my shirt to pinch my nipple and that set me off.

"Cole!" I screamed, convulsing hard, a wave of pleasure washing over me, dragging me under as I rocked unevenly against him, riding it out. I was panting hard, and only when I felt my shorts being tugged down, did I realize what was happening.

"Wait, stop," I said quickly, shoving against him. Sense and reason floated back to the surface of my mind, and with it the horrifying realization of what had just happened, what I had *allowed* to happen. "Get away from me!" I ordered, shoving harder when my previous attempt did nothing. Cole stepped back slowly, and I tried to adjust my clothing to prolong the moment when I'd have to look at him.

What the fuck, Mika? You seriously just dry-humped a King of Hell and got off… you're a fucking moron!

My inner reprimand only made my cheeks burn hotter.

"You just came using my leg, and now you won't even look at me?" Cole drawled, his voice thick with smug amusement. The heat in my face intensified and I dragged my gaze to his face. That stark hunger was still there, but so was that annoying smug satisfaction that made me want to drag my nails across his face.

"Now… what did you want?" he asked calmly. I glowered. I was humiliated, and extremely pissed off at my own lack of self-control.

"You know what, no. I won't feel shame for that," I began, lifting my chin stubbornly. "You're stupidly hot and I think you know it. I'm not ashamed to admit it, nor am I ashamed to say that I wanted a piece of you. But that's done now, and this does not excuse what you did to me. You marked me, and you can go and undo it," I pressed, determined to own my shit. I'd never blamed anyone else for my own screw ups before, I wasn't about to start now.

Cole stared back at me, and I was waiting for his smart-ass reply. But it didn't come. Slowly the heat in his eyes dampened and he looked serious for the first time.

"I don't know how I did that. Nor do I know how to remove it," he uttered. I stiffened.

"You're lying."

He shook his head and ran a hand over his head, sighing heavily. "I'm not. I do not know how I marked you, or why. I don't know of any other Demon who has done this, so I have no frame of reference. But I…" he trailed off and glanced down at his palm again. I frowned and he slowly came towards me. I watched as he showed me his palm and he brushed his thumb over it. In the center of his palm, a mark just like mine, minus the symbols, appeared before it faded once again into his skin as if it had never been.

"That wasn't there before?" I asked, already knowing the answer.

"No."

I swallowed hard and tried to think of what this meant. If he was telling the truth–and some part of me knew that he was–then we were royally screwed. Because marks like that? Brandings like that? They couldn't mean anything good, not for a Witch now tied to a Demon.

"Can you find out?" I asked softly, almost defeatedly. I glanced at the wall of books and back at him. Cole studied me for a moment and nodded slowly.

"I'll try to find something. I'll speak to my brothers and see what they know," he explained.

Nodding slowly, I wrapped my arms around my waist and shuffled sideways slightly. Cole's dark eyes never left my face and I glanced around a little awkwardly.

"This isn't over," he said softly. My eyes shot back to his face, and he was smiling knowingly. "What happened there against the wall was just a teaser, a prelude to what we are capable of and what will eventually happen."

"I don't think so," I added, glad to be feeling that fire coming back.

He flashed that half-smile I was quickly finding to be irresistible and shrugged a shoulder.

"You're a human, it's your prerogative to be wrong. And I look forward to making you see that."

"Screw you, Cole" I sniped as I spun and marched away from him, taking several long strides to my room.

"Is that a promise?" he called after me.

Gritting my teeth, I waved my hand behind me, and the door of thorns reappeared.

I was in so much trouble.

CHAPTER FIVE
COLE

The Little Witch was trouble. I knew it as well as I knew my own name.

But she was trouble I wanted to get into, trouble I wanted to play with. I had no fucking idea what it was about her that set me off like that. I could go from wanting to strangle her to wanting to fuck her in a nano-second, and the strength it took not to compel her, not to sink into her hot, wet, welcoming body was much more than I ever thought I'd need.

How the hell could she set my blood on fire like that? I felt an almost painful ache to touch her whenever she was within reach. I wanted to stroke her skin, explore every smooth, vast inch of it. I wanted to sink my fingers into her thick black hair and watch her emerald eyes blaze with passion or anger. I wanted to taste her mouth more than I wanted my next breath. She was addictive, tantalizing, totally sucking me in. I'd lost control before, determined to feel her. And having her come using my leg had been better for me than I would have thought. I'd been in her mind, feeling her pleasure alongside her. Experiencing her orgasm through her mind was enough to almost make me shoot my load in my pants. Thankfully, being as old as I was, had earned me at least that much restraint.

But fuck me, it had been a battle.

What the hell was going on? What was it about this mortal, this Witch, that had me so messed up? And what the fuck was up with that mark on her neck? The exact same one was on the palm of my hand, but it disappeared when I wanted it to. I had to have been the one to do it, there was no escaping that. My palm had itched and burned when I was talking to her in the warehouse. When I'd grabbed the back of her neck to kiss her, that pain had seared my skin. Somehow, I'd marked her. But how... why? What did it mean?

I hadn't been lying when I told her I wasn't sure what it meant or where it came from.

I turned to look at the wall of books beside me and decided to try there first. If I could figure this out without involving my brothers, I'd prefer that. At this point, Nova was the only one who knew I had a Witch in my realm, and I wanted to keep it that way a while longer. I needed her to want me, to rely on me before my brothers got within reach of her and tried to offer her something else. A deadly fury bubbled up inside me at the thought of my brothers trying to take her.

She was *mine*.

Sucking in a deep breath, I exhaled and shook my head. That right there was a perfect example of the fuckery that was this situation. What the *hellfire* was that about? My brothers had my loyalty, absolutely, but the thought of one of them putting their hands on her had me more than willing to tear their throats out. Scrubbing my hands over my face, I started pulling books from the shelves.

Absently, I checked in with Tomika. She didn't yet know I could do this, and I was going to keep it that way for as long as possible. She was undressing and preparing to bathe. I dropped the book in my hand at the image of her naked and beneath the waterfall I'd created in her room and groaned.

Fucking hell, I was going to have to take matters into my own hands tonight in order to get some relief. I may be a bloody King of Hell, but there was no joy in taking an unwilling partner to bed. Half of the enjoyment came from chasing. Although, I would still love for her to have a little fight when we did end up in bed. And that was a damn guarantee. I'd feel what it was like soon to sink into her hot little body, and I'd make it an experience she wouldn't soon forget.

Picking up the book up from the floor, I stared down at the old, worn cover at the circular symbol. It was the same one that was

now branded onto Mika's neck and emblazoned upon my palm—
I knew I'd seen that symbol somewhere before. Growing up, our
mother, Lilith had demanded we know all about our heritage and
what it entailed. My brothers and I had tried to do as she
ordered, but none of us had much cared. Now, I was kicking
myself; because something in my gut told me there would be no
getting rid of this mark Mika and I now shared. It was old, older
than old. It had been around since the dawn of Demons, and it
meant something dangerously important.

Apprehension was a new feeling for me, but it was creeping over
me now as I traced the symbol on the cover. Knowing what it
was, what it entailed would only help me in handling it and
accepting it. But did I really want to know? Shaking my head at
my own cowardice, I sat back on the overstuffed chair and
opened the book, determined to know what I was up against. But
more than that, I needed to know if there was a way for Mika to
remove the mark. Because if she could, the book had to go. I
refused to look too closely at *why* the thought of her removing
my mark set my teeth on edge and an almost panic to set in. I was
just going to put it down to her being a Witch and that they were
stupidly rare. Yes, that's what this was. She was nothing more to
me than a power and status boost, and maybe a hot body to bed
in between battles. That was all.

Finally happy with my mental pep-talk, I got down to reading.

~

I glanced around the rainforest I suddenly found myself standing
in and frowned. Okay... this was strange.

"Even in my dreams you won't leave me alone."

I turned to see Mika standing a few feet away, her black hair
loose and tousled, her green eyes glaring. My body came to
attention immediately.

"And you look as ravishing as ever," I responded, dragging my
eyes over the boy-short underwear she was wearing and loose
white tee. The woman was almost in rags, but she was hot as

fuck.

"And you're cocky too," she glared. "Sexy as hell, but cocky." I grinned slowly and watched her eyes heat and her cheeks pinken. Oh yeah, the woman wanted me.

I took a few seconds to look around us, noting the detail and the feel of the *dream*. The thing was… this wasn't a dream; I knew it wasn't. This was a psychic realm, another dimension, but it was *not* a dream. I had been in a psychic realm a few times in my life, and they all had the same slightly dizzying side effect. Somehow, Mika had dragged me into a whole other plane of existence within her head. Which meant anything we did here was just as real as in my realm. It would feel real, and our physical bodies would react. If she cut me here, I'd bleed in my realm. But she thought it was a dream… interesting.

I bit back a smirk at that realization. It was time to test the waters.

Slowly, I stalked toward her, keeping my eyes on her as I moved. Mika's eyes widened and I watched the pulse in her neck pound away, I heard the way her breath hitched, and I could taste the sweet scent of her arousal that spiced the air. Yes, my Little Witch wanted me, despite what her pretty mouth said.

"At least in this dream, you can tell me what you think of me without repercussions. I find you sexy, Mika. Incredibly sexy and alluring," I told her, moving closer to her. She swallowed hard and her lips parted slightly. Lips that were made for kissing… among other things.

"Dreams have meaning," she answered, her words more a whisper than anything else.

"So, what does this dream mean to you?"

She shook her head and licked her lips. I bit back a groan, feeling that one innocent gesture all the way to my aching cock.

"Probably that I'm attracted to your body. Your personality leaves something to be desired. It also probably means that despite using you earlier to get off, I need more," she explained. I knew that if she thought this was in any way real, if she thought I was in any way *actually* me, she'd never admit any of this. I smirked and edged closer, slowly reaching out to touch her face.

"Then take advantage of me here," I suggested. She smiled and shook her head.

"I should wake up now and stop entertaining ideas like this. You kidnapped me. Sinfully sexy or not, you're still an asshole Demon who is refusing me my freedom," she answered. I wanted to laugh. Even in what she assumed was a dream, she was practicing restraint.

"I don't know… the kidnapper and his victim can be a sexy roleplay," I murmured, waving my hand.

She gasped and looked down at her wrists that were now bound in a complicated knot with a silk rope. She raised her gaze to my face and the heat in her eyes had me throbbing painfully.

"Maybe it does. But this isn't a good idea, and it isn't exactly a role-play when it's my reality," she gasped, looking flustered and needy.

"Do we have to make good decisions here?" I tempted her, grasping the tail-end of the rope and lifting her arms above her head. Her lips parted in surprise when she realized I had slid the silk rope over a hook in the stone wall that hadn't been there before. The wall hadn't been there before either, but we could create anything here.

"Cole."

My name on her lips was an aphrodisiac I hadn't expected, and I clenched my jaw to stop from groaning.

"Be a good girl and stand still. You can struggle a little if you want, I like fire," I suggested, smiling at the way her breath caught in her lungs and her pupils grew so large they almost eclipsed the green. Yeah, my Little Witch liked being forced into submission, whether she thought so or not. Her body's reaction told me everything I needed to know.

"Cole," she tried again, and I ran my hands down the length of her tight little body to spread across her abdomen.

"You are mine. Bound and helpless, you're here for my pleasure. And I can guarantee you that I can give you yours. You know that already, don't you, Tomika?" I drawled softly, leaning close so that my lips brushed the side of her face. My hands slid around her back to cup her luscious ass, and this time I did groan. She was the perfect size. Her gasp was mingled with my moan, and the echo of our combined sounds had my body tightening uncomfortably.

I scraped her ear with my teeth and worked my way down her neck, sliding slowly to my knees as I snapped my fingers and her shirt disappeared. She was left shirtless, in nothing but a pair of panties that I had a wild desire to rip from her body. *Fuck!* Her breasts were the perfect size, rosy nipples hard and awaiting my attention.

No, I had no idea why *this* Witch had me hard enough to hammer nails, I didn't know why just the scent of her, the sound of her voice or the fire in her eyes was enough to make me want to bury myself in her, over and over again. But right now, I didn't need to wonder why. I just knew that my body was aching for hers, demanding it, and I was feeling helpless against it. No woman, mortal or otherwise, had ever driven me so wild with lust. This wasn't just a desire, it was a need, a compulsion that I didn't understand. But I didn't want to, didn't care to understand even when some part of me said I should question it. I just needed to indulge the need and take her while I could. I tentatively brushed across her mind and found the same desperate need inside her, the same mounting demands, too powerful to ignore.

My lips brushed over her stomach to the underside of her breast before I sucked a nipple into my mouth, suckling strongly. She cried out, the sound like fucking nectar to my ears. Her skin tasted like honey-suckle, a hint of jasmine intermingled with it, and the taste was enough to drive me crazy. I gripped her ass in a hard grasp as I moved to her other breast and she whimpered, dropping her head back as I toyed with it, nipping gently before sucking strongly to take away the pain. She moved restlessly, her breathing uneven and her scent becoming stronger the longer I played with her. I wanted to take my time, but this was a psychic realm, and she could wake up at any point. I needed to be inside her, to feel her hot and tight around my cock, and I didn't want to take the chance of her waking before I'd had a chance with her.

I gripped the edges of her panties, and just as I wanted to do earlier, I tore them from her body in a swift yank. She gasped and I grinned. Yes, I could have waved my hand and they would have disappeared, but she liked me dominant and taking what I wanted. She just wouldn't admit it to herself.

"Cole," she whimpered again, and I leaned in close to her, running my hands up the inside of her thighs before I gripped one leg and draped it over my shoulder. The scent of her had my mouth watering and my body tightening painfully, my cock heavy and leaking. Fuck, I needed to be inside this woman. But I needed to taste her first. It occurred to me that once I did this, it would be impossible to get the taste of her out of my head. That she'd become a craving I could never do without. But it wasn't something I needed to worry about now. Every other thought and possible worry I had was muted, muffled, distanced, so that all I could think about was claiming my woman's body. And that was exactly what she was and what I was doing. I'd already marked her, tied her soul to mine—this was me staking my claim on her body.

"Hang on, Little Witch," I warned before I buried my face between her legs. She threw her head back and cried out, her voice echoing around us.

The first flick against her pussy had me groaning in pleasure. She was spiced honey and intoxicating. The taste of her on my tongue was something I'd never forget. I teased her for a few seconds, running my tongue up her slit to her clit where I teased her relentlessly until she was almost sobbing for release before I clamped down over her and devoured her. She screamed and I gripped her thighs tightly to keep her legs open as I lapped at her, teeth, tongue, and lips put to work to send her to that pinnacle.

"Cole, please," she whimpered. I grinned against her and speared my tongue inside her and increased my efforts. She chanted my name like a talisman, and every second of it was ingrained in my brain forever as her pleasure built higher and higher.

"Cole!" she screamed, and I felt her topple over the edge as she came on my tongue, her hips bucking wildly. I didn't relent, I continued my assault until she stopped moving and I'd dragged out every possible second of her orgasm. She was panting hard, and I took a moment to kiss her thighs and up her abdomen before I stood before her again. I didn't give her time to breathe or come to terms with it. I slid my hand down her stomach to her pussy where I pushed two fingers inside her. I groaned as she moaned. She was so fucking hot, drenched and tight. She would be the closest thing to heaven I'd ever get. I continued to finger her, picking up in speed before I slid a third finger inside, stretching her. I had to prepare her. I was not a modest man by any estimation, and I knew I had a large cock. While I wanted her, and while pain could sometimes be fun, *that* kind of pain wasn't on the table here. I didn't want to cause her real pain. Fuck, I was getting *soft*—figuratively, not physically. If anything, feeling her velvet folds clamping around my fingers and not my cock was a kind of torture I hadn't experienced. And that was saying something.

"You're ready, Little Witch. Hold on," I warned her.

"Cole, let me down first."

"You're my captive," I reminded her. She spared me a small smile and shook her head.

"Keep my hands bound, but I want to touch you," she suggested. I grinned and did as she suggested.

I lifted her easily, and she gasped as I wrapped her legs around my waist and draped her bound hands over my neck. I watched her as I slid my hard length against her slick entrance and her eyes darkened, her lips parting. And then without warning, I positioned myself and slammed hard inside her. She screamed, her head thrown back, her breasts like tempting treats. I swore loudly at the feel of her velvet sheath squeezing hard against my cock, her tight channel parting reluctantly as I forced my hard length inside her. I drew back and surged forward again. I had to do this three more times before I was fully inside her. Mika was panting, her chest and forehead misty with sweat, her dark green eyes almost black. I gritted my teeth and began driving into her, walking forwards until her back was pressed against the stone wall I'd created. She moaned as I plunged into her again, the wall helping me to go deeper, harder.

"That's it, Little Witch. Feel my cock inside you, feel me fucking your pussy," I panted, my grip on her hips tight as I held her still, drilling into her. My words seemed to spur her on, make her ripple around me. A fresh wave of her wetness coated my dick, and I gritted my teeth as I hammered into her, over and over. Every surge had her breasts bouncing and I wanted to suck on them again, but I had other things to do first. I knew we wouldn't last long; we were both burning too hot, too fast. This powerful pull I felt to have her, to claim her, was not allowing for time to indulge my every whim. We were about to go up in flames, but it would be fucking spectacular.

"Oh, God," she whimpered, and I grinned.

"Not God, sweetheart," I reminded. Her mouth parted again, and I claimed her lips with mine, forcing my tongue into her mouth where she answered with equal need, her nails digging into the back of my head. I don't know what it was about her that made her so damn intoxicating, but I never wanted it to end. I'd fucked my fair share of women over the millennia in every position imaginable, but none of them drove me as insane as this one.

"I'm going to come," she moaned, panting hard. I could feel her pussy tightening around me, rippling as her orgasm drew closer and closer. I gritted my teeth and thrust harder and faster, my hips snapping against her, my cock coated with her wetness, our combined scents filling the room. Our sounds of pleasure echoed off the walls and in my ears as we both drew closer to that end zone.

"Fuck me, Cole," Mika begged, and I shouted wordlessly in triumph at hearing those words from her lips. I ground my pelvis against her as I drove into her harder and she sucked in a sharp breath as she tightened impossibly around me, coming so hard her sheath was strangling my cock.

"Fuck!" she screamed as I came, her pussy sucking me dry, draining every drop from me –

And then I suddenly found myself staring at the ceiling as I lay sprawled on my bed.

I was panting hard, my stomach coated with thick ropes of cum, my body shaking hard from the force of my orgasm, my chest and forehead slick with sweat.

Holy. Fucking. Hell.

CHAPTER SIX
MIKA

"Fuck!" I screamed, shooting up from my bed, my body still convulsing from the powerful orgasm, my skin slick, my hair sticking to my face and neck.

I panted and shoved my hair away from my face and took a moment to get my bearings. Struggling to regain my breath, I remembered I was in Hell with a Demon King, and this was where I'd slept. I groaned and squeezed my thighs together again as a final wave of pleasure rolled through me. Falling backwards onto the ridiculously comfortable mattress, I tried to calm my heart.

What the hell?

Did I really just come because of a dream? I mean—I knew I had. My body was still throbbing and pulsing with pleasure. I felt like I had just been thoroughly fucked... but I was alone. That dream had been... I shook my head and sighed. I had to stop entertaining the idea of that Demon. No good could come from sleeping with him, no good could come from forgetting that he was a King of Hell and was holding me here against my will.

This was not Beauty and the Beast. I would not be bought into complacency by a fancy library, crazy-cool fireplace, and a sexy beast. No. Nope... hopefully not.

Groaning, I scrubbed my hands over my face and turned to look at the waterfall. Okay... so the waterfall in the mini-rainforest in my bedroom *might* be the thing that buys my complacency. But I was trying to be better than that.

In any case, I needed a bath and to rinse the dream away because wow, that had felt *so* real.

Shaking my head at myself, I stripped off and walked straight into the water. It wasn't cold, but it wasn't hot. It was somehow the perfect temperature, and I sank right into it. I slid all the way under the surface, wetting my hair and letting the water cleanse me of my dirty dream. I had to get him out of my head. And I was going to demand some freedoms. I needed to know if he had discovered anything about The Mark, and if he didn't, then I was going to go to his brother and ask him to figure it out. Nova seemed more than willing to help me, whereas I got the feeling Cole wasn't above lying to me to keep me where he wanted me. While I believed he really didn't know anything about The Mark or how it had ended up on my neck, I didn't think he'd remain ignorant forever. He'd figure it out, but I wasn't sure if he'd tell me everything he knew either.

I broke the surface of the water and pushed my wet hair back, wiping the water from my eyes.

"As sexy as I remember."

I shrieked and spun around to see Cole standing at the edge of the water, his heated gaze watching me. I swallowed so hard I almost swallowed my tongue at the sight of him standing there shirtless, tattooed chest and arms bare, his body encased in nothing but a pair of grey sweatpants. Yes, this sexy as sin man had to go the extra mile and wear *the* grey sweats. I was positive he knew what it did to women to have a man like him wearing them. I tried to school my features but judging from the satisfied smirk he sent my way, I hadn't been successful.

"What are you doing in here?" I demanded, finally coming back to reality. I crossed my arms over my chest to hide my breasts. He grinned slowly, and I cursed myself that seeing that sexy smirk had my stomach doing a slow roll.

"I came in to see if you were awake. And to see how you were after... everything," he added.

"You mean how was my first night in Hell? After being kidnapped and refused my freedom?"

"Yes, and the dream," he added. I frowned and then stilled, my heart thudding hard once in my chest.

How did he know about my dream?

"The dream?" I echoed, a part of me pleading with the universe that he did not know what I had dreamed about. He raised an eyebrow, his lips curving into a half-smile as he shrugged his impressive shoulders before crossing his arms over his chest. I was momentarily distracted by his strong forearms and the veins I could see in them. Seriously, what was it about a guy's forearms and hands when I could see veins? Why was that so damn hot?

"Yes, Little Witch. I, myself, found it very pleasurable, even if I did wake up with my release on my body and not inside you where I wanted it," he explained.

My eyes shot back to his face, and I gaped.

"H-how?"

Cole grinned, his expression knowing. "It wasn't a dream in the strictest of senses. Somehow, you pulled me into a psychic realm," he answered.

"Okay…" I trailed off, waiting for the other shoe to drop. Because there was more here that I was missing, I knew it.

"And whatever happens in a psychic realm is as real as if we were right here and now," he added.

I swallowed hard.

"You mean last night… last night we…" I trailed off, seeing the answer already on his face, feeling it in the throbbing and aching of my body. *Holy shit!* I'd just had a fuck-session with a real-life King of Hell!

"You knew," I whispered, suddenly realizing. "You knew it wasn't a dream."

He shrugged.

"You're an asshole!" I shrieked, spraying water at him with my magic. Well, that backfired epically when his bronzed chest glistened at me, tempting me to lick every drop off his skin.

"Do not pretend that you didn't like it. If I remember correctly, you were begging me to fuck you," he reminded in a deep, low voice. My sex spasmed at that tone and I glared, trying to hide my body's reaction.

"Liking it or not, I deserved to know it was real. You knew I wouldn't have gone through with it if I had known," I snapped, clinging to my indignance. Because damn it! I was not going to be one of those women who fell in lust with their captors... even if he was sexier than the legal limit and knew how to use his body to bring pleasure to a woman such as she'd never known.

"I am a King of Hell, Mika. I am not a saint, nor am I a hero, and I will never pretend or strive to be one. It's best you get that through your head right now because it will not change," Cole answered, not a speck of remorse or guilt in voice. I glowered at him.

"That was beyond wrong, Cole. It was tantamount to rape."

"You can lie to yourself all you want, Mika, but I was in your mind last night. I could feel the same compulsion to share our bodies as you did. I couldn't have stopped it any more than you could. You wanted it as much as I did, despite what you need to tell yourself this rising," he added in a matter-of-fact tone.

"Why?" I asked, deciding to push past his deception. I could unpack my feelings about that at a later date, but some part of me already knew he was right.

Cole shrugged. "I have never felt such desperate need before. It was new," he admitted. My stomach clenched tight at that, and I felt like a rock settled in my gut. That couldn't be good.

"It's The Mark, isn't it?" I guessed. Cole's black eyes flashed at me before he looked away again.

"I believe it is," he answered.

"What did you find out last night?" I asked, waving my hand for my towel. Cole caught it mid-air and opened it up for me. I glared but shook my head. Whatever, he'd already seen me naked.

Throwing my shoulders back, I dropped my arms to my side and walked out of the pool of water, watching the way his sharp gaze slid over my naked body and heated exponentially. I stepped into the open towel and took it from his hands. His glittering eyes came back to my face, and an answering need sung out in my body.

No. I needed answers. I needed to know why this man could make me a liquid mess of desire just by looking at me like that. I'd never experienced that before, and I was convinced it wasn't normal.

"The Mark is old, older than me even. It is very rare, and very potent. And from what I read, there isn't a thing we can do to remove it or lessen its effects. Marking someone is something Archangels and Kings of Hell can do. But it is rare, as in, we have no records of it except for Lucifer himself with our mother, Lilith. I don't know if an Archangel has ever Marked someone," he explained. His words rang with honesty, but it did nothing to quell the fear that had taken root within me.

"So... what else can we expect?" I asked, almost afraid of the answer, but needing to know.

"Do you *really* want to know?"

"No. But I need to," I answered.

Cole considered me carefully for a moment before he nodded slowly and turned as I passed him, thinking of the outfit I wanted to wear. I pictured every detail in my mind, the feel of it, the weight of it, the texture and material. When I opened my eyes, I was wearing a faded pair of jeans, my favorite combat boots, and a black tank top.

"When I Marked you, I bound us... soul to soul. There is no way to undo it," he began.

Hearing those words was like a bucket of ice water had been thrown in my face and I stiffened, a shiver running down my spine.

"You bound my soul to yours?" I repeated. He nodded, staring at me unflinchingly as he waited for me to digest the news.

Having sex with a King of Hell was one thing. I mean, it had been hot, even though I knew it was wrong. He wasn't just a Demon; he was a Hell King. He was deadly and brutal and... evil. Wasn't he? If I was going to get down and dirty with someone from the paranormal world, wouldn't it have been smarter to have jumped into bed with an Angel? I'd met them before, from a distance, they were beautiful, divine. So why had I never found myself a trembling mess of desire when I looked at one, but I did when I looked at Cole?

I shook my head. Sleeping with him had been one thing. That was my body... but my soul? If what he was saying was true—and I couldn't see a reason for him to lie—the very essence of who I was, everything about me, was now bound to a King of Hell.

"I cannot undo this; the only way out is death," he continued, obviously seeing the growing horror on my face. "But from what I read; it will not be easy to achieve. The Mark can only be given to one, and never again repeated. It works as a branding, and it ties the two as mates. We will be forever fighting our body's need for one another if we don't succumb and appease the need often. The chemistry will never die out. If anything, it will only grow, the pleasure will double and even triple, ensuring the bond stays strong," he continued.

I slowly sat back on the edge of my bed, my head spinning.

"Wait, so we're like… mated? And what you're telling me is, that Mark has acted as some kind of permanent Viagra, where we will both want each other forever, and it will never go away. Ever," I rephrased, needing to wrap my head around it.

Cole's lips twitched, and he nodded.

"I would not have put it like that, but that is the basis of it. There is more, but at least that explains why I could not have stopped myself last night any more than you could have," he explained.

"What more?" I groaned. He smiled and shook his head.

"Along with the physical pull, will be a psychic pull. You will need the touch of my mind often, and I will need yours. It will be virtually impossible to lie to one another. I get the feeling if we're away from one another for too long, things will get uncomfortable. This at least explains why, after you woke up the other morning, there was a new pathway forged between our minds, allowing for us to speak telepathically," he explained.

I swallowed hard and dropped my head into my hands, struggling not to freak out. I was usually pretty good at compartmentalizing, at putting things in a box and taking them out small sections at a time to examine and come to terms with. But this? This wasn't something I had the luxury of time to explore.

"What do you want to do, Mika?" he asked. I slowly raised my gaze to meet his, frowning slightly at the look of almost… concern on his face. Who knew a Hell King like Cole could experience that emotion?

I shook my head and drew in a deep breath.

"I want to go hunting," I answered. He frowned.

"Witches abhor hunting. You value life," he reminded me as if I did not know. I rolled my eyes.

"Thanks for the mansplaining there, Cole. No, I was in the middle of an investigation when you kidnapped me. I want to go and pick up the trail," I explained. His frown deepened.

"The ritualistic killings?" he asked. I glared at him. He held up his hands in mock surrender and smiled. "I didn't go wandering in your mind. I saw the paperwork and the photos spread out on your table at your house. I figured you were trying to narrow down the culprit," he answered.

"Well, that's what I want to do," I answered. He frowned again. I was beginning to like that I could put that expression on his face. I got the feeling he wasn't challenged often.

"That's not what I meant when I asked what you wanted to do," he stated.

I shrugged. "But it's what I want to do right now. From what you've told me, there's no going back on what you did when you Marked me. It's done. There's no escape, even though I fully intend to research that for myself. I can't handle looking too closely at it all right now, so I want to do something I can control," I explained, standing and smoothing out my shirt. He was still frowning, and I huffed impatiently.

"Come on, what else did you have planned for today? You can even come with me?" I suggested, even though in the back of my mind I was putting together a plan of escape. Because despite what he told me, I couldn't believe that this was my new life. I needed to get the heck away from this guy at my first chance.

~

Cole relented and wrapped us in shadow. He explained that this was a form of transport that only Demons used. I was pretty sure it was his way of telling me that it would not be something I could do myself, and therefore leaving Hell was not an option unless I was with him. With every new thing I learned, I felt the cage he'd put me in when he Marked me get a little smaller, the bars a little thicker. I was having trouble breathing already, but I pushed the sensation away and concentrated on the here and now. I would find a way to get away from him. I would regain my freedom. I just had to bide my time.

We picked up the trail where I left off the other night before I'd healed Cole, and while we walked, I asked questions. It was better to know your enemy, and I wanted to know all there was about Cole and the inner workings of Hell, so I knew what I was up against.

A part of me wished I'd never asked.

Nine of them. There were *nine Kings of Hell!*

As if Cole wasn't enough? He explained the process in Hell and how souls ended up down there in the first place and how they were sorted. Nothing he told me even hinted at a small weakness I could exploit, which darkened my mood further.

"Where to now?" Cole asked as I finished canvasing the last scene. I closed my eyes and blocked everything out around me. I needed to pick up the trail of violence and hatred, and being that the trail was now several days old, I had to concentrate even harder.

Everyone left an impression wherever they went, a footprint that reflected their personality and emotions at the time. I had always been sensitive to the more volatile emotions, and that made Demons and evil humans easier to track. I knew this was Demons, though, which was also why the human authorities were having so much trouble finding the culprits.

I sent my senses out around me, feeling the other life forces surrounding us. I could feel Cole, he was a huge beacon on my radar, and I tried to ignore him. There was a small brush against my mind, and I knew he was there, experiencing what it was I did. Again, I had to concentrate harder to ignore his presence as he experienced this with me. I could have pushed him out, I could have fought, but the sickening truth was; I didn't want to. The moment I felt his consciousness brush across my mind, I felt at ease, as if I could take my first real breath since the last time he'd been there. I hated it. I did not want to be reliant upon anyone for anything. And in one selfish, thoughtless act, he'd taken my independence and my freedom from me.

"*I am in your head, Little Witch,*" he reminded, male amusement clear in his words.

"*It's my head, I'll think what I want. If you don't like it, get out,*" I snapped, gritting my teeth.

There was the echoing sound of his laughter before he fell silent again. I dragged in another lungful of air and concentrated on my surroundings, the impressions left behind by those who had walked this ground. Plenty of humans had been here, mostly the homeless or the hopeless, those who felt too far apart from the normal people in the world. My heart bled for these people, those who felt like they were the castaways of society, forced to live in shadow and filth, having to remain hidden so as not to call down unwanted attention. Some days, I didn't feel as if the human race was worth saving.

Again, there was a gentle brush across my mind, soft, intimate, almost comforting.

I located the fading trail I was looking for and started forward. I opened my eyes and followed it, the sensation of seeing in my mind as well as through my eyes were dizzying, but bearable. I'd been doing it my whole life. The anger and malevolence that was left behind stood out among the human impressions. It was like an inky, sticky substance that oozed out, trying to infect everything around it.

Almost against my will, I turned my head slightly to look at the impressions Cole was leaving behind, and was momentarily shocked that he was not leaving a trail like the Demons I was hunting. I frowned. Cole was a King of Hell. By right, he was more evil and destructive than these lesser Demons I was looking for. How did he not leave a dark, sinister impression?

Shaking my head, I focused once again on my task, knowing I was getting closer.

CHAPTER SEVEN
COLE

What in Lucifer's name was wrong with me? Since when did I feel a need to comfort *anyone?*

Mika had been suffering needlessly. I'd merged our minds to feel what it was she was doing, to experience and get an idea for it so that maybe I could do it too. But then I realized why I would never be able to do what she did. I wasn't sure if it was a Witch thing, or if it was a Mika thing, but she was purity.

Alright, she was a little sin, especially when I got her hot and bothered, but her soul was pure and untainted. She was everything good and light in the world, which made it possible for her to pick up even the slightest shadows of evil and track them. I *was* the shadow, which made it impossible for me to track the evil traces as she was doing now. But I could share her mind as she did it and see what she saw, feel what she felt.

It bothered me only slightly that she thought I had taken away her freedom, but I shrugged the guilt away. The truth was Mika's freedom had always had a ticking clock on it. She was a Witch, and it was a miracle she'd made it to twenty-eight without being discovered.

Twenty-eight.

She was a new-born. She was practically fresh from the womb when one compared her age to mine. Then again, almost everyone was that way. Unless I was interested in hooking up with another Demon, humans were all that were available to me, and they would always be ridiculously young when compared to my age.

Anyway, Mika had been living on borrowed time. If I hadn't

found her that night, someone else would have. And who knows what they would have done or how she would be treated.

Granted, I had taken away her freedoms and I was feeling next to no guilt about that. If taking away those freedoms kept her safe and protected from being taken away by dick-bag Angels or another Demon, then that was just how it was going to go. I would make no apologies to her for that, and she would either accept it or she wouldn't.

What had me reeling was the moment of despair and sadness that had swept through her when she considered the number of people, homeless and alone, who felt helpless and lower than dirt. She had far too much compassion to be in the line of work she was in. She felt too deeply for those around her. And I had been unable to bear her feeling so desolate. I'd reached out to her without even thinking about it to offer her comfort and support. It had been a compulsion, a need, something that I had no say in doing. She was hurting, and I had to help her. Either relieve the burden or take it away all together.

What the fuck? What was this woman doing to me?

We continued to walk in silence, and I remained a shadow in her mind, following the trail of evil she was looking for. Meanwhile, I was keeping my senses alert around us. We were very exposed up here, and while I had no doubt that I could wipe out any creature who came at me, I was still on edge thinking about them taking Mika.

And there it was again!

It wasn't just about having the only known Witch in existence. It was about *her*. I refused to relinquish her for some reason, refused to allow her to slip away, not because she was a Witch, but because of who she was as a person.

Oh, damn it all to Lucifer. If my brothers could hear me now, I'd be beaten on so fast for being such a fucking wuss. I shook my head physically to try and shake off the need to be whatever this tiny Witch wanted me to be and searched harder around us for any sign of trouble.

"We're getting closer," Mika murmured just as I began to feel the presence of Demons ahead. A group of them, more than eight. I could taste the blood, sweat, and death in the air and inwardly sighed. Mika was not going to like this. The echo of pain and fear rang out around me the closer we got to a dilapidated old house. It looked like one good gust of wind would send it crashing in on itself. They were in there, and they weren't done playing with the mess.

She paused for a moment, and I knew the second she felt the pain coming from that house. Her breath hitched and her chest tightened painfully for a moment before she started up again, picking up her pace to reach the house and maybe save whoever was still alive inside.

I put my hand out and pulled her to a gentle stop several houses away.

"You wait here, let me go in first," I told her. She frowned.

"No, this is what I do. Someone is still alive in there and in pain. This is my job; there's no way I'm going to let you go in there and take over," she replied sharply.

"The Demons are still in there. They'll take one look at you and want to tear the flesh from your bones. That is if they don't realize you're a Witch first," I explained. That was something else I'd never bothered to do before, never *had* to do before—explain myself.

"Then don't let them touch me. But I'm not waiting here. I can sense the humans in there too," she replied and before I could come back with a reason for her to stay, she was already jogging towards the house. I didn't point out that all but one of the remaining living humans in there were about as evil as the Demons they stood with. They'd all be making their way down to Hell very soon. The only one that was any good was dying a slow agonizing death. I sighed. I could keep her safe, I knew that. But she wasn't going to be happy about the way I went about it. Oh well. I won't apologize for who I am, and I'd already given her all the warning I was going to give that I was not about to change. Not for anyone. Not even her.

I followed behind her as we reached the house, and I felt her apprehension grow. She could feel the strong vibrations of evil, sense the pain that had occurred, and could smell the acrid smell of death. All of it hit her hard, and she had to steel herself and strengthen her mental shields so that she could continue on without doubling over in pain. Witches—or maybe just Mika—were far too sensitive for this.

I closed my eyes and sent my senses out searching, taking note of where each human and Demon were and how many I was up against. It was hardly going to be a fair fight; they were too few in numbers. But I didn't care about fair, I cared about ending this shit so that I could take Mika back to Hell with me and probably refuse her to come here ever again. Seriously, if her being on the surface hurt her so much, and I had to go with her, we were never coming back. It was stupid to allow her to do something which would only cause her suffering, and I *detested* the way I wanted nothing more than to soothe her hurts and make it all better. I wasn't the *soothing* type. Fuck that, she could just stay in Hell and be my personal nurse. This whole *feelings* thing was a major draw-back in this claiming shit, and I was not interested in letting it continue.

So, I needed to wipe these fuckers from the face of the Earth and then I could take Mika back to Hell. I'd had enough of this shit for one day.

Opening my eyes, I set Mika to one side without looking at her and faced the door. I kept a mental map in my head of where all of those inside were standing and then I kicked in the front door. Yes, I could have waved my hand and had the thing disappear—it wasn't magically guarded or anything—but I needed to vent some frustrations.

"Cole!" Mika hissed, but I ignored her and strode in. I tried to wave a hand to place a command on her to stay right there, but she was prepared. My command barely had a chance to take hold before she began unraveling it and I shrugged. I was a Demon; I was a motherfucking King of Hell. It was time she remembered that and got a small taste of what I was about. If that meant she was going to witness me destroy a room full of evil, then so be it. I knew it would take her a minute, maybe less to take apart the small ward I'd thrown at her to keep her out of the house, I could do a little damage in that time.

Noise echoed from the room down the hall where they were all gathered. The scent of blood, death and decay reached me, as well as the sounds of warning, of weapons and a shuddering cry for help that was cut ominously short. I counted one less heartbeat and knew that the human who had been dying painfully and slowly for their amusement was now dead. At least they had done that job for me. I would have had to dispatch the human myself, and no doubt Mika would have reprimanded me for it because she would have tried to heal him. But I could feel that his intestines were on the outside of his body, and since she currently took the wounds of those she healed onto herself, and I wasn't about to let that happen.

I'd have to talk to her soon about learning to heal others the real way. Other Witches knew how to do this without suffering the effects of those they chose to heal. Mika was self-taught, which meant her knowledge on how to use her magic was crude and rudimentary.

I reached the doorway of the occupied room and took stock of what was around me. Eleven Demons and three humans. They were all covered in blood and tattoos with burns etched into their skins. They had branded themselves in their belief.

Contrary to what many believed, not every Demon was under our control. There were those who had peeled off over time and created their own little group. We'd never bothered with them because their numbers were so abysmal that it was hilarious to even consider them a threat. But it was clear to see that these Demons in front of me now belonged to that small group. Every cluster had their overzealous individuals, and these Demons were some of those.

"Hmm… looks like you got carried away with the guests at your party," I mused as I looked around at the three dead humans on the floor, their insides spilled out around them.

"We have no issue with you, Demon King. Let us leave," the one I assumed was the leader piped up. I turned back to look at him and raised an eyebrow.

"You and yours are creating a problem for mine. Until now, my brothers and I have been more than fine to leave you alone to wreak havoc for whatever purposes you had. It did not concern us and was no issue. But these recent killings have created some new... problems," I answered.

"What problems?" another spat, and I tipped my head to the side as I considered him.

It had been a while since I'd joined in on the torture that took place in the Pits. There were several levels of torture a soul went through before they became a Demon, but then there were several levels of torture new Demons went through before they could be considered a high-level Demon. I could tell by looking at these few that their suffering was limited compared to what mine went through. Their tolerance for pain was lower. Their knowledge of how to kill or hurt another Demon would also be diminished.

"Cole," Mika panted as she came skidding into the doorway.

I immediately waved my hand to keep her immobile, ready this time for her intrusion. I may not care if she witnessed my depravity, but I would not allow her to put herself in danger in some ill-conceived plot to attempt to save the worthless humans in this room. They were eviler than some Demons.

The Demons around us looked at her with avid interest, hunger, and need.

"The Witch," one sneered

"She's mine," I ground out.

"But she will be ours," the leader growled. I cocked an eyebrow and smiled.

"You're welcome to try and take her from me. I'd like nothing more than to remove your head with my hands."

I bowed slightly, my blood singing with the chance to fight. True, this would hardly cause me to break a sweat, but I could use a little something to vent my anger on. And this would be the perfect time and place. I could wave my hand and have this room combust with hellfire. I could use my power to grip their hearts in my mind like a vice and slowly bring them all to their knees before exploding the organ in their chests. A number of fast and creative ways to kill them ran through my mind, but I ignored them all. I wanted a little bit of a fight. I needed messy and painful and drawn out. Being a King of Hell meant that I held a lot of power over all lesser Demons. But using it right now felt too easy. I had to make a point.

The first Demon rushed me, and I threw a barrier around Mika that both protected her and kept her in place before I flicked my wrist and sent the Demon flying into the wall across from me. The room burst into action.

There was a flurry of fists, fangs, and claws. I side-stepped as two Demons tried to rush me at once, their heavy bodies slamming into the drywall before spinning to face me again. I gripped another Demon by his head as he rammed me with his shoulders and twisted hard. There was a loud, wet, snap followed by a squelching rip as his head twisted and I ripped it from his neck, tossing the bloody mess to a corner.

Mika's cry of horror was drowned out by the shouting of the Demons. I felt her disgust and pain, but after assuring myself that none had touched her, I turned my attention back to the fight.

I was hit on the side by one of the humans. I smirked down at him, his strength barely registering to me as he swung his fist at my face. His eyes widened and his face paled visibly as I grinned down at him. For a moment, I let him see the hellfire that burned in my eyes before I raked my now elongated black nails across his face. My claws dug in deep and ripped. I felt his eye tear from its socket, blood sprayed up my arms and across my chest. His agonized screams pierced the air and I turned to the leader who was hanging back, allowing his minions to do his bidding. Two more Demons stepped forward and I twisted them both harshly, one after the other so that their backs snapped like twigs. Simultaneously, I grabbed at their throats with either hand, dug in my nails and wrenched their windpipes from their throats.

This would not kill the Demons, no. They would exist in agony for a time. The only things that could kill them were Angel or Demon blades. Demon Blade worked on lower-level Demons, and even Knights of Hell. But not me. Not the Kings. Only an

Angel Blade would do that.

Sliding my knife from its sheath at the small of my back, I stepped forward as another Demon rushed me. I ducked and struck out hard, slicing my dagger across his abdomen so that his insides fell out before I raked it upwards, twisting it in his heart, tearing it apart.

I faintly registered Mika calling out my name, begging for me to stop, asking me to spare the humans. But I was not going to let a single being who had participated in this massacre loose. I may be a fucking King of Hell, but we had rules, we had integrity, we had a *reason* for killing. We got a bad rap from those fucking feathered assholes. They made us out to be creatures of murder and mayhem without a cause. It was what we were created for—torturing the damned and the deserving. Who gave a shit if we found a way to get enjoyment out of it? We always had a reason. And taking out innocents without a cause was still wrong for us. We *tortured the evil and the damned*. We didn't create them. We punished them.

Again and again, I swung my knife, my eyes still on the leader as I made a bloody mess of his followers. The two humans took little more effort than snapping their necks.

The two Demons I'd shoved into a wall came at me together once again. I gripped one by the neck as I struck out with my blade at the other, ripping it across his jugular. The Demon in my grip clawed at my forearm and I lashed out, the dagger digging deep into his chest and raking up to his throat. His lungs and heart were exposed, his ribcage breaking open. Over and over, I slashed and grabbed, ripped and tore. The sounds of blood and innards hitting the floor was music to my ears, drowning out the shouts and sobs from Mika as I turned the already bloody room into a slaughterhouse.

I stood before the leader when the last of his minions had fallen and he sucked in a steadying breath. After a moment he bowed and dropped to one knee.

"I offer you my allegiance, my King. Please forgive my errant ways and accept me as one of your own," he said quickly, his eyes downcast. I gripped him by the shoulder and urged him to stand. His dark, emotionless eyes met mine and I shook my head.

"You let your men fight for you, die for you, and then you save your own hide by offering to defect to my side?"

The two Demons on the ground who still lived but were in horrible pain, made gurgling noises as if in protest of my words.

"I realize now that I was wrong to try to do this without being under the command of my master. Please allow me to rectify my mistake and make you a vow of loyalty," he begged. I tipped his head up with the blade of my knife under his chin.

"Cole," Mika warned in a choked voice from the sidelines.

The Demon before me flicked his attention her way, and I saw them heat in hunger and greed. Her small, stifled sobs seemed to echo in the now deathly quiet room, but I gave no thought as to what she was crying over. She knew these Demons were evil, there was no need to cry over their deaths.

"No," I answered through gritted teeth. The Demon's eyes flew back to my face in horror before I slammed the blade upwards through the bottom of his jaw, holding it there as I watched the life drain from his eyes. When he was truly gone, I yanked the blade out and let him fall to the ground in an unceremonious heap. Shaking my head in disgust, I then turned around and made quick work of the other Demons dying, finishing them off with little more than a few slices of my blade. There was blood spatter and innards everywhere, the scent of blood and death soaking into the air and the floorboards.

Wiping my blade on my pants leg, I slid it back into my scabbard before turning to face Mika. Her face was ashen, her cheeks wet and her already big eyes wider than ever. A strange pang twisted in my gut, but I ignored it and waved my hand, releasing her from the ward I'd trapped her in and removed the barrier. She was clean, even though the wall and floor before her were caked with Demon remains.

Silence reigned for a moment, and I steeled myself. I told myself that I didn't care what she thought or said. Because in the end, I was who I was and there was no changing it. She needed to know and get used to it. I'd told myself that before the slaughter, and I was clinging to it now. But somewhere deep inside, a place I didn't want to acknowledge, her thoughts mattered to me.

"Cole," she whispered, her big, green eyes glued to me, her thick lashes spiky with tears.

"Don't think about reprimanding me," I glared.

"He begged you to spare him, to allow him to join your side," she protested, her voice wavering slightly as she fought to bite back another sob. I snickered and shook my head, stepping closer.

"He begged me to spare him in order to save himself. He never would have been loyal to me," I explained.

"You don't know that—"

"I do," I cut in with a growl. "I have been a King of Hell longer than you can possibly fathom. There is nothing I do not know about Demons and their capabilities. There are a few who do not follow my brothers or myself, they defected, and we have allowed it because their numbers have been small, and they are little more than a nuisance. But now they are encroaching on our territories. They are making a move, and we cannot tolerate it," I snarled.

"He asked—"

"Had I let him go, his first move would have been against you. Make no mistake about it, Mika, he wanted you."

She glowered and I sucked in a steadying breath. The fight had been quick and nowhere near enough to exhaust my reserves of frustration and rage.

After a few seconds, she glared and breathed out slowly, trying to control her emotions. "And the humans?"

"They were as evil as the Demons they served."

"They were human. There are human laws to deal with them," she argued in exasperation. I shrugged. She made a noise of frustration and blew out a large breath.

"You're hurt," she pointed out, her voice resigned.

"That happens sometimes," I shrugged. The claw marks were already healing. Things like that didn't stay around for long.

"Let me heal you," she offered, although she didn't sound happy about it. I glanced up at her and frowned. Why would she want to heal me when she was so obviously angry at me?

And then I saw her wince and I understood. All at once, I understood why she'd been screaming, why she'd begged me to stop. Rage at myself had my chest tightening and I stilled, unable to believe my own stupidity

"No," I shook my head and focused on my pain. I ignored it, pushed it away, and her shoulders visibly relaxed. Regret was a bitter taste in my mouth and one I was not used to feeling. Guilt was new too, and I didn't like it one bit. But I had just hurt Mika when I only wanted to protect her.

"I'm sorry, Tomika. I should have remembered that you'd feel the pain here today. I was thoughtless," I added, closing my eyes in dismay. Of course she would have felt it all. The pain I put those Demons through, their deaths. Her soul would have been on fire, demanding that she heal, that she save their lives. And I'd locked her in a ward she could not break free from to do as she was meant to do. Fucking hell—I was an asshole of the first order. I already knew that, but my thoughtlessness had been a torture for her.

I ran a hand through my hair in agitation.

"Fuck!" I roared and slammed my fist through the wall. I hated that I had forgotten, hated that I'd come in thinking that I was protecting her, when in fact I'd caused her the most pain. Silence fell between us again and I brushed the plaster from my hand, refusing to meet her gaze for the longest time.

"Are you okay?" I mumbled.

She wiped at her wet cheeks and nodded, avoiding my eyes. Fuck.

"You know those men deserved it, right?" I tried again, desperate for her anger instead of her tears.

"Cole, you can't just kill people!" she shouted, outraged. Relief hit me hard at seeing her fire and I bit back a grin.

"Yes, I can. I just did."

Mika glowered and kept very still. She was standing within a perfect half-circle, untouched by the blood and gore that now covered every inch of the room.

"Cole." Mika sighed and shook her head. "It's wrong to kill like that. There are other ways to handle things. Three of those men were humans. There are human laws and punishments, and it would have been a perfect way for the humans to wrap up this case," she tried to explain with all the forced patience of an adult explaining something to a child. I cocked an eyebrow.

"How is it wrong? They were evil men, and nothing was going to stop them. Your human laws have too many flaws, too many loopholes, and the truly evil and wicked often walk free. Yes, they get punished when they die and end up in Hell, but there's no punishment here on the surface where they deserve it also." She gritted her teeth.

"They needed to be punished, and they would have been had you let me do my job," Mika ground out.

"And they will be punished. Trust me, where they're going, they're being disciplined," I explained, seeing no fault in my logic, but many holes in hers. Why was it so difficult for her to understand? The humans tried, but in their need to make sure the innocent were not wrongfully convicted, they made it all too easy for the corrupt to walk free of their crimes. At least now, these men will go to Hell where they will be properly punished.

Mika threw her hands up in the air in exasperation and planted her hands on her hips. My attention turned to her perfectly rounded hips and that curve in her waist that led to the swell of her generous breasts, and I felt that familiar fire begin to kindle in my groin.

Mika's eyes flickered with warning but there was an answering heat that made me grin.

"Alright smart-ass. You wiped out a whole clan of Demons, a few corrupt humans and managed not to get me dirty in the process. Thank you for that by the way," she began.

"You're welcome."

Silence fell between us again and I still felt odd... like I was walking on eggshells. I had hurt her. Unintentionally, but all the same, her pain had been caused by me. I was a bastard, but I wasn't cruel without cause, at least not to her.

Never her.

Of that, I was oddly certain.

"We should go... I don't think there's anything more we can do here," she said after a moment. I nodded and waited for her to step out of the doorway before I joined her.

"You may want to do something about... that," she pointed to my clothing. I glanced down and grinned. Yep–I was covered head-to-toe in blood, guts, and other matter. With a wave of my hand, I was clean again, not a speck of blood on me. Before she could protest, I swept her up in my arms and strode out of the house and away from the death and decay behind us. She might not admit it, but I knew the vibrations of violence were suffocating her, making her uncomfortable.

"Cole! Put me down," she hissed, wriggling in my grip.

"I don't mind carrying you. It makes me feel all dashing," I answered mockingly.

She scoffed and shook her head, but I caught the smile that tugged at her lips and felt an answering tightening in my chest. For fuck's sake, why did making this woman smile, laugh, or just making her happy in general, give me such a sense of pride and satisfaction? I've never given a shit about anyone besides my brothers... not really. We weren't programmed that way. Sure, there'd been the odd person here and there who had elicited a little of my loyalty or whatever passed for friendship from a Demon King, but there had never been anything close to this. It had to be The Mark. It was beginning to be a pain in the ass. Because if caring for this woman was going to become as important as I feared, then she was a huge threat to me. She would become a weak spot, somewhere for my many enemies to attack to bring me down.

And I *hated* having a weakness.

I got us out of that house and set her on her feet once we were clear of the gore. I'd put a group of Demons on clean up duty. While normally it wasn't a top priority, we did tend to keep the existence of our kind quiet.

"Cole," Mika's voice dragged me out of my spiraling mood. I glanced up at the frown on her face and I looked into her mind again to see what she was seeing. Another trail of evil, this one still fresh leading past several broken houses.

"More?"

She nodded. "More."

Well, fuck.

CHAPTER EIGHT
MIKA

I could tell Cole wasn't happy about there being another trail to pick up on and that there are more Demons or evil inclined humans to follow. I didn't think he was bothered much by the prospect of killing a few more as he did in that house. He hadn't even broken a sweat when he reduced the other Demons and humans to their bloody insides. In fact, he'd appeared down-right bored. A shiver worked its way down my spine. This Demon could lay waste to hundreds of Demons or humans without straining himself. What would happen if he actually tried? And would I be a bystander of such destruction, or would he force me to be a part of it?

Seeing him in there, had been like seeing his true face. I'd thought I knew what he was capable of, and I guess on an intellectual level, I did know, but watching him dispatch eleven Demons and three humans in less than three minutes and walking away with little more than a couple of scratches had been eye-opening. More than that, I had seen the joy he'd taken in their deaths. I'd seen it burn within his eyes, seen it etched into the lines of his face as he ripped them apart with little more effort than it would take me to put up my hair.

I shivered and pushed that thought aside for now, aware that he was continually slipping in and out of my mind. I wasn't even sure if he was aware that he was doing it. It was almost like he was reassuring himself that I was still there, absentmindedly brushing against my consciousness as we went about our business.

The pain.

I forced myself not to feel it again. Standing there, helpless, forced to watch and endure the pain in my soul as he tore apart the beings in front of me had hurt in a way I'd never known. The Angel Blade wound I'd taken on from Cole when we first met had been the most painful thing I'd ever endured, but being forced to remain immobile and not help had been a burning in my soul that still hurt. I was a Witch. I may be new to the label, but I had always known that I was meant to heal, no matter the side I was on.

How had he forgotten that? Or maybe he hadn't. Maybe he'd meant for me to feel it in order to remind me who was really in power. He wanted me to know he was the boss, that what he said was the law, and I had no say in anything anymore. Was this outing, which I had assumed was done out of generosity on his part, really just a way for him to teach me some kind of lesson?

"Mika," Cole said my name softly, his voice like a velvet caress. I could feel my body react to that tone in his voice and I hated it. I'd just watched the man butcher a room full of people less than five minutes ago. How the hell could I ever look at him with desire again? But my body didn't seem to have gotten the memo because I could feel that familiar pulsing and pounding begin deep in my core.

"I don't really want to talk about it, if it's all the same to you," I answered without looking at him.

"Tomika—"

"Look," I cut in, pointing to the trail that only I could see, but I knew he was sharing my mind, I knew he'd see what I could see. I flicked him a quick glance and caught the dark frown, the small growl before I faced forward again. I followed the fresh trail, moving quickly in the hopes of saving someone. Anyone. If Cole

wasn't worried about what we'd face in the next house, then
what had put that dark look on his face? I could have delved into
his mind to find the information, but I shied away from the
thought. I wasn't sure that was a habit I wanted to get into.

The stain of evil on this house was worse than the previous one.
Where the last house looked like it would topple over with the
next gust of wind, this one was better kept. It was still a house in
the slums, but someone had obviously tried to keep the house in
order. The yard was mowed, the gardens kept and maintained
with cute little flowers. The paint was peeling in places, but it
had obviously been painted within the last ten years, which was
more than I could say for the neighbors. But the feeling of death
and pain that came off this house in waves was almost enough to
bring me to my knees.

It was the same kind of pain I'd come to associate with the
others, where a true innocent's blood had been spilled, their life
snatched away.

"Mika, wait," Cole called as I raced for the stairs. Maybe I could
save them. Maybe, if I hurried, I could save this one. Turning his
trick on him, I threw a Ward up behind me. I knew it would only
slow Cole down for a few seconds, but that was enough time for
me to make it over the threshold of the house.

I ran down the hall, following the echoing sounds of screams that
seemed to live inside the walls. I skidded to a halt outside the
living room and gasped.

There was a tall man facing me, his long thick hair was black as
night and tied neatly at the nape of his neck with a leather cord.
His face was a work of art, all carved edges and strong features.
He looked like a warrior of old. I took note of his thick black coat
and the large sword in his hands, and then my gaze trailed down
to the woman at his feet. Her blonde hair was stained red with
blood, the gaping wound in her chest revealed the place where
her heart had been cut from her.

The cloaked man raised his gaze to mine, and I reacted without
thinking. I was angry, furious, utterly disgusted and I was tired of
evil winning every time.

I drew power from my core and threw it at him with all my anger and hate, but to my complete and utter shock, it passed right through him and dissipated into the air.

He cocked a regal eyebrow at me; a King looking down at a peasant. I was gathering more energy, preparing to try again when I was yanked backwards. Cole stood before me, his broad shoulders blocking my view of the room. I waited for him to move forward, to Ward me out, to start throwing his blades, but to my surprise, he stepped to the side and allowed me through. I looked between the two men and cocked my head to the side when Cole sighed.

"I am sorry, Mika. I wish we had been on time to save her," Cole murmured. I frowned and peered at the robed man who was watching me curiously.

"But you're not going to try and kill the man that took her life?" I asked. Cole frowned.

"What man?" he asked. I turned to him in shock and then back to the gorgeous being in front of me, still standing over the dead woman.

"He cannot see me," he explained.

"I gathered that," I replied. Cole's head snapped up, his sharp eyes looking around the room. "Why?"

The man shrugged.

"I am neither evil nor good. I am neutral. I am an inevitable part of life, of existence, and I am only here when needed," he replied cryptically. I scrubbed a hand over my face and tried to conceal my exasperation.

"Did you have to sound so much like a fortune cookie?" I asked. The man's eyes lit with amusement for a moment before they were once again cold and flat.

"Mika." Cole brought my attention back to him.

"I'm pretty sure I'm talking to Death, or a Reaper," I answered. It was the only thing that made sense. The whole *inevitability* thing clued me in. Cole's face cleared in understanding, and I felt him merge his vision with mine so that he too could see. At once, Cole's gaze focused on the other man.

"Reaper," Cole confirmed.

The Reaper stepped back in surprise, his eyes swinging between the two of us in shock.

"I must say… I have been around for a long time. Longer than you, King of Hell, but I have never had anyone but Lucifer and God see me. Or those who have recently died, and I have come to collect them," he told us in shock.

"So, you were not the one who killed her," I said, nodding to the dead woman. The Reaper's eyes did not leave me, and he shook his head.

"No. I took her soul when she died, as is my duty," he answered. "I can sense a connection between the two of you, but how can that be? You are a Witch, he is a King of Hell," he asked. I shook my head and shrugged.

"We're still working that out ourselves," I answered.

The Reaper studied me more closely and then stepped forward. I felt Cole tense beside me, but he made no other move to intercept. The Reaper was neutral, so there shouldn't be any need to shield me from him, but I could sense that Cole was like a snake; coiled and ready to strike should the need arise.

"May I see The Mark?" he asked.

I pulled back slightly. How did he know? My question must have shown on my face because he smiled gently.

"As I said, I have been around a long time. The only other I have known to have a connection like the one I sense between you two, was between Lucifer and Lilith. With these types of connections, there is always a Mark," he explained.

"Cole?"

I detested it the moment I reached out for him, but I wasn't sure about this man.

"He may know something that we do not. You wish to know all there is to know about this Mark, do you not?" Cole replied, his eyes on the Reaper. *"Do not worry, Little Witch. I will not allow any harm to come to you,"* Cole added with a small smug voice.

I mentally groaned and his chuckle brushed across my mind.

"If I show you, you have to tell me everything you know about it," I decided.

"I will divulge all I can," he replied. That wasn't exactly the same thing, but it was something. Sucking in a breath, I nodded and turned my back to him while lifting my hair. I waited for several seconds before I turned back to face him.

"This Mark is not the same as the one Lucifer and Lilith have, but it feels old, as old as I am, maybe older still. It is powerful, and I daresay it is impossible to reverse. It will tie you both together for eternity, and I greatly suspect its benefits will outweigh any limitations it may set on you both," the Reaper explained.

"That's it? That's all you have to say?" I asked, frustrated. It was a whole lot of cryptic nothing. His eyes smiled, but he said no more about it. His gaze swung to Cole, and he once again was all business.

"They will come for her. All of them. Any of them. She is precious, and a symbol of things long lost," he added.

I felt Cole go still. Not outwardly, he was already quite steady, but inside, where no one else could see, he was as still as the mountains, his eyes focused. I felt his outright refusal to allow me to slip away, the flash of pure fury at the thought of anyone taking me away. His possessiveness, his need to keep me safe. All of it happened in a second, maybe two, before he was once again a blank slate.

"They will not get her," Cole answered evenly, but there was a threat in his words. The Reaper shook his head.

"You will have a fight on your hands unlike any you've faced before. You're going to need allies, others at your back. You need ones you can trust because they will use everything they have to take her from you," the Reaper continued.

I felt Cole's slow resolve to do whatever was necessary to keep me, to have me safe. It was a heady feeling, having a being so powerful decide so adamantly that you were going to be protected above all else. For a moment I even found myself softening towards him. But then I remembered that he had Marked me. He had taken away my freedom, and he wanted me for his own personal uses, not because I was someone he could not live without. He had his own agenda for keeping me, and I had to remember that.

"Any advice?" I asked, hoping my voice hadn't sounded as small as I was sure it had.

The Reaper turned his black gaze back to me and he shook his head.

"Stay safe. Do not allow yourself to be fooled by those who would use your vulnerabilities against you," he replied. Again, another cryptic answer. I don't know why I'd expected anything different.

With another nod to both of us, the Reaper vanished into thin air. I let out a long breath before my eyes rested once again on the dead woman. She hadn't been dead long. I stepped closer, my heart heavy at the loss of life. This group of Demons and humans were killing true innocents in order to further their own abilities and powers. This loss of life hurt me on a level that was different than from my need to heal. I ached with their loss, and with my helplessness to stop it. I was angry at myself, frustrated at being unable to do a damn thing. How many had they killed now? How many more would have to die?

"Mika," Cole's voice brushed my mind, and I could feel his need to comfort me, a need he wished he did not have.

I had caught his earlier thoughts, the ones he had unintentionally pushed into my mind. He thought of me as a weakness he could not afford. Yeah, I was a burden. A problem. And he was going to lock me away somewhere so that no one else could take me, no one else could use me against him.

Unless I could find a way to break away from him, to run and hide and stay safe.

I carefully kept that thought in the back of my mind, as far away from him as possible. I needed to do my own research and gather all the knowledge I needed. Running now would get me nowhere but locked away for good. I had to bide my time, play it smart. I'd let him think I was happy being his prisoner, but I would need to use my time wisely to find any and all vulnerabilities in his realm so that when I ran for it, I could stay gone.

"Let's go," I said out loud, turning away from the dead woman and marching quickly out of the house. I didn't want to be here anymore. All I could see was my failure, my inability to find whoever did this and stop them. I knew now that it was more than just a handful of Demons, it was an entire faction determined to wipe out purity and innocence. I knew enough to know that the heart of a true innocent was a powerful organ that, once consumed, gave the one who consumed it immense power and control. Was it as simple as that? Were they simply after power?

Sighing, I closed my eyes and turned my face up to the sunny sky, letting the warmth heat me, but no matter how long I stayed out here, I knew it could not warm me where I needed it most.

I blinked and glanced back at Cole as he stepped from the house to stand in front of me. I wanted to know more about my past, my family, my ancestors. I needed to know more about them and how to control my powers and use them. And Nova was the only one who knew.

"I'd like to speak to Nova," I told Cole. Hellfire flickered in his eyes for a fraction of a second and then it was gone. He turned away from me for a moment, his jaw clenched, but he nodded.

"Let's go," he suggested, holding out his hand to me. I slipped my hand into his and let him pull me in close. I closed my eyes as I felt the wind whip around us and tried to ignore the way I felt wrapped in Cole's arms. The longer I stayed here, the more I could feel my resistance to him slipping.

I needed to get out.

CHAPTER NINE
COLE

I reluctantly let Mika go when we arrived back in the entrance hall of Hell. She pulled away, her eyes averted, and her arms wrapped around herself as if in comfort. She had retreated into herself, her natural shield back in place in her mind. It didn't matter anyway. Thanks to this connection, I could slip in and out of her mind at will. This time, however, I didn't need to be in her mind to know what was going on.

She wanted out.

And why wouldn't she, really? What did the life I had forced her into have to offer her? She got to know more about her ancestors and now knew what she was, and if she'd let me, there'd be some really hot fucking sex in our very near future. But other than that... What else did she have here?

Running was the logical thing for her to want to do. Everyone would be coming for her, everyone. And I'd already claimed her for my own reasons. She was intelligent enough to realize she was in danger no matter where we were, and that the most logical way of keeping her safe was to keep her here. It would only be a matter of time before word spread that a Witch survived, and not much longer than that for them to know I was the one who had her. She thought she could keep a low profile and look after herself if she were out on her own, but if she really thought about it, she would know that wasn't right at all.

She was a Witch. If she used her magic in defence, it would linger in the air. And when one of us got hurt, she would be desperate to heal, which would reveal herself in the end.

Beside me in Hell really was the safest place for her.

I watched Mika go through my door without turning back to me. Frowning, I shoved away the need to go to her, to wrap her in my arms and give her whatever comfort that I could. She'd only been a part of my world for a day, and already it felt as though she was fast becoming the most important thing in existence to me. The Mark had worked fast to entrench her into my life, my soul, and my mind. She now factored into everything I did and said, she was always a grain of every thought. And what was more, I felt as though I had known her forever. Thanks to our minds constantly reaching for one another, I knew her unlike anyone else.

Snarling to myself, I spun away from my door and paced the length of the marble room where we all arrived after traveling by shadow.

I detested this new vulnerability and the feelings it brought with it. Mika was going to be an asset; I knew she would. But in the meantime, I was left with a neon sign pointing at the best way to injure me. No one besides a Reaper knew that we were bound together. So at least no one *really* knew that I had a vulnerability, but the truth would be revealed in time, and then Demons and Angels alike would be coming for her at all angles to take her from me.

I had to find a way to nip this in the bud. I needed to cut off my emotions from her, to not really care about her feelings. If that meant numbing my desire for her, then fine, I'd do that too. Even though I'd *never* felt such a pull towards someone in my entire existence, and that even the psychic sex had been the most satisfying I'd ever had the pleasure of participating in, I needed to be done with it. Because I was *not* going to suffer through the rest of eternity with these fucking knots in my stomach at the very thought of her in pain or hurting. I detested that I cared about her emotional health as much as her physical safety. I needed to remain indifferent to her in every way. She had to be a tool to use to end this endless fucking battle between us and the Angels, and she was a way for me to win. That was all.

An image of her tear-stained face filtered across my mind, and I hissed in displeasure.

"Fucking hell," I snarled. I drew in a deep breath and laced my fingers together on top of my head. What the fuck was I going to do?

I glanced down the long hallway at my brothers' doors and sighed. Nova already knew about Mika. I wasn't sure if he'd told the others, but I didn't think he had, or I would have been inundated with telepathic messages from them demanding to see her for themselves. They'd no doubt find out soon. Maybe they would know something more about this Mark. And more than that, maybe they'd know how to numb its effects so that I wasn't a giant target to my enemies.

"Brothers. I have need of you. Meet me in the entry room, we have some things to discuss." I sent the call out with a resigned sigh. Waving a hand absentmindedly, I created a stone table and nine chairs for us to sit at. We'd probably be here a while, and I needed some bloody answers.

"Mika, I will be with you soon. I have some things to discuss with my brothers. Please do not come out unless I ask—I do not know how the others will react to you, and I wish to keep you safe," I reached out to her. It was true. I knew that Nova wanted her because of some long-ago vow and connection to a Witch he considered a sister, but I had no idea if the others would take her because they saw a chance at power where none other had it. I'd like to think that my brothers would help me protect her, but I had no guarantees. This was unknown territory for us, and everything in me screamed to protect Mika... even from them.

"I will await your orders, oh masterful one," Mika replied, pure sarcasm in her voice. I bit back a grin and, without giving it another thought, I imagined sliding my fingers through her hair and brushing a kiss across her lips. I felt her instant reaction.

"Careful, Little Witch. That kind of attitude will have consequences you are not ready to pay," I reminded, feeling my pants get uncomfortably tight at the thought of punishing her. I hissed when I felt a brush of fingers across my crotch and her echoing laughter in my mind.

"It looks like you are the one suffering the consequences," she teased.

"You are braver now that you are out of sight, Witch, but you will not always be so," I warned, shocking myself that I was teasing her. But I couldn't deny that it felt amazing to know that I had brought out that small moment of playfulness in her despite how she was feeling.

There was a small silence and then I felt her humor die off slowly and she gave a small, resigned sigh.

"I will not come out while they are present unless you say it is safe," she agreed, and I cursed at the lack of humor or fire in her spirit. I hated the despondency in her voice, the lack of fight. And I hated that I hated it even more. I should not care how she felt, and yet it seemed to matter a great deal to me, my instinctual reaction was to be what she needed. Gently, I imagined brushing my thumb across her cheek and kissing her forehead before I withdrew from her mind completely.

I could feel my brothers approaching, and I did not want to be thinking of Mika and her feelings when I faced them. I needed answers, and so I needed my head on straight.

"What is so urgent that we had to talk right now? I was training my Knights," Adrik asked as he strode towards the table with long strides.

"Did you get struck by an Angel Blade again?" Malik asked with a mocking smile.

"Nah, I bet you're finally bored enough to throw yourself in the Pit," Harkyn added as they all came towards me. I smiled and waited as they each took a seat.

"Well?" Tamas asked as he too joined our brothers.

"I'd rather wait until all of you are here to begin," I answered.

"It's about her, isn't it?" Nova asked as he took his seat, his blue eyes flicking to my door and back to me. I knew he was worried about Mika, knew he was worried I'd mistreat or harm her. The knowledge that I'd already fucked up began to nudge at me and I shoved it away. What Nova didn't know wouldn't hurt.

"Who is 'she'?" Cassius asked.

"And should we have brought weapons?" Devlin added.

The funny part was, he was serious. We'd all, at one time or another, gotten ourselves caught up in a situation where a female had wanted us dead for some perceived betrayal. I mean, usually it was because they caught us in bed with another woman, but that was a finer detail that wasn't really important.

"No weapons necessary," I answered.

"Then why are we here?" Corvin asked, and the mood in the room instantly changed. Corvin didn't come out of his realm, not ever, not in the last few hundred years. His temper was something we were all cautious of, and he had little time for frivolous activities, not even with us.

"Okay, now that you're all here, we'll get to it," I began, sucking in a breath. It was now or never. I had to trust someone, even the Reaper had said so. And if I were to trust anyone, it would be my brothers. I was mostly sure they would support me, help me, but I wasn't absolute in my certainty, and so I was still hesitant to speak.

When the silence dragged on while I tried to find a way to phrase things and how much I wanted to give away, Devlin shifted, his expression darkening.

"Cole found a Witch," Nova volunteered.

"Donovan," I snapped, instantly angry.

"What? You were wasting our time, and we have shit to do. Is she okay?" he continued. I glared.

"If you mean is she breathing and unharmed, then yes," I ground out. "We had a rough day, but she'll be fine."

"You found a Witch?" Devlin asked, sitting forward, his eyes locked on me with intense interest.

I nodded.

"Look, there is a lot of information here, so I need you all to remain silent for a moment while I tell you everything I know. And then hopefully, you assholes can help me figure out a way to handle it, because I'm beginning to think this is a little outside my wheelhouse," I admitted.

One by one, they nodded and waited, but the tension in the room was high. Sighing, I started at the fight in the warehouse and explained everything that had happened since. I may have skipped the juicier details about kissing her, her riding my leg and our psychic dream. But I was pretty sure they understood our relationship was beyond that of kidnapper and victim.

"So… you've somehow bound her to you?" Malik asked, looking skeptical. I nodded and leaned forward to show the palm of my hand. I skimmed my thumb over it and The Mark appeared. One by one, they all looked at it and then I took my own seat.

"Mika has one that matches on the back of her neck where I grabbed her that night, only hers does not disappear like mine," I explained. Silence fell over the table, and I waited as everyone absorbed what I'd told them.

"So, Witches are still among us," Adrik murmured softly. Harkyn frowned down at his hands, looking lost in his own thoughts. I frowned. He hadn't looked all that surprised at finding out that Witches were still in existence, and he'd since retreated in on himself.

"How did she go undetected for so long?" Devlin asked, seeming perplexed. I shrugged.

"I don't know. The fact is, she did. But she's here now, claimed and still in need of tutoring. But we're both needing more information about this Mark. I mean, are there ways to numb or at the very least, dull it's effects?" I asked.

"The sexual pull too much for you, brother? Maybe she needs a real King?" Malik suggested with a grin.

Without thought and without pause, I sent him flying backwards with a flick of my wrist. He hit the wall hard, and I stood, fury flowing through me, harsh and violent at the very thought of any of my brothers touching her in that way.

"What the fuck?" Malik shouted.

"Don't talk about her like that," I ground out, fully prepared to beat him to within an inch of his life.

"This fucking bitch has you turning on your brothers now?" Malik snarled in outrage. I opened my mouth to tell him what I'd do if he even mentioned touching Mika again, when I felt her gentle touch across my mind, a soothing balm that made it easier to see past the red haze of fury blinding me.

"It's The Mark," Corvin muttered, looking unperturbed at the fact that I was willing to beat on my own brother. Why the hell was he so calm about the news that Witches still walked among us?

"Fuck The Mark. Since when do we turn on each other?" Malik demanded, striding back to the table.

Corvin exhaled heavily as if we were no more than troublesome little kids.

"The Mark is obviously more than a branding. It ties them together, or weren't you listening? His soul and hers are forever intertwined, and from what you have told us, Cole, it does not look as though there is a way out of the binding, nor would there be a way to dim the effects it has on either of you," he explained in a matter-of-fact tone.

"So… what? I'm just supposed to accept this?" I demanded, not so much upset that Mika wouldn't be able to find a way out of this binding, but more than I was going to be left vulnerable with all these… *feelings*.

Corvin shrugged.

"It would appear so."

"Maybe you should have practiced more self-restraint and not marked her," Harkyn suggested with a raised eyebrow. I shook my head.

"You don't know. You have no idea of the overwhelming feeling that came over me. It wasn't a desire. It was a need, desperate and as integral to me as breathing is to a human. There was no way for me to stop it. As soon as she was within my grasp, I found myself ensuring she'd want me. I had no real clue what I was doing when I did it," I answered, remembering how it had felt to Mark her.

"And you haven't felt that way since?" Corvin asked with a small frown.

I dropped my gaze for a moment, thinking of the psychic dream and how desperate we'd been, how impossible it had been to pull back

"I have," I finally admitted. "She pulled me into a psychic realm. And I could not have stopped the events that unfolded there even had I wanted to. I felt the same need in her, the relentless demand," I answered.

"You fucked her in a psychic realm?" Malik asked with a raised eyebrow. I shrugged.

"Like I said, it was impossible to stop for both of us," I answered. Nova shook his head and clenched his jaw angrily. I knew he felt like he had some prior claim on her due to her bloodline, but if he thought for even a second that I'd let him take her from me, he had another thing coming.

"So, you felt the need to tie your souls together, then your minds. I should expect heart and body are next," Devlin said thoughtfully. I swung my gaze back to him and frowned.

"Excuse me?" The thought of anyone having any impact on my heart whatsoever didn't sit well with me.

"This Mark is old, Cole, ancient beyond even us. Those kinds of bindings are for eternity, and they must tie two beings together in *every* way possible for them to be complete and withstand the test of time without disintegrating," Devlin continued.

I sat back in my chair and closed off my expressions. I didn't want to consider what he said to be true, but some part of me already knew that it was. Of course it was, it was the only thing that made sense. To ensure two beings were bound together for all eternity, and that they would not resent each other but only grow to care and *need* each other, they would need to be tied together completely and irrevocably. Mind, body, heart and soul.

"Cole, I have found something I think you should see," Mika reached out.

I closed my eyes on the feel of her once again in my mind, at the feeling of relief. I hadn't realized how much I'd needed to hear her voice, how much she had become a part of me.

"Can it wait? I do not know how I feel about you coming out with my brothers here," I answered honestly, blinking to bring the room back into focus.

Corvin was watching me closely, and I had the distinct feeling he knew I was talking to her.

"I think it is something you all should see. I think I found a prophecy," she replied.

I stilled. A prophecy? Fuck.

"You speak to her, even now. And her touch soothes you," Corvin pointed out. I hesitated and then nodded. There was no point in hiding it.

"I would like to meet her," Corvin announced.

"Yes, I think we would all like to meet her," Devlin added. I frowned and sighed.

"Mika thinks that she has found something you should all see, anyway. A prophecy of some kind," I answered.

"Then bring her out and let us hear it," Devlin answered.

Again, I considered the repercussions if any of my brothers made a move toward taking her from me. But these were my brothers. If there were ever any beings on this planet I could trust, it was them.

"Come out, Little Witch. But do not go near my brothers. Come out and come straight to my side, and if you feel something off that I do not, you must tell me at once. If I order you back to my realm, you must go immediately. I will have your word on this before you come out," I told her, determined to keep her safe. My gaze roamed over the faces of each of my brothers. They were beloved faces, men who had stood by me throughout the ages. And yet in this one thing, they could possibly be enemies.

"Yes, master. Should I also speak only when spoken to?" she asked in a falsely sweet voice.

"If only you would obey such an order," I replied, biting back a grin.

"On my way. Don't let any of them kidnap me," she replied sarcastically, but there was an edge of seriousness. She feared being taken away from me, almost as much as I feared her being taken away. She would die before admitting such a thing, but I could feel it when she spoke.

"Worry not, my woman. I will protect you, even from my brothers. None will harm you or take you away," I replied, and I flooded her mind with every bit of resolve and determination I had. She had to know that I took her safety seriously.

"Well?" Devlin asked when I remained silent.

"She is on her way. None of you are to touch her or approach her." I made it a decree. Malik rolled his eyes, but a smile tugged at his lips. He was secretly enjoying my torture, and I couldn't blame him. Had this happened to any of my brothers, I would have taken great joy in making him squirm and getting a rise out of him.

The door to my circle of Hell opened, and Mika stepped out. Silence fell over us, and I could feel the sudden tension in the room as each of my brothers got their first look at my Witch.

CHAPTER TEN
MIKA

I'd never really wanted to know what it was like to be an animal in a zoo. I mean, I'd always had great sympathy for them, even recognizing that most of them were there because they were endangered, but I'd always felt bad that they were stuck in these cages or enclosures that couldn't possibly be big enough for them, with hundreds or thousands of faces pressing in on them all day.

I knew how they felt now, though.

The Kings of Hell were... woah. I mean, if a woman ever wanted to know what it was like to be the object of interest to the sexiest men in existence, I could give a real and honest account of how it felt.

Nine gigantic, muscled, dangerous looking men all locked in on me as I stepped out of Cole's realm. I noted some of the astonishment and confusion, but I wasn't sure if it was because I used his door on my own or because they hadn't expected an actual Witch.

My gaze automatically found Cole's, as if drawn by some invisible force. He was sitting in his high-backed chair and angled sideways towards me with his legs stretched out in front of him. He looked deceptively lazy, but I knew he was coiled and ready to strike if any of his brothers made a move towards me. All of the brothers, I noted, were tattooed, large, and had an air of danger about them that made walking steadily difficult. Gripping the book in my hands tighter, I lifted my chin and straightened my shoulders as I approached the table, my eyes flicking over every face there. I found Nova's startling blue eyes and gave him a gentle smile.

"Hello again, Nova," I greeted. He smiled immediately, and I heard Cole growl low in my mind, although his face showed none of what he was feeling.

"Pipe down, Hell Boy. I was being polite," I reprimanded.

His dark eyes smoldered at me in warning, and I tried to prevent my body from having a physical reaction to that look.

"You do not need to smile at him like that," he replied darkly.

"You mean politely?"

"At all."

I rolled my eyes and came to stand right beside him as he requested. Not a single one of the brothers blinked or spoke, but all of their eyes were on me. I was used to being invisible. I didn't have friends or family, so having this much attention on me at once was daunting. I did a mental check over what I was wearing, suddenly insecure.

"You look delectable, Tomika. You need not worry about how you look," Cole's soft voice whispered across my mind. I ignored him and then looked around the table again.

"So, I know who Nova is. Would the rest of you kindly introduce yourselves? Or would you prefer I come up with my own names? Hell Boy here knows I can be quite inventive," I began, wearing my false bravado like a security blanket.

Nova grinned and ducked his head, and I kept looking around the table. A few looks were shared among them, and then Cole tugged at my free hand.

"In order of the circles of Hell, we have me in the first circle, Adrik, Malik, Harkyn, Tamas, Donovan, but we call him Nova. Then there is Cassius, Devlin and Corvin," Cole introduced, indicating to each brother as he went. I repeated their names to myself my head and nodded slowly, hoping I'd remember them all. I knew they weren't exactly the kind of royalty I was thinking of with my mortal mind, but they were a kind of royalty, and I didn't want to think about how rude it would be if I forgot one of their names. And like hell I was referring to any of them as "your majesty" or any other kind of phrase which would make them feel superior to me. I mean, they kind of were, but I didn't need to feed that idea.

Cole snorted and then coughed, and I glared down at him.

"Stay out of my head."

"But then I would be deprived of such interesting thoughts," Cole responded with a laugh.

I sighed and then looked around for a chair.

"Could you do that wave thing you do and whip me up a chair?" I asked aloud. Cole's eyes glittered mischievously, and he cocked his head to the side.

"You can always sit on my lap."

"I'd rather sit on the floor."

When he made no move to help, I shook my head.

"Perhaps Nova will offer me his chair," I threw out, moving as if to walk around his seat. Cole's hand shot out quickly, his grip on my wrist tight but not painful. He raised glittering black eyes to mine, and I refused to back down. With another warning look, he waved his hand and a chair appeared beside him.

"Thank you, oh masterful one," I said, giving the impression of a bow. He growled again and I bit back a smile and took my seat before turning to look back at the brothers. They were each watching us with avid interest and speculation. I shrugged. I didn't know them, didn't care what they thought, and in the end, I was hoping to get away from all of them. Cole didn't seem worried about what they might think, so I refused to be either.

"What is this prophecy you came across?" Nova asked, breaking the silence.

I smiled my thanks to him and opened up the book, ignoring the small jab I felt from Cole. He could go sulk in a bloody corner. I wasn't going to stop smiling at his brother just because he had a possessive streak that could outdo a room full of hoarders.

"I haven't finished reading this book yet. I was just skimming over it when I dropped it and found the prophecy in the back pages. It refers to the Brothers Nine, which I assume is you guys," I began, opening the book to the page. I sucked in a breath and began to read.

THE PROPHECY OF THE NINE

From the first to the last, the Brothers Nine will fall...

The first will face death and prevail,
The second shall follow her blood trail.

The third will endure his deal of time,
The fourth need only await his sign.

The fifth will betray his woman of binding,
The sixth will save she he must be finding.

The seventh will take her to keep her safe,
The eighth will have to rely on Faith.

The ninth alone is left to find,
She who was taken, now hidden by design.

From first to the last, the Brothers nine must fall,
Or chaos reigns, and they will destroy it all.

I looked up as I said the last word and they all sat in silence, their faces removed of all expression.

"Cole?" I reached out, not knowing if I'd overstepped.

"None of us have ever heard the prophecy before," Cole explained.

"What do you think it means that the Brothers Nine must fall?" Devlin asked, looking around the table.

More silence.

"I think we need to do a lot more research into this prophecy and see what each line could mean to us individually. Maybe similarities will give us an idea of what it all means," Cassius suggested with a frown. They all nodded, but no one spoke, or at least not aloud.

"In the meantime, I'd like to know more about you, Mika,"

Tamas called. I frowned but nodded.

"Okay, what do you want to know?"

And then the next hour proceeded to be one of the most frustrating.

I knew almost nothing of what they asked. I didn't have family, I didn't know where I came from, I hadn't even known I was a Witch until a few days ago. I knew I had power, obviously, and I knew about the existence of Angels and Demons, but not anything else. Anything I had learned, I had learned on my own and in secret. I showed off my birth mark, and a few of them who had met Tabitha agreed that this was proof I was from her bloodline. That news made me happy, and only too eager to learn more about them, any of them. Nova seemed stuck on my family, asking me if I had access to my birth records. His questions had me on edge, and I made sure that I buried every reaction deep so that Cole would not sense it and go digging. Some things had to remain a secret. Some things I would die before revealing. And Nova seemed to know enough to ask the right questions, which made me nervous and a little unsettled.

"Okay, that's enough for tonight," Cole called when I began to feel tired.

"I think we can all agree that we need to get to the bottom of this prophecy," Adrik reminded.

"And we can each work on it on our own. Work out what the line in the prophecy that refers to you means to you, and then we'll begin to put the pieces together. In the meantime, Mika is tired. We have had a long day, and she could do with the rest," Cole returned, standing from his seat.

I might have put up a fight any other day, but I was exhausted and wanted nothing more than to curl up and sleep. But I also wanted to learn more about my family, about my magic.

"Nova, would you mind putting aside some time and telling me about Tabitha and her family? I'd really like to know more, and if there's anything extra you can teach me about my magic, I would be very grateful," I asked. Cole growled low and I scowled at him.

"What's your problem? You're determined to keep me locked up. The least you can do is make it so that I can learn about my history."

"I'd be more than happy to spend some time with you and tell you all I know, Tomika," Nova replied gallantly, his blue eyes shifting to Cole with something like humor in them. "I can be ready in an hour if that suits you?" he added. I felt my heart leap in excitement, all thoughts of sleeping evaporated.

"That would be amazing, thank you," I told him.

There was a loud growl and before I knew it, I was upside down. It took me a second to realize Cole had thrown me over his shoulder and was marching me back to his realm.

"Put me down, you big oaf. I can walk! You don't own me," I snapped, placing a well-aimed punch to his kidney. Or at least I thought it was. Did Kings of Hell have kidneys?

Cole stepped into his realm and the second the door was closed he put me back on my feet before backing me up against the door, his body crowding mine, his glittering black eyes filled with heat and possession.

"Mine," he growled.

Fucking. Hell.

Did he have to sound so bloody sexy when he said that? Why did him taking ownership of me make me want to melt into a giant puddle or let him have his way with me?

"Say it," he demanded. I shook my head. The smile the curved his mouth was all sin and sex. Oh, holy mother of all lady boners. Did my knees just go weak?

"One day soon, Little Witch, you will say it. And you will mean it," he promised, his hands gripping my hips tightly in his hands. I swallowed hard and shook my head.

"No one owns me," I responded, but my voice was a husky whisper.

"Yet. But I intend to rectify that very soon," Cole replied, grinding into me. My mouth fell open and I barely managed to hold back the moan that wanted to sound from my throat.

"I want to know more about The Mark. I need to know more about it," I forced out, managing to form the words behind the lusty cloud of confusion that was currently fogging my brain. Cole's forehead slowly came to rest on mine, and I could feel the shudder that went through him as he tried to contain his need. I didn't realize how heady a feeling it would be; the ability to bring a being like Cole to the brink of his control. And a part of me liked it. A bigger part wanted him to lose control, to ignore what I said and take me anyway. My body damn-near ached for it, cried out for it.

I sucked in a breath, desperate and needy, but I needed to gain control of myself. Jumping into bed with him right now, while ridiculously tempting, was probably also a very stupid idea. We had no idea about the possible repercussions. Cole had already bound our souls; his brothers believed the psychic dream had bound our minds. All that was left was body and hearts. While I felt secure in thinking he would not gain my heart anytime soon, if at all, my body was begging me to give in already. I couldn't do that. Not yet.

"I will allow you to escape me this time, woman, but believe me when I tell you—you will not be able to hold out against me forever. You will want me to take your body soon, and when you do, you're going to beg me," he promised. The heat in his eyes scorched me and liquid heat pooled low. With another searing glance, Cole pressed a hard kiss to my lips before he pushed away and strode with long, purposeful steps to a door on the opposite side. I stood there against the wall, unable to move, my body trembling with desire. I had to fight my mind against my body which was urging me to run after him. Pride be damned.

I shook my head and sucked in another breath, and then another until I had more control over my body. I needed more information.

~

"Oh, this is not good," I whispered to myself as I looked around the forest setting.

I recognized this feeling as a psychic dream. I'd thought it was just a regular dream last time, but now I knew the difference.

"You can tell me you don't want me, but every time you pull me into one of these dreams, I know otherwise," Cole's voice called, and I turned to see him make his way through some thick trees.

"I don't know how I'm doing this," I admitted. He grinned.

"It's a subconscious thought. It's not something you go to bed intending to do. You want me, but have denied yourself, so your mind provides it while you sleep," Cole explained. I shook my head.

"We're not doing this again. I didn't find out enough information," I told him, holding out a hand as if that would ward him off.

I'd spent four hours with Nova, talking about my family and learning how to heal properly. Apparently, Witches weren't supposed to take the wounds of others onto themselves, they had to draw the energy from around them, not from within themselves. So, I'd spent a good amount of time healing shallow cuts on Nova. It was harder than I thought, retraining my brain to heal the right way and not the way I'd always done it. But I had made progress. Then Nova had left after telling me more about Tabitha and her family, and I'd spent time reading the textbooks. They were old and the writing so small it was taking forever for me to read it. So far, I hadn't learned anything different, but it was nice to know that Cole hadn't lied to me about anything yet.

"Why can't we do this again? We've done it once, we can't be anymore tethered in our minds than we already are," he suggested. My body shivered at that, wanting me to give in.

"Cole," I warned, but I knew I wasn't strong enough to resist him, not this time.

"Just feel, Mika. We both need this. Denying ourselves does not help anything," he urged as he came to stand in front of me. I closed my eyes as he edged closer and tried to find a reason to say no. I mean, there were plenty. He'd kidnapped me, he was keeping me here against my will, he was a tyrant, he was merciless, he was dangerous and a *King of Hell!* But for whatever messed up reason, none of those dampened the flames of desire raging within me. I was all kinds of messed up, I had to be to even be considering this.

Cole tipped my face upward with a finger, his black eyes heated and hungry.

"Tell me that you want me," he murmured.

I shook my head. His grin was slow and hot. There was a challenge in his eyes, daring me to keep pushing him. He brushed a kiss across my cheek, down to my jawline and to the spot on my neck where it met my ear. He sucked gently and continued a languid exploration down. I closed my eyes, pure bliss overriding my good sense.

"Tell me you want me," Cole demanded again, his breath hot against my neck.

I shook my head. No, I couldn't give him that. He had too much control already. His hands slid to my hips, and he gripped me hard, his mouth working down the front of my chest, and I found myself already bare. Oh, shit.

He moved lower, his hands sliding to my backside while his tongue circled my nipple before he blew cool air onto it. I moaned, my hands sliding into his hair that was just thick enough for me to cling to.

"Tell me you want me," Cole said again, refusing to put his mouth where I wanted him.

"No." The word came out choked and desperate.

He chuckled against me, his fingers gently sliding down the backs of my thighs as he drew one taut nipple into the hot cavern of his mouth. I moaned, needy, bordering on desperate now. I could feel hot liquid pooling low for him, readying me, but I refused to give in.

His fingers were light on my bare thighs, so different to the assault on my breasts that I didn't know where to focus. He traced down to my knees and then up to my front, making small, slow circles up my inner thighs.

"Cole," his name was a whimper, but I didn't care right then. I needed... I just *needed*!

"You know how to make it better," he murmured, lavishing attention to both breasts, his fingers moving ever closer to my center. My thighs almost shook, my hips rocking without my permission in an attempt to feel him there. But he stubbornly refused to give in, refused to give me what I wanted. One of his hands disappeared, and I glanced down to see it wrapped around the long hard length of his cock. I stilled, my breath catching in my lungs at the sight of him stroking himself. My temperature went up again, a hot flush washing over me at the erotic sight. I'd never thought I'd see something like this and find it so damned sexy, but holy fuck!

His other hand crept closer to my core, *so damn close!*

"Cole," I almost begged, needing more.

"Tell me you want me," he repeated, his tone never changing. I was mesmerized by the sight of his hand moving over the velvet length, his strokes tight and slow. I could remember how it felt having him inside me, stroking me, thrusting hard, over, and over.

"Please," I pleaded as his hand moved featherlight over my pussy. I made a sound of frustration when he moved too quickly for me to do anything.

"Tell me, Mika. Tell me," Cole urged, his voice thickening with need. His dark eyes glittered with heat and hunger, almost as desperate as me.

"I want you," I almost shouted the words at him.

He was on me in a second. I found myself flat on my back, his mouth and fingers between my legs as he licked and sucked, thick fingers plunging in and out of me. I was so on edge that it barely took more than a few seconds to send me careening over the edge, screaming his name. Cole dragged out my orgasm for as long as possible before he was kneeling between my legs and with one long, hard drive of his hips, he was inside me.

I cried out again as pleasure and pain mixed together at his rough intrusion, but I didn't hate it. No, if anything, it made me burn for him even more. I opened my eyes to see him hovering over me. He was like a man possessed, a man on the edge of sanity, and I had been the one to drive him there. His fingers twined with mine and he lifted them up, pressing them into the ground at either side of my head.

"You want me," Cole ground out, pulling out to drive forward again roughly.

"Yes," I panted, even though I knew he wasn't asking.

Triumph lit his eyes, and he began moving faster, harder. I tried to move with him, to meet his every thrust, but he was the man in charge. All I could do was let him use my body for his own pleasure while bringing me to orgasm a second time. I wanted him to use me. Right then and there, I wanted to be the instrument of his demise, the one thing that could make him lose his cool, lose his sanity in his desire to reach that finish line and come crying my name.

"Come with me, Witch," Cole demanded as his cock thrusted faster and faster. I was getting closer, barely able to concentrate with the pleasure building within me.

"Cole," I cried, my back arching.

"Now!" Cole shouted harshly. As if my body obeyed his command, I came in a hard crash screaming his name, my back arched, my body throbbing and clenching tight around him. I felt him come hard, felt him lose himself in me as he called my name—

I found myself alone and awake in a tangle of sheets, soaked with sweat, my body thrumming and throbbing, pleasure still cresting over inside me. I could hear a low moan and panting from outside my bedroom and closed my eyes when I realized what had happened.

A smile tugged at my lips. I just couldn't find it within myself to regret it.

CHAPTER ELEVEN
COLE

I'd expected to get reamed this morning for the dream. It wasn't me who was doing it, it was all her. But I still expected her to call me out and say I took advantage of her. To my surprise, she only smiled knowingly at me and went back to the books to read more about The Mark.

To say I was shocked was a huge understatement. I watched her throughout the day, half expecting her to be mad at me. But after a few hours, I realized she had accepted what had happened and was... okay with it. It was a little unnerving, yes. A part of me was waiting for her to try and gut me with my own blade. But mostly, I was just glad she was accepting it.

"This would be funny to see if it weren't so pathetic," Nova commented, dragging me out of my thoughts of Mika. I frowned at my brother, and he was watching me with a mix of amusement and disgust.

"What?"

"You've been sitting here, mooning after her for the last several minutes and haven't heard a word I've been saying," Nova replied, rolling his eyes. The gesture was so juvenile that I laughed.

"What were you saying?" I prompted, not wanting to comment on the fact that he thought I was 'mooning' after Mika. The truth was, he was probably right. My mind was on her constantly today and we were often brushing one another's minds, reaching out to feel each other, share a random scrap of information or touch each other in a way she wouldn't let me physically. She wouldn't let me *yet*, anyway.

"And there you go again," Nova snapped.

"Okay, I'm listening. Something about your Knight?" I conceded.

Nova glared and shook his head.

"I was saying that he wasn't with the bodies in the warehouse. He got out, but I haven't been able to get a lead on him. He wasn't taken, I'd feel it. So where is he?" Nova repeated. I frowned. There would be no reason for a Knight to stay gone from Hell. They were not pawns to be sacrificed. A lot of years and pain went into making a Knight. He would be welcomed home as a survivor after that massacre.

"Unless…" I murmured, thinking back to that night.

"What?" Nova asked.

I thought back, remembering where I was in the fight, who was there. I got stabbed with an Angel Blade on my side. I hadn't seen who'd done it, only that they had been on my left. Could it be? No. Why would he? What would he get out of it?

"Cole," Nova snapped. I blinked and frowned.

"I think your Knight stabbed me," I answered. Nova sat back, clearly shocked. Krae wasn't only a good Knight, he was one of Nova's best and most trusted.

"Why?" he asked. I shrugged.

"Maybe he thought that by taking me out, he'd get my throne?" I suggested. Nova shook his head.

"That doesn't make any sense. He's one of mine, he'd need… oh fuck," Nova groaned. Now it was my turn to wait.

"It was a trap for me," Nova clarified.

"What?"

"I was meant to go up there that night. Me, not you. But you were bored and begged me to let you go instead. I had other issues to deal with, so I let you go. He was expecting me, not you. He wants *my* throne," Nova explained.

I sat back, disgusted. It shouldn't surprise me. Demons were always scheming little assholes who were after power. But this was an unexpected betrayal.

"How would that even work? We don't know what will happen when one of us dies. What if the circle closes and there are only eight circles from there on out?" I reminded.

"Maybe he thought he would take the chance. Being the highest

ranking Knight, maybe he assumed he'd ascend the throne?"
Nova speculated.

"So, what? He thinks I know it was him and that's why he hasn't
come back?" I asked.

Nova nodded. "It's the only thing that makes sense. He would
have heard about it had you died. Since you're still around, he
knows it didn't work."

"Oh shit," I whispered, a sudden thought flaring up in my mind.
"What now?"

"Mika. Krae has got to know that Mika exists. Think about it.
Nothing can cure a Demon of an Angel Blade wound except for
the blood of the Angel it belongs to, or a Witch," I added. Nova
sat back; his face impassive as he thought about this.

Mika was in more danger than we originally thought. If there was
a possible coup going on down here, we'd just spotlighted the
fact that a Witch still lived because I was not dead.

"I'm going to send my Demons out to look for him. You should
send any of yours that you can spare. We will get him and find
out what he knows and how far this plan of his goes. We'll keep
her safe, brother," Nova declared.

I frowned down at the table and nodded. It was a good plan,
somewhere to start. We didn't want to raise too many questions
on who we were hunting and why, so only those most trusted to
us could go. Whatever that meant anymore.

I put out the call immediately, my orders exact. Find Krae, bring
him back alive. There would be a reward for whoever did this.
And they had to keep it quiet.

"Have you noticed Mika... holding back?" Nova asked after a
moment. I raised my gaze to meet his blue eyes and cocked an
eyebrow.

"How?"

"Just... she seems to be holding something close to her chest.
Like she'd guard it with her life," Nova observed, looking at Mika
from the corner of his eye as she made notes. I considered what
he said and looked at my Witch too.

He was right. I had noticed her being careful in her thoughts, but
only when the topic of her adoption was being discussed. I

guessed she was feeling vulnerable, but maybe I was wrong. Maybe she knew more than she was letting on and was hiding it for some reason.

"Why would she hide something from us?" I asked instead. Nova shrugged and glanced down at the blade he'd been admiring, his face carefully blank.

"Why do I get the feeling that *you* know more than you're letting on?" I pushed.

Nova sat in silence a few more moments as he considered my words. I waited; I'd learned patience. And my brothers and I were the same in that, if we were rushed, we were not going to answer. We didn't answer to anyone, each of us a law unto ourselves. But this was about *my* Witch, and he would answer me no matter what.

"I think I know something. But until I'm sure, I don't want to say it. It could cause your Witch to clam up or attempt to flee if I'm right. If I *am* right, then the best thing to do is to gain her trust and wait her out," Nova finally answered. I frowned and wanted to push for more answers, but I knew he wouldn't tell me anything more.

Nova sat with me for an hour more as we put together a plan to find his Knight and end this coup before it had a chance to really take hold, and I watched Mika scour through the books. She was determined to learn; I'd give her that much. Whether it be about her own family, about being a Witch, or about anything to do with The Mark. She was tenacious. I still felt like an asshole for the jealous streak that shot through me every time she smiled at Nova for telling her more about her family than I could. I hated that they had that connection, a bond. Mika fought me tooth and nail, but Nova she seemed willing to accept with hardly an effort. Of course, Nova hadn't bound them together without her consent nor had he kidnapped her.

Nova had promised me his help in protecting Mika should the need arise. As far as he was concerned, his Demons were at my disposal if I needed them for Mika. It both annoyed me and made me grateful that he would offer. Nova and I were unable to agree on the best way to protect her, and it was causing problems. But at least he had offered to help in any way he could. I could look after her myself. She was safe with me, and my Demons were strong enough to do the job. But the thought of anyone taking her from me left me feeling empty and cold, utterly helpless. I can guarantee you that in the time I have been alive, helplessness was not something I felt.

Ever.

Knowing I had my brother's Demons at my hand if the need arose helped to dissipate a little of that helplessness. Not get rid of it all together, but it was something.

Several hours later, I was still watching Mika as I cleaned my weapons and dealt with the day to day of running my own circle of Hell. I'd gone to the Pits a few times to make sure everything was running smoothly down there, but my mind was constantly on the Little Witch.

I still hated that Mika's safety was such a priority in my mind. Not just simply because she was the only Witch we knew of, but because she was beginning to mean something *to me*. I loved her fire, the way she snapped back at me and never gave in to me without a fight. I loved that she wasn't scared of me. I liked that when she got mad, her eyes crackled green, and her cheeks flushed. I loved watching the sweep of her lashes when she realized I caught her thinking dirty thoughts about me. Hell, I loved the sound of her when we fucked, the way she reacted to me, the way she couldn't resist me any more than I could resist her. She was funny too, and smart. She had a fearlessness to her that I both loved and hated. When it came to matters of her safety, I would not allow for her to break or bend my rules, but her compassion and need to do the right thing would tempt her to do so.

She wasn't *just* a Witch to me. And that thought was terrifying.

~

MIKA

I felt his fingers brush the nape of my neck, despite the fact he wasn't even here. He said he had some business to take care of in the Pit, whatever that was. Nevertheless, I could feel his fingers skim the right side of my neck, his lips on the left. I shivered and closed my eyes for a moment.

I hated that I loved his touch. When had I accepted my fate? Why did I look forward to seeing him, to hearing his voice and feeling his consciousness brush my own? What was it that made it feel like he was such a vital part of my life now? Despite the fact that I wanted my life back, wanted my freedom... the very thought of going back to a life where Cole wasn't there left me... hollow.

I groaned and fell backwards into the giant, cushioned chair in front of the fire. When did I become one of those women? The ones who needed a man? The ones who were no one without the person they were dating? I was disgusted with myself and we weren't even dating! I was his captive.

As if called by my sudden drop in mood, I felt Cole brush my mind, felt him envelop me in the warmth of his arms and flood me with security and comfort. I closed my eyes on the stinging tears and dropped my head forward into my hands. What the hell was I supposed to do? I shot up off the chair, unable to sit still. The man was an actual King of Hell. He wasn't just a Demon. He was a *King* of Demons. And here I was, craving his touch, his attention, and his sinful words. Why was this happening? Was it all because he'd bound us? Was it because of this prophecy I'd found? Or would this have occurred had none of those things happened?

"Do you need me to come to you, Little Witch?" His voice whispered in my head, soft, warm, comforting. I shook my head and stood up, wrapping my arms around myself.

"No, I'm fine."

Male amusement lit inside me, and I bit back my own urge to smile.

"I can feel your emotions, Mika. I know you are in distress. Do you need me?"

Need. He'd used the word *need*, not *want*. That was telling.

Because I felt that I did need him. But did I want him? Did I really want to be around him? Did I really want to be in his life and have him in mine?

I didn't answer because I didn't know what to say. I felt like I needed him, but I didn't want to. At the same time, my body ached for him, my mind was constantly trying to reach out for him. I feared it would not be long until my heart demanded I go to him as well.

Warm arms slid around me, real this time, and Cole pressed his body against mine from behind. I closed my eyes as his familiar scent hit me, comforted me, settled something deep within me. I both resented and treasured that feeling. No one and nothing had ever given me that sense of belonging. And yet this man, no, this Demon King made me feel whole again.

"You suffer needlessly," Cole whispered against my ear.

"I'm not suffering," I denied, even though I knew he was right. I felt him smirk against me, and he held me tighter.

"Why does it bother you so much to admit that you want me?" he asked.

"Why does it bother *you*?" I returned, turning in his arms to look up at him. Shit. That was probably a mistake. How did I manage to forget just how bloody gorgeous the man was until I was looking at him?

"I've admitted that I want you," Cole told me. I raised an eyebrow and felt the truth of his words. But it wasn't a full truth; there was more.

"You've admitted that you want me, but not why," I guessed. His dark eyes flickered for a moment, some unnamed emotion shining at me for a second and then it was gone.

"It seems we both need to be a little more honest with ourselves and each other," Cole replied, his hand gripping my waist. I nodded and cleared my throat.

"In the spirit of honesty, I think you should know that I want to kiss you," Cole added, his low tone igniting that fire within me.

"I don't think that's a good idea," I warned.

He cocked an eyebrow but leaned in closer, his burning gaze focused on my mouth.

"We get carried away. And we don't want things to go too far before we know what the prophecy is about, and don't forget The Mark and all its ties," I added almost desperately because I could feel myself falling forward.

"Mika," Cole interrupted.

"Hmm?" I said absently, my attention sliding to his lips, remembering how they felt against mine.

"Shut the fuck up and kiss me."

I didn't even have a chance to think of a response before his lips were on mine. I don't know who moved first, all I knew was that I was helpless and swamped with longing almost at once.

My hands slid up his chest and he gave a low moan against my lips at my slow exploration, feeling every dip and mound of his well-defined torso. His fingers dug into my hips, and he hauled me closer to him as if he couldn't get close enough. I clutched his shirt in my hands and Cole slid his hands to my backside where he lifted me up. I wrapped my legs around him and didn't stop kissing him as he backed up, and then fell backwards onto the chair I'd recently vacated. We sat so that I was straddling him, his hands on my ass, my fingers already loosening the buttons of his shirt to feel his skin.

We'd been this hot for each other several times now, and I was yet to feel him properly, to explore him. I got his shirt undone and let my fingers slide over his heated skin. He had the perfect amount of chest hair, tattoos that I had a mad desire to lick, and ridges and muscles I couldn't wait to touch. Images of kissing down his chest, his abdomen and exploring below the belt melted into my mind, and I wasn't sure if they were my desires or his. But suddenly I wanted to take his cock into my mouth and torture him, run my tongue down the long hard length of him and take him into my mouth, down my throat, have his fingers tangled in my hair, his groans of pleasure filling the room, the taste of him on my tongue.

Cole swore against my mouth as the images in my mind became more and more vivid. I could feel him hard beneath me, and I rocked gently, dragging another moan from his throat.

I was working on the belt of his pants when he suddenly stilled and I pulled back, panting, overwhelmed with how much I wanted him.

"What?"

He groaned and closed his eyes, his head falling back.

"We have to stop," he bit out.

"Why?"

"Because I put some Demons onto a job earlier, and one of my Knights just reached out. They think they have the one I'm after, and I need to get up there to find him," he answered.

Oh.

I let my head fall forward, my hair curtaining my face as I worked slowly at buttoning up his shirt once again, trying to steady my breathing and erratic heartbeat. It was probably for the best. I mean, really, we weren't ready for this. I mean, we were *ready*, but it was better if we did nothing. I still wanted to find a way out of the binding.

I had to remind myself that he was a King of Hell, and that he could be a complete and utter asshole sometimes. And yet...

"Hey," Cole said softly, leaning forward to cup my face. "I would really like to continue this when I get back," he added. I frowned.

"Can I come with you?"

Cole paused and seemed to consider me for a moment. I hated this. I didn't want to have to ask for permission to leave, I didn't want to have to wait for him to decide to take me along like I was a kid on a field-trip.

"Tomika," he began slowly, and I prepared to give him a mouthful if he so much as thought about leaving me behind. I needed to get out of here, I needed to feel like I wasn't a prisoner. Because if he continued to leave me here while he went gallivanting along wherever he desired, then I knew that was exactly what I was.

"Your safety is the most important thing," he started. I shook my head and started to climb off him, but his arms came down around me, holding me in place. "I wasn't done talking," he snapped.

I glared.

125

"Why bother? I know what you're going to say," I replied, crossing my arms over my chest.

Cole's eyes lit with a smoldering fire, and he leaned in close.

"Your safety is the most important thing," he continued in a low voice. "So, if I tell you to stay, you stay. If I tell you to ignore a trail or someone in pain, you *will* listen. And if I say we're leaving, then you will come to me immediately. Do I have your word on this?" he rumbled, his voice deep and gravelly, sending a shiver down my spine.

I considered him for a moment. I wanted to defy him, to fight him on it. But right now, he really was my only chance to get out of Hell.

"Tomika. I will not take you with me if I do not have your word on this," Cole repeated, his expression darkening.

"Fine," I replied quickly. "I'll do as you ask when we go up when it's about my safety," I replied. He cocked a brow, and I was sure he noted my phrasing. Before I could say anything else, he leaned forward and kissed me again. What the hell was it about him that made him so damn hard to resist?

"Let's go," he whispered unevenly. I nodded and he stood, setting me on my feet.

~

COLE

I was already kicking myself for bringing Mika along. What had I been thinking? The truth was, I hadn't been. At least not with my damn head.

She was to be protected above all else, and she would be of no use on this job anyway. I had to see my Knight because he was sure he'd found where Krae was hiding. I didn't need to be worrying about her safety on top of everything else, but fuck it all—I'd caught her thoughts back there, the desolate feeling she had at being left behind, feeling like a prisoner.

She *was* a fucking prisoner. Okay, so maybe we were something more now, but I'd marked her, she was *mine*. Which meant she went only where I wanted her to go and did only what I wanted her to do. But then she looked at me with those goddamn eyes and I was fucking powerless.

I held Mika close as I wrapped us in shadow and directed it where to take us. My Knight hadn't said whether or not there was a danger, but I didn't think there would be one. As soon as we arrived, I sent my senses flaring out, looking for any danger to Mika. I could sense several Demons, but they were all mine. I looked around, ready to send Mika back to my realm if it came down to it, but we seemed to be alone for now. Reluctantly, I let her go and allowed her to step away from me.

"Where are we?" Mika asked, looking around the abandoned warehouse quickly. It was empty, except for us.

"My Knight is outside. I'd like you to stay here while I talk to him. No one outside my brothers and a Reaper knows about you, and I'd like to keep it that way. I could pass you off as some random mortal I was entertaining myself with, but I'd rather they not see you at all, if possible," I explained.

Mika didn't look impressed. In fact, she looked ready to go to war with me about this.

"Mika, you gave me your word. This is a matter of your safety. For the time being, the less people who see you or know about your existence, the safer you will be," I reminded. She glared and after a moment huffed in annoyance and nodded.

"Fine. I'll wait here unless you call for me, oh masterful one," she agreed, bowing slightly. I stalked towards her and watched as her eyes widened and her breath caught. I pulled her up against me and leaned in close, loving the way her heartbeat picked up, her breath hitched, and her gaze narrowed on me.

I drew out the anticipation, feeling the way her body reacted, loving the way her mind went fuzzy with desire.

"Good girl," I whispered before I crushed her lips with my own, slipping my tongue between them. She answered the kiss with one as desperate as my own before I pulled away. Her breath was ragged, her pupils dilated, and her face flushed. Smirking with satisfaction, I left her standing there as I headed for the massive double doors that would lead me to my Demons.

Sliding open the door, I took note of all who were there and where they were. We were in an industrial area, very few humans nearby.

"My King," Durras, my favorite Knight, greeted, bowing his head, his black eyes dark and focused. He was dressed in traditional Knight-ware. Black armor, pants, and a shirt. His hair was kept short-cropped, a sword in the scabbard between his shoulder blades and another at his hip.

"Where is he?" I asked, getting right to the point. Durras stepped aside and pointed to a warehouse four buildings away. "You're sure?" I questioned.

"I tracked him here myself several hours ago. I watched to see if he met with anyone in case we needed to prepare some more. But he has been there alone all this time. He made one call, but I didn't hear it. No one else has shown up. He seems to be waiting, but for what or who, I don't know," Durras answered. I nodded slowly as I scanned around us once again, used my other senses to feel out the environment, intentions, and life forces. Durras was right; Krae was alone.

"I want you guys to go back to the realm and wait for me there. If Krae decides to scan, he'll see you all waiting here and I don't know what else he has planned," I explained.

"But Cole, you might have need of us," Durras protested, and the other Demons nodded, frowning at being sent away. Mostly, I didn't want them to chance seeing Mika. But there was also the fact that Krae had tried to commit treason, he had tried to have my brother murdered and had almost killed me. We didn't need word to spread that there were cracks in our ranks. No, we needed the other Demons to remember their place, and I would make an example of Krae for all those who thought to betray us or dethrone us.

"I will call out if I have need of you, and you can be here in an instant. I would like to deal with him alone," I explained. When he looked ready to complain once more, I straightened up and pinned him with a glare. I did not explain myself, and never twice.

"Of course. Call and we shall be here," Durras finally relented, bowing his head slightly once more. The other Demons followed suit and I watched as they all wrapped themselves in shadow before disappearing.

Sighing heavily, I looked around me again. I wanted to find out why that fucker had decided to overthrow my brother. I wanted to know where the hell he got an Angel Blade, and I needed to know if he knew about Mika and if so, who else he'd told. He had some talking to do before dying, and I was going to get all the information out of him that I could.

I strode towards the building, my anger building and boiling over the more I thought about it. A number of things kept running around in my head; the fact that he had planned to kill my brother, that he had almost succeeded in killing me, and that he might be a danger to Mika. Over and over, those thoughts fed my anger until I was ready to explode the building he was in. I realized when I was several paces from the warehouse he was hiding in, that he had become aware of my presence. He was on his feet, waiting, anticipation coming from him.

Was this some kind of trap? Anger flared and I embraced it, allowed it to run through my veins, to fill me up so that I almost exploded with it. This fucker had tried to kill my brother, and when Nova had not shown up, he had instead tried to kill me. He wanted the throne, the title of King.

I was going to enjoy causing him pain.

The door to the warehouse burst open as I reached it, my power sending it flying inwards in a spray of splinters. Krae was standing, facing me. I knew we were alone, but he was far too confident standing there. I looked for traps, reasons that he was so calm.

"Cole," he greeted.

"What a mess you have gotten yourself into, Krae," I answered, not moving any closer.

"I admit, things could have gone more smoothly," he continued without preamble.

"Where are the others?" I asked.

"Others?"

"Yes, your little friends who are going to attempt to help you escape your death. You are not powerful enough to defeat me on your own, so where are your friends?"

"Don't you worry about them, they'll be along shortly," he answered.

Silence fell and I remained where I was. Krae smirked smugly and started walking slowly towards me.

"I hear you have a Witch at your disposal. How fortunate for you that she arrived when she did," he started. I didn't confirm or deny Mika's existence.

"It had to be a Witch, right? Because I stabbed you with that Angel Blade, and there is no way you would have survived it without her. We all know the Angels are averse to giving us their blood when it will save our lives," Krae continued, a little closer now. I tensed readying for the attack, wherever it was going to come from.

"So, where is she?"

"What I want to know, Krae, is how you expect to survive this. You must know that when myself or my brothers get their hands on you, you'll spend an eternity in the Pit being tortured," I said instead.

He smirked and shrugged, looking unconcerned.

"*If* I get caught," he corrected. I cocked an eyebrow.

"And you think you'll survive, how, exactly?"

And then all at once, I was surrounded. I glanced around at the eight angels that now encircled me, Angel Blades at the ready. Their eyes were all narrowed on me, their bodies tensed and prepared for action. Well, at least this was an explanation as to how he got an Angel Blade. The backstabbing bastard had betrayed his own kind.

I glanced past them to Krae and he smiled arrogantly at me.

"My liege," he farewelled with a mocking bow before he turned around and started to walk away. I lost sight of him as the group of Angels moved closer and I took in their numbers and their positions. I was prepared to fight. As surrounded as I was, I'd been in worse positions before. At least these were all lower-level Angels, hardly top tier, which made me frown. How the hell did Krae think these fluffy fuckers would keep me occupied for long? Why was he so smug?

And then I felt her—Mika. She brushed my mind, her concern washing over me. My gaze shot to Krae again. He didn't know she was here, did he? She hadn't used her magic, there was no signature for him to pick up on.

But this had to be a trap for her.

"Nova," I reached out to my brother, the only one I would trust with Mika if for some reason Krae managed to get one over on me here. It was unlikely, but I would not take any chances that the Angels would get their hands on her. And if I did make it out of here, Mika was going to hate me a lot more because I was not bringing her out on any more outside visits—fuck that. This wasn't about keeping her locked up for my own personal use anymore, this was about protecting her from those fuckers.

"Brother, you have need?" Nova reached out.

"Your Knight is here, working with the Angels. I am surrounded by eight lower-level Angels, but Krae is too smug. He has something else up his sleeve. If for whatever reason I do not get out of here, you are to come for Mika. She insisted on coming," I told him, sending him Mika's location.

"I will come to aid you at once," Nova replied as the Angel's began to circle.

"No. I need you to be there for Mika in case this goes wrong," I answered.

The first Angel struck, and I threw my arms out, creating a firestorm of Hellfire around me, whirling like a tornado and burning anyone it came in contact with. Well, almost anyone. Perks of being a Demon. It was hot, but it would do no damage to me. It kept the Angels back while I worked out a battle plan, though. The problem with Angels, even lower-level ones, was that they were lethal bastards. I wasn't going to underestimate their abilities; it was how you ended up dead. But I was a King of Hell–I could handle it. I just had to be smart.

I came to a stop and got my bearings, preparing to fight when I heard her call my name. I turned just as the Angels did and caught sight of Mika in the doorway, her face a mask of concern, etched in pain.

Fuck.

Krae roared and ran for her, the Angels started for her.

I had one heart-stopping, aching moment of terror, fear that they'd get her, fear that I'd lose her. I sprang into action, moving faster than I ever had before. My eyes were only for Mika as she stood frozen in place, but I was one step ahead of them all. I launched myself after her, reaching her milliseconds before the Angels, wrapping her in shadow and sending her back to my circle of Hell. The Angels came to a stop, realizing she was gone. Silence filled the warehouse, nothing but our combined uneven breathing before Krae turned to me, fury flooding out of him, surrounding us all.

"Time to die, King."

And then the fight began…

CHAPTER TWELVE
MIKA

I was suddenly standing in front of the bookcase in Cole's circle of Hell. I staggered a step, dizzy, breathless, but the burning in my soul had finally disappeared. I dragged in several breaths and looked around only to realize Cole wasn't with me.

He hadn't come back with me.

I spun around uselessly for a second, hoping I'd see him standing somewhere else in the room, but he wasn't anywhere to be found. My worry for him increased and I sucked in a deep breath, forcing myself to calm so that panic wouldn't overrule my clear head.

First of all, the amount of worry I felt for him right now should not be happening. We were still... off kilter. I didn't care about him like that... did I? No, not at all... maybe.

Either way, this level of worry was out of proportion, but it was there.

I had already started looking for him when I'd felt the stirrings of suspicion and anger coming from him. I'd needed to see what he was seeing, hoping to be of some help if at all possible. I hadn't been able to stay back when the burning in my soul had started. I knew someone was hurt nearby. I could have reached out to see if it was Cole, I knew that. But I'd worried about distracting him if he was in a fight. And then when I'd reached the shattered entrance to that warehouse, I'd seen the tornado made of fire and knew Cole was in there. He was a Demon King, of course he knew how to control fire. And when it had died down, he'd been surrounded. At least eight Angels were there. I'd seen the other Demon, but I got the impression that he wasn't on Cole's side. The pain the Angels felt at being burned so badly was still affecting me, urging me to go and heal them.

Then, all at once, Cole caught sight of me, as did every Angel in that room. Startled by their speed, even though I shouldn't have been, I'd been frozen to the spot, unable to move as they all flew at me with supernatural speed. Panic and pain mixed so that I couldn't decide what action to take against them.

And then, before I'd had time to properly breathe, Cole had wrapped me in shadow and sent me back here. I hadn't known that I could travel without holding on to him, but apparently, I could.

I bit my thumbnail as I began to pace, needing to know if he was okay. My chest was tight with worry, and I couldn't stop seeing how close all those Angels had been to Cole when he'd sent me away.

Please be okay. I whispered the plea to the universe, trying not to look too closely as to *why* I needed him to be okay.

Unable to keep my distance any longer, I stilled and closed my eyes, reaching out tentatively to see how he was, if he was in pain, if he needed help. Maybe I could get his brothers to help. But when I touched him, I knew that Nova was already there. I flinched at the violence swirling in him, the hatred, the rage, and was surprised by the sliver of fear. But I had the feeling that fear wasn't about himself.

Pulling back, I opened my eyes and breathed a sigh of relief. Nova was there, Cole wasn't alone. And if he was badly injured, all they had to do was get back here for me to heal him. I kept pacing, wrapping my arms around myself as I tried to come to terms with what I was feeling. I hadn't known him all that long, he was a Demon, he was happy to cause pain and bloodshed to others. Granted, it seemed to be limited to the truly dark and evil or Angels, but he liked causing pain. I abhorred it.

Groaning, I shook my head at myself. Why was I trying to justify my feelings for him? Did I really see us having any kind of future where I'd be happy? Because if I wasn't free, then I would never be happy. And I didn't feel like Cole was going to be the type to allow me my freedom any time soon.

But then… there was the way he touched me. The way he smiled at me with that look I was sure he only gave to me. I'd felt his surprise at his growing feelings, I knew this was new territory for him just like it was for me. I closed my eyes and remembered the way he said my name, my *full* name like it was a caress. We barely knew each other, but I felt like I'd known him forever. How was that even possible?

There was a sudden *whoosh* sound, and I spun around at the heavy footsteps and found Cole already striding towards me, his glittering black eyes pinned on my face. His shirt was torn and a little singed. There was blood on his face, hands, and spattered over his clothing. But he didn't look badly injured, I couldn't feel any severe wounds.

"You're okay," I gasped, starting for him.

"What the hell did you think you were doing?" he shouted, gripping my upper arms and shaking me slightly.

"I—"

"I told you to stay put, and then you came out in the middle of a fucking fight and were almost taken. The Angels almost got you. If I'd been even half a second slower, you wouldn't be here right now. You'd be in the clutches of those dick-bags, and I might never have seen you again!" he shouted, angry… scared.

"I could feel the pain, I was worried it was you," I replied feebly. His fear and anger were swirling together, swamping me, drowning me so that it was hard to breathe. Was he… did he actually *care* about me? Or was he worried that the Angels would have a Witch on their side and not him?

"Is it me you were worried about, or your Witch?" I decided to ask.

Cole dragged in a steadying breath and slid his hands up my arms to my neck to cup my face. He pressed his forehead against mine and growled low.

"I wish like fuck I only cared about my Witch being in the middle of a deadly fight. I wish to fucking Lucifer that I only cared about the other side getting their hands on you," he answered low and deep. I swallowed hard, feeling the intense and confusing emotions rolling off him, drowning him, making it hard for him to breathe or think clearly. He was as much out of his depth as I was.

"I wish I didn't feel fear at the thought of losing you."

His voice was so soft, so low I almost missed it.

I pulled back slightly, studying, needing to see the truth on his face.

"I was worried about you too," I whispered, feeling as though I was stepping out onto a ledge without any real assurance that it would hold me. Cole's black eyes searched mine for one long, intense moment before he was suddenly kissing me. I didn't hesitate to wrap my arms around his neck before I plastered myself against him and kissed him back for all I was worth.

He groaned, his tongue brushing mine, plundering, ordering. I kissed him hard, my nails digging into his scalp as he moved his hands down my back to cup my ass. He squeezed hard and then lifted me up. I didn't bother to look around as he walked, I was pretty certain of where we were headed. And all I could think was—*finally!*

Nothing else mattered right now, not The Mark, not a prophecy, not Angels and Demons or anything else.

There was just us and this intense, demanding need.

I found myself thrown backwards onto one of the most comfortable beds I'd ever been on. Cole stood over me, and with a click of his fingers, we were both naked.

There was no going slow and steady here, we were going right for it. And I wanted it, I needed it even. It was like the first time we'd shared a psychic dream. There was an intense urging for this, a need almost as vital as the one for oxygen. There'd be no backing out now. My heart, my soul, my body was screaming for this and there was no way to ignore it, no way to block it out. The longer we waited, the more it hurt. He waved his hand over the length of himself, and he was clean of all blood and gore. I caught sight of a few of his wounds and sat up immediately, running my hands over them.

Cole moved to back away, but I pinned him with a glare before I closed my eyes, sending my healing energy into his body. I searched over every part of him, healing every wound, even the small ones. When I was done, I opened my eyes to look up at him and I slid my hands down his ripped abdomen and trailed my nails down the front of his thighs.

"Hurry," I whispered as Cole dragged his gaze over my naked form. He didn't smile as he pushed me backwards onto the bed and climbed over me, his imposing form blocking out the light above, his intense eyes boring into mine. He dipped his head but stopped just short of kissing me.

"Say please," he whispered against my mouth, flicking his tongue out to lick my lips. I tried to lean up to kiss him, but he wrapped my hair in his fist and pulled my head back. I gasped, the small sharp pain sending a thrill through me.

"Cole," I whimpered, unable to stop my hips from moving against him with need. I knew I was ready for him, more than ready. I needed him inside me, or I was going to die, I knew it.

"Say please, Little Witch," he ordered, biting down on my lower lip for a moment. I moaned, arching my back. Everything in me was screaming at me to do or say whatever I had to so that we could do this, so that he would be inside me and this burning that was radiating throughout my body would go away. His hands moved down to cup my breasts and his fingers pinched a nipple lightly, but hard enough that there was another little zap of pain that only spurred me on.

I raised my gaze to meet his and licked my lips to wet them. His black eyes were glittering at me, heat and need shining back at me. I brushed his mind and could feel the same desperate urgings riding him that were on me. Something between us was demanding we do this, but he was holding out, waiting for me to beg, to plead, to give him that power.

And how sick was it that I wanted him to have that power? I wanted him to make me beg. I wanted him to drive me to the edge of insanity with needing him before he let me have it. And I wanted to do the same with him. But not right now. Now, I was at my limit. I needed this more than I needed my next breath. And so, I said the one word he needed to make it happen.

"Please."

Triumph lit his eyes, his desire flared so bright, the roar of demand in his head so loud that he couldn't hold back any longer. He drew back, positioned himself between my legs, and while watching my face intently, he thrust hard inside me.

I screamed.

I'd never screamed during sex in my life. But this time I did. Pleasure so intense engulfed me, pain sharpened the edges of it creating a mixture so powerful that I almost convulsed on the spot. I was so full, so fucking full that I wasn't sure I was going to survive this. He stretched me almost to the point of pain. Despite how ready I'd been, how wet and needy, he was still almost too much.

I heard the same roar in Cole's head, the feeling of sudden completion as our bodies became one and he sank all the way inside me.

I clutched at his biceps, my nails digging in as he paused for a moment, savoring this sensation. I shared his mind as he shared mine, and the combination of my pleasure and his was overwhelming.

Cole's eyes opened and he looked down at me, a man possessed with need and lust.

"Mine," he growled, the word pushed into my mind as well as from his mouth. I panted, ached, desperate to move but pinned down with the weight of him.

"Say it, Mika. I want to hear you say the words," he repeated, low and harsh, his face etched with such brutal intensity and need. Until a man looks at you that way, there are no words to accurately describe the confidence I gained from it.

"Make me," I whispered. Excitement lit his gaze, and he drew back before driving forward again. Our loud moans intermingled, and he gripped my wrists in his hands before slamming them down on the mattress on either side of my head. "Say it," he repeated.

"No," I gasped as he pulled out and then slid inside me harder. I moaned and he did it again, and again. Burning black eyes drilled into mine as he continued to thrust into me with almost brutal intensity, but I liked it, needed it, craved it more than anything else. I began to raise my hips to meet his movements, the air in my lungs burning.

"Say it," Cole growled again as I felt myself begin to climb. I got higher and higher and just as I was about to tip over that edge, Cole pulled back.

"What?!" I shouted. He smirked and waited a few beats before slowly sliding back inside me.

"Say that you're mine," he demanded in a soft pant. I glowered. "And I said, make me," I returned. Cole's smile widened and crushed my lips with his, his tongue moving in time with his cock, his hips snapping hard against me. I tried tugging at my hands, wanting to touch him, but he held me down, kept me pinned. Again, I liked it, needed it, the thrill sending me up again almost to the top.

But Cole pulled back again.

"Fuck! Cole, stop doing that!" I shouted, frustration mounting. He leaned in close and gently kissed my lips.

"You. Are. Mine. Say it," he commanded, his voice low. I kept stubbornly silent, and he changed his grip, holding both of my hands above my head with one hand before he slid the other down my body to my knee bent around his waist. Then he slid lower to my backside. Watching me with male amusement, he raised his palm and then brought it down over my ass-cheek with a sharp sting. I gasped and tried to wiggle away, sending him deeper inside me. He did it again, the sting of his slaps causing me to tense and writhe against him, dragging moans of pleasure from both of us.

"Say it," he panted. I shook my head, breathless now. My ass cheek stung but he raised his hand and brought it down again. I cried out and he groaned, rocking harder against me. I rolled my hips against him, again and again, feeling the way his cock throbbed and swelled within me. He was close to the edge, barely holding on. I could make him come before he broke me. After a moment, Cole gave up spanking me, the demand in his mind, the complete and utter compulsion to complete this moment was overriding his need for dominance. I was grateful for that because I wasn't sure how much longer I could hold out. Cole began to pick up speed, his long, hard cock drilling in and out of me with wild abandon. He released my wrists, and I slid my hands around his back to dig my nails in. He made a low, rumbling sound of pleasure and I realized he liked a little pain too.

"Fuck me," I moaned, and I felt his increased desire at hearing those words.

"You're so wet, Little Witch. So wet and tight," he ground out, and I knew he felt the thrill that went through me at hearing him speak like that. "Come for me, Little Witch. Come on my cock," he instructed, his teeth gritting as he came closer and closer.

"Cole," I whimpered, feeling myself climb towards that peak again. I was so ready for this, so desperate for it. I could feel it building as he fucked me harder, better than anything I'd felt before.

"Say it again."

"Fuck me."

He groaned again, his orgasm building and building, his cock thickening impossibly.

"I can feel you almost there. Come for me, Mika," he ground out. *Shit, shit, shit!*

"Cole!" I screamed as I hit that peak and finally came, clenching tight around him. My back arched and I screamed his name.

"Fuck!" he bellowed, his cry of release following mine by a second. I felt him come, felt every hot jet shoot from him. His climax set off another within me, a smaller one but no less intense. He shook above me, gritted his teeth as he strained. I watched his face through half closed eyes, his face carved into sensual lines of pleasure and relief, his chest and forehead coated in a misty sweat. But I didn't care. In that moment, nothing had ever looked as goddamn beautiful as Cole.

He didn't move, and I was grateful. Little aftershocks were still going off inside me, and he moaned every time I tightened around him. He kept up small, gentle thrusts as we both came down from our high.

It seemed harder than before to draw oxygen into my lungs. Little black dots had appeared before my eyes for a moment, my throat was raw, and my lungs were starved for air.

Holy. Fucking. Hell.

CHAPTER THIRTEEN
COLE

Mika and I didn't leave the bedroom for three days.

We stopped in between sessions, mostly because Mika needed to eat or sleep, and Nova contacted me to see how things went. I had to leave for an hour to give him an update, but then I'd come straight back here and fucked her against the bookcase.

And then the wall. And in the pool. And on the couch. On the rug in front of the fire. I'd spent the last three days fucking her in almost every position I knew how, and I knew a lot. It was a good thing she was a Witch who could heal fast, or I might have fucked her to death.

To say my Little Witch was a fiend was putting it lightly. I wasn't even sure that she knew how dirty and rough she liked it until now. And pain. That had been an interesting addition for her. We'd found how much was too much, and that had opened up so many new doors. I didn't like to cause her real pain, just enough that it set her off. And we hadn't even gotten to using toys yet!

I couldn't seem to keep my hands off her. Or my mouth. She tasted so damn addictive; I wasn't sure I'd ever get enough of her, and it seemed she felt the same way about me. My enjoyment was as important to her as hers was to me. It wasn't just a point of pride, either. When we came together like that, our minds automatically merged. Her pleasure was mine, and my pleasure was hers. Desire was enhanced one-hundred-fold, and we were addicted. I felt like a damn rat in a maze, given the choice between an orgasm and food, and I always chose the orgasm.

She had a dirty mouth when I pushed her far enough, and she

loved the way I spoke to her during sex. I liked to push her boundaries, to see how far she would let me go, to see what she would let me do to her. It was utterly intoxicating knowing that she was letting me do these things to her where I knew she'd trust no other.

Trust.

Yes, I'd realized at some point in the last few days that she had come to trust me. To let me do these things to her was the ultimate show of trust. There were times when she was utterly at my mercy. I had to know when she really meant stop or no, and when she actually wanted me to keep going. And I knew my Little Witch and what she wanted *very* well. She liked to be forced into submission, and I liked to be the one to make her do it. She liked to be dominated and tossed about like a rag-doll, and fucking hell did I like to be the one to manhandle her like that. She craved it, needed it. She wasn't a dominant, not in bed. In real life she liked to call the shots, absolutely, and there was hell to pay when she was told what to do and expected to obey. But when it came down to sex, she'd put up a fight, but only because it made things so much sweeter when she finally gave in.

Despite all this, I still hadn't gotten her to admit that she was mine.

I'd get her there, though.

Interspersed with all the sex, we'd talked. Interestingly enough, I *wanted* to talk to her, to have her know me. Even thinking that way made me want to punch myself in the head for being such a wuss, but it was true. I told her about each of my brothers in more detail, told her about Hell and went deeper into the inner workings and how we were perceived by the outside world. I detailed several of our past wars for her and what role I'd played. She'd been interested in it all, asking intelligent questions and learning everything. I, in turn, asked her about her life. Mika was still closed off when I asked about her adoption. She was adamant that she knew nothing more about who her parents were or where she came from, but I still felt that small twinge of fear from her, that part of her that was concealing something. I didn't push it, not yet. I'd get it out of her eventually. But Mika was as

I'd guessed her to be. She'd lived a mostly solitary life, keeping her talent to herself and trying her hardest to solve cases the regular police couldn't.

After speaking to her so much these last few days, I began to wonder if we could actually handle this new bond amicably. Would we be able to work together without constantly wanting to put the other on their ass? Could this actually be something... real? Just thinking of it made me want to distance myself from her. I didn't do relationships or vulnerabilities, but Mika was a lot more than she appeared to be. She wasn't just a firecracker in bed, she wasn't just a whirlwind of sass and attitude, she was intelligent and funny too.

And sexy as all hell.

I woke to feel her hot, wet mouth wrapped around my cock and couldn't suppress the low rumble of pleasure that escaped me. I opened my eyes to see her dark, sinful gaze already on me, her lips around my cock and I groaned again, hardening, thickening. *Fuck.*

I still hadn't had enough of her. Her tongue swept across the sensitive head of my dick, and I bucked slightly. I slid my hands down to her hair and gripped her tight, thrusting my hips gently until she got the feel of it, the rhythm. Her throat opened and I felt myself slide deeper inside.

"Fuck, Mika," I growled, still waking up but totally awash in desire and lust. She hummed around my cock, the vibrations causing my eyes to cross for a moment. She did it again and I drove forward a little faster, careful not to hurt her. Her hand slid between my legs to cup my balls and I raised my hips against her, tightening my hold on her hair.

"Good girl," I praised roughly, and I felt her body react, the instant rush of heat between her legs.

Oh yes, my Little Witch liked to be praised.

"Just like that, Mika. Suck my cock." I encouraged; my voice thick as she sucked harder. I wanted to come, I needed to come, but I wanted to be inside her more. I savored the feel of her mouth around my dick one last time before I gripped her arms and yanked her up over me. In the same motion, I rolled and crushed her lips with my own, sliding my tongue along hers, grinding myself against her wet pussy.

She moaned louder, and so I did it again, driving her as wild as she had gotten me.

"Cole," she whimpered.

"On your knees," I demanded, my voice deeper, rougher. But she just did that to me. She could drive me to the edge of my control and smile while she did it.

With a smirk, she did as I ordered and gripped the headboard. Nudging her legs apart, I positioned myself behind her and thrust hard into her hot, wet pussy. She cried out, tossing her head back. Her body reluctantly gave way to mine, opening up when I gave it no other option.

I gripped her hips hard with one hand and fisted her hair with the other, holding her exactly as I wanted her while I pounded into her. Over and over, she whimpered and begged, but I wasn't stopping this time.

I was coming hard and fast, and I needed it. Her sheath began to tighten, and I gritted my teeth, holding on until I felt her come, heard her scream and only then did I allow myself sweet fucking release.

As we came down, I buried my face against her neck for a moment and shuddered, twitching and groaning. Mika was panting, her body still convulsing, and I brought her down with me. I tucked myself around her so that I wouldn't have to leave the sweet, welcoming heat of her body and she sighed with satisfaction.

"If you wake me up like that every morning, we'll never leave," I told her. And I meant it. Because then I'd want to return the favor. And then we'd end up fucking again, all over the place. She was like a drug. Once I started, I never wanted to stop. The world could be ending outside, and I wouldn't know until one of my brothers called out for help.

I watched as she smiled happily, tiredly, her lashes fluttering closed as exhaustion overtook her.

We hadn't been asleep long when she woke me up with heaven

around my cock. Or at least, that's what I imagined heaven to be like. If it wasn't, then why the hell was everyone so eager to get there?

I let my mind wander for a moment, feeling myself hardening again even while I was still inside her. Would I ever get enough of her? And was this just The Mark or was this what it would have always been like between Mika and myself? It hadn't escaped my attention that we'd completed the third part of the ritual.

Our souls had been bound by The Mark. Our minds had bonded with that first psychic dream. Now our bodies had well and truly been bound—metaphorically and literally. A smile tugged at my lips when I remembered the first time I'd tied Mika up and driven her crazy for an hour, constantly bringing her close to her release, edging her for what seemed like forever to her. The pleasure she'd felt when I finally allowed her to come had almost caused her to pass out.

I sighed and looked down at her. Now, if my brother was to be believed, the only thing left to bind was our hearts. The thought of that still made me uneasy. I was fine with admitting that the Witch owned my body. Absolutely, one-hundred percent was not worried about admitting that. And the souls—well, mine was pretty damaged as it was, and that was my fault as I was the one who bound us.

But my heart?

I frowned. I didn't want to think about someone owning that, and the kind of damage they could do if they wanted to. Despite what I wanted others to think, what me and my brothers *all wanted* others to think, I knew we were capable of loving someone. But I'd spent my entire life making sure I had no weaknesses. I loved my brothers, but we all understood that if one of us died, we had accepted the risk and it was obviously unavoidable. No one was stupid enough to try and capture a King of Hell, not since Nova had destroyed a battlefield of Angels. So, no one could use us against each other, therefore they were not a weakness. However, to give someone the power to destroy me and leave me a husk of the Demon King I was now was... unnerving. I didn't like it at all.

My gaze roamed over Mika as she slept, and I gently pulled away from her. She definitely had the potential to bring me to my knees. This Little Witch was an addiction now. I'd always need her body. Fine. I would constantly seek the reassurance of her mind. Okay, I could deal with that.

But to look to her for my happiness? How could I allow her to become a weakness that others could exploit? How was I supposed to live for eternity with the constant, nagging fear that someone could take her from me, and I would be... alone. Vulnerable. Easy to manipulate.

I had to be brutally honest with myself. The Witch had begun to burrow her way beneath my skin. She'd started to become a part of me, and I needed to dig her out now before it was too late. We could be friends. We could share our bodies and use each other for physical pleasure. But if she wanted more than that... I shook my head. I had to make this absolutely clear to her. There would be no love between us. In fact, from now on, when we had sex, we would do it in her bed and then I'd leave. I didn't want her thinking she *belonged* here. And outside world excursions would be kept to a minimum, and only when I was with her. I couldn't risk the Angels getting their hands on her. Fuck. The other day they had come so close. Too close. She was too valuable to accidentally hand over to the other side. I had to be more careful. From now on, I had to start putting some distance between us. We'd both been going mad with physical desire for one another. We'd done that, gotten it out of our systems for the most part. It should be easy enough to ignore now that we were well aware of how it felt. We could keep a handle on it. And at the end of the day, now that she knew what it was like to fuck me, I could use that to manipulate her decisions.

Yes, that would be acceptable.

~

MIKA

I woke up in bed alone for the first time in almost four days. I stretched carefully, slowly, my body aching in such a delicious way. I rolled onto my back and inhaled slowly, smiling contently. Okay, so I'd been right about Cole. Sleeping with him would have been an experience I'd have hated to miss. And the cocky bastard definitely knew a thousand different ways to touch a woman to bring her pleasure.

I blinked a few times and allowed myself a few minutes to wake up. My mind automatically reached for Cole, but I kept the touch feather-light, not wanting to interrupt him if he was busy. He was talking to Nova, and they both seemed in a very serious mood, so I retreated and let them be. That would give me time to find something to eat and relax in the hot springs for a few minutes. I needed to soak a little to help ease the aches and pains sleeping with Cole had left me with. Despite my usual speed for healing, I was still feeling sore.

I climbed naked from the bed and sighed. I wanted to get back on the surface and finally put away the assholes who were responsible for the ritual killings on the surface. The killing of an innocent woman and consuming her essence—not her soul, two different things—was a power move.

I had always known that it had to be something important, but I hadn't known what. Having been confined here in Hell for a while, I'd had a chance to do my research. And whoever this guy was who was killing truly innocent humans, he was taking in their essence which was boosting his power. We needed to find him and stop him, because even without the fact that killing innocent people was wrong, no one wanted a Demon out there who was consuming people's essences to make himself more powerful.

My mind traveled back to Cole as I made my way to my bathing pool, and I felt a smile tug at my lips. Okay, so the guy was arrogant beyond measure, but he was also incredible in bed, caring even though he didn't want to be; protective, bordering on possessive, and he had a sense of humor I couldn't ignore.

The brutal, bare fact was, he'd put his Mark on me. I knew he was telling the truth about not knowing how he'd done it because I'd shared his mind plenty over the last week. We were bound together, and there seemed to be no way out of it. I'd scoured every book available, but there was no way to undo it. That part sucked, but I could either sulk about it, or accept it and try to make something out of it.

While Cole sometimes drove me to violence, I couldn't say that I was disappointed about the physical specimen I was now stuck with. He definitely knew his way around the female body, and I was deliriously happy about that. We butted heads when it came to him bossing me about outside the bedroom, but he was learning.

He'd taught me something new about myself, though.

Apparently, I liked to be dominated in bed. Who knew?

It was something I couldn't get enough of. But outside in the real world, we still had a few things to work out. I needed freedom, I needed trust. I needed room to breathe and just be me without him watching my every move.

All in all, though, I felt like we could work these things out between us. For as long as I was alive anyway, which was more or less a long weekend to him, I needed him to give me a little room. And I was going to enjoy every damn minute of the sex while he still found me attractive. Soon enough, I'd be old and wrinkled while he still remained the perfect image of the male form. That thought made me sad, and a knife of jealousy twisted in my gut at the thought of him with someone else. In fact, it was my heart that ached painfully at the thought of being replaced, of him not wanting me like that anymore.

I wish I didn't feel fear at the thought of losing you.

He'd said those words to me, the look on his face had been ravaged with fear and anger. He'd feared losing me, not just because I was a Witch. He was worried about *me*. That insinuated deeper feelings here. I knew already that I had started down that road, I cared about what happened to him. Lately, I'd even looked to him for comfort and protection. An uncontrollable urge had taken root inside me; I wanted to make sure he didn't get hurt and I hated that he took so many risks with his safety. I cared about Cole, more than I had thought possible.

I wasn't sure if it was just the afterglow of the sex marathon we'd just had… but I was pretty sure I was falling for him. We had a lot of potential. When he wasn't talking out of his ass, he was funny and intelligent, and we mixed well on a lot of things. We would have a lot of bumps in the road. But I could see myself falling in love with him one day soon.

While I'd originally tried to fight it, now I was making the best of a situation I'd originally hated. Maybe Cole wasn't so bad to be tied to for the rest of my life after all. And if he could feel the same way about me, then things could actually go very well for us.

Half an hour later, I was freshly washed, my hair was tied back and I was dressed, ready for action. I reached out to Cole, and I saw that he was in the entrance room. I glanced around to see him and Nova talking. They looked up as I exited Cole's realm. Cole's dark gaze raked over me from head to toe, and I felt the heat of his stare down to my bones. Despite the days we'd spent together in his bed, despite the things I'd let him do to me and the things I'd done to him, I still felt my face warm as I approached him. My gaze flitted to Nova for a moment, and he was considering us both with interest and a little suspicion, but said nothing. I glanced back to Cole and his lips twitched.

"Good morning, Little Witch," he greeted, and I felt his fingers brush my lips even though he wasn't near me.

"Hello, my King," I replied, making sure to make him feel the brush of my lips against his.

Cole's eyes lit with my greeting, and I bit back a smile.

Nova cleared his throat loudly and I looked at him with wide eyes.

"I don't need to read your minds to see the eye-fucking. Can we leave that for when you're alone, please?" he begged. Cole grinned and I ducked my head.

"Hey totally off topic and I'm not bringing this up at all to change the subject—but why do your brothers call you Nova? Is it because

Nova fits into the name Donovan?" I asked. Nova's gaze turned inward for a moment, and he shrugged a shoulder.

"We started calling him Nova after your ancestors were killed," Cole explained. I frowned.

"Why?"

"Because he decimated pretty much every Angel on that battlefield like a goddamn supernova. None of the rest of us were even needed, so none of us intervened. He earned his name," Cole continued.

A muscle in Nova's jaw twitched for a moment but he slowly raised his gaze to meet mine.

"Like I said, Tabitha was a good friend. Her death unleashed something in me, and every Angel within my radius died for it," he said softly. I nodded, my heart going out to him. He really must have cared about my ancestor for him to have had such a strong reaction. I wondered briefly if Cole would ever be capable of feeling so strongly about me.

"I found the Demon's responsible for the ritual killings," Cole announced.

"Really?"

"Yes. I was about to go up and deal with them."

"I'm coming," I demanded, eager to put this case to bed. He was already shaking his head and I frowned.

"Why not?"

"Because you don't need to be there. There is no use for you in that situation. Besides, you're too sensitive. You'll feel the pain they feel when I dispatch them, and I'd rather not have a repeat of what happened last time," he explained with a small shrug. I frowned, feeling the distance he seemed to have put between us. He wasn't as merged with me in my mind, although he seemed incapable of fully extracting himself. He was holding back; barriers were in place to keep me from feeling his emotions. My stomach felt funny at the lack of emotion I could sense in him now. What was going on?

"I need to be there to see this end," I protested.

"No. It's not worth the risk, especially now that Krae and the Angels know you exist," he reminded.

"Cole—"

"Nova is going to help you practice your magic while I'm gone. I'll be back as soon as this is over," he added in a tone that told me this conversation was over.

"Wait," I tried again, but before I could take a step towards him, he'd wrapped himself in shadow and was gone.

I stood there, my mouth agape and my mind in a state of shock. That rat bastard. I had thought we were past this, past him dictating what I could and could not do. I thought we were past him being an asshole and me having to knock sense into him. He knew better than to just *demand* my obedience. How hard was it to change his phrasing?

"What the hell?" I gaped, looking at Nova.

He sighed and shook his head before looking at me with a resigned expression.

"I can't say I disagree with him," Nova admitted. I glared and he smiled slightly. "He's right, Mika. You are a Witch. Your natural inclination is to protect, to heal. The minute he starts to dispatch justice up there, you're going to feel it all and your entire being is going to demand that you do something to help them," Nova continued.

"Why does he have to kill them? Why can't he bring them down here for punishment?"

Nova looked at me as though I was strange and shook his head.

"They are Demons," he said as if that were enough.

"Gee, thanks Captain Obvious."

Nova chuckled and shook his head.

"They're Demons who have gone rogue, and are creating problems for us. There is no such thing here as prison. Not really. They can withstand a lot of pain; it would hardly be a punishment. We need to make an example of them so that others don't try to repeat this," Nova explained.

"An example," I repeated slowly. Nova nodded.

Oh. He meant that Cole was going to kill them bloody, slowly, painfully. He was going to make such a mess that no other Demon would wonder what kind of pain they'd been in before they died. My stomach knotted again at the thought of Cole being the one to distribute that kind of punishment. Why did it have to be him?

Was this how it would be from now on? Cole decided what was best for me or what I could handle, and I had no say in it? Would I always be left alone under the guise that I was "safer" down here? A chill started to creep over me, deep down, and reality began to settle. The rose-tinted glasses, the hopefulness I had woken with this morning was slowly fading, and I was realizing that this was how it would always go.

"Come on. Let's practice your defensive magic again," Nova called, interrupting my thoughts.

I nodded reluctantly and moved to the other side of the entrance hall so that we could get in position.

~

Hours later, I heard that familiar *whoosh* and peered around to see Cole standing before the fireplace.

He wore his usual black jeans, tight black shirt, and dark brown leather jacket. His eyes were dark and guarded, his jaw set. Despite how mad I was at him, how disappointed I was, I couldn't help but appreciate his sheer masculine beauty.

I'd finished practicing with Nova a while ago and he had decided to let me finish for the day when he could tell my heart wasn't in it. From the moment Cole left, I had felt odd, almost numb, and it had drowned all my feelings. It had been the wakeup call I'd needed to finally understand my place and my use around here, and it wasn't a pretty future. Not really.

I would be Cole's on-hand healer. I would be a body for him to use when he needed a release, and I would stay in his realm all the time, waiting to be used. That was just the way it was, and it felt almost useless to attempt to change things.

He was a millennia old King of Hell, and I was a Witch still learning her craft. I could not leave this place on my own... I had no power. What would fighting him get me other than locked up? He was a King of Demons. I needed to come to terms with that and all it entailed. If I ever had any insipid ideas that he would change his ways or become something else just because he may or may not have feelings for me... well, those thoughts were dead now. Even if I did manage to escape, how could I ever hope to stay hidden? Not just from him, but from all of them, Angels and Demons alike? Would leaving here just be escaping one cage to enter another? What was the point of feeling all that anger and frustration when the reality of my situation would not change? No, feeling nothing was the better option.

I had decided after Nova's lesson ended to come back to Cole's realm and do some research and reconsider a few things. I needed to examine my feelings for Cole more clearly, post sex-athon.

And annoyingly enough, I'd come to the same conclusion. I was falling for a damn Demon.

Was I insane? Probably.

Was I suffering from Stockholm syndrome? Most likely.

Had Cole somehow managed to buy my compliance with earth-shattering sex and orgasms by the dozen? I was beginning to think that was the sad and unfortunate truth.

I hated the idea of it, but it seemed like I was out of my depth and falling hard and fast for a King of Hell, despite his villainous ways and Demon nature. Even after touching on his mind earlier and seeing the brutality of his killings, the blood and gore, the pain he was handing out and more than that, the pleasure he took in doing it... Despite feeling sick about it, I couldn't shake how much he meant to me.

Damn it. Was I in love with a frigging King of Hell?

And what was more annoying; was that he was right. The Demons were his domain, and he knew how to doll out their punishments. And when it came to that, I just couldn't be anywhere near it because I felt everything, and it was torture. So, it didn't make sense for me to get annoyed at him for leaving me behind. I was frustrated at him handing out the order rather than explaining it to me and us agreeing. But maybe we could work on that in time. The truth was, there wasn't a lot I was going to be able to change about Cole, not to make my life more bearable, and not to make him see that not everything had to be dealt with in such a violent and dominating way. Cole had been this way forever; I wasn't even thirty. If anyone was going to have to change and accept things, it was going to be me.

I took one last look at his dark eyes glittering at me, daring me to say anything. He had to know I checked in earlier, he had to have felt my horror and disgust at what he'd been doing, he had to know I wasn't happy with him for it.

Instead of saying anything, I turned back to the book on my lap and ignored him.

"So that's it?" he asked softly. "You're not going to label me a monster after what you witnessed?"

I shrugged but remained silent.

"Seriously? You're not going to tell me how you could never be with someone like me, that I was too brutal and harsh? You're not going to try and make me out to be the most horrible creature to ever exist?" he demanded.

"No," was my simple reply.

He snickered and stepped to the display where he kept his blades. I could feel the faint traces of wounds on him, but they'd already begun to heal and there was nothing more for me to do there. He was home safe.

Home.

Yep, that was what I thought of this place now. Because no matter how hard I fought it, I knew there would be no going back. I'd never be allowed to roam free; I'd never be out there on my own, I'd never be trusted and never not be guarded. This was my life; this was where I was going to live out the rest of it. I might as well get comfortable.

"I can feel your disgust of me from here," Cole snapped with his back to me as he cleaned the blades.

"No, you can't," I replied, and I was right. Because I wasn't feeling disgust right then, I was quite apathetic to it all.

"I can. You're just doing that female thing where you say you're fine," he growled.

Again, I ignored him and continued to read. There was no point in arguing with him; he'd do what he wanted and believe what he wanted to anyway. And then he'd walk away feeling all superior and righteous. It was better not to feel.

"Just say what you want to say already," Cole snapped, turning to face me. I glanced up from my book and shook my head.

"I have nothing to say."

"Bullshit!" he sneered. "You want to condemn me for punishing those Demons. You want to name me a monster and hurl your insults and remind me that I am lower than dirt and that I belong down here. Get it over with already."

"I don't want to say any of that."

Cole scoffed.

"Tell me what you want me to say, Cole," I replied, closing the book softly to look at him more clearly.

"I don't want you to say anything."

"Then I won't. The truth is, I don't have anything to say to you. I'm not feeling anything in particular, and I have no intention of condemning you. You are who you are, and I am who I am. There seems to be no changing either of us, so why bother arguing about it?" I explained, making sure to keep my voice even and reasonable.

Cole frowned, his eyes narrowing in suspicion.

"That's it?" he demanded.

"That's it."

"I don't believe you."

I sighed and slowly sat up, making my way towards my bedroom.

"Look, I am a Demon, Mika. I am a Demon *King!* I have responsibilities and duties here. And trying to keep a bunch of Demons in line is not easy. They don't respond to harsh talks or threats. They understand violence and pain, that's all. I can't let a band of Demons like that go around killing and do nothing about it. It makes me look weak," he argued, following me as I walked.

"I am aware," I replied without looking at him.

"I have been alive for eons, longer than you can even conceive. I have a way of doing things. I am not about to change because you got your panties in a twist," he snarled as I reached my doorway.

"I wouldn't dream of you changing," I murmured, refraining from rolling my eyes.

"I'm not changing for anyone, least of all you!" he roared.

I stopped just inside my room and stared up at him, still oddly empty and unfeeling. I took note of his angry eyes, the rage coming off him and caught the edges of guilt and regret. He expected condemnation because a part of him felt like what he'd done was wrong, and he didn't want me to rub it in. I could see that on his face, but no matter what I said to him right now, he'd use it to attack me.

"I understand. If you don't mind, I'd like to sleep on my own tonight. I'm tired after the last few days, and practicing with my magic this afternoon made me even more so. If you would like, we can continue with you telling me everything I think in the morning. But for now, I'm tired," I replied softly.

Cole stiffened, a frown creasing his forehead.

"Goodnight, Cole," I added before I waved my hands and a wall of thorns grew rapidly across the doorway, separating me from the Demon King. I knew he could destroy the plant in a second, but I was also hoping he'd give me my space tonight.

When he didn't come charging right in, I let out a slow breath and turned to look at my little oasis. I wasn't used to not fighting back. I wasn't used to bowing out of a fight. But it was time to accept that my future was no longer my own, and that the sooner I gave Cole whatever answers he was looking for, the smoother our living situation would be.

I found myself shockingly close to tears and blinked them away. I didn't even know where they'd come from, but it had to be from exhaustion. Kicking off my shoes and stripping off my jacket, I crawled into bed, imagining myself wearing a pair of gray, soft cotton shorts and a tank top.

By the time I slid under the covers, I was dressed to sleep, and struggled to get a hold of my emotions. Tears continued to threaten to spill, and I closed my eyes, hoping to sink into oblivion.

THE KINGS OF HELL
COLE

CHAPTER FOURTEEN
COLE

"What the fuck is your problem?" Nova snapped a few days later.

"Nothing," I growled, watching as Mika buried her head in yet another book.

"Something is. You've been in a fucking pissy mood all day, and I'm tired of being the one to deal with it," Nova returned, tossing the blade on the pile of ones we'd already cleaned.

"I said it's nothing. Mind your own business," I almost snarled, barely reigning in my anger.

Mika flicked her gaze to me, obviously feeling my irritation. When she saw us looking at her, she turned back to her book, her face a mask of indifference. I couldn't even feel anything coming from her. No hatred, disgust; no fear or annoyance. There was just... nothing. Why wasn't she feeling anything? Last night was the same way, and the night before that. Besides the two minutes of overwhelming sorrow and the feeling of being suffocated, Mika hadn't felt a damn thing since I'd come back from dealing with the rogue Demons.

Not one. And that was days ago!

"Trouble in paradise?"

"I said mind your business," I snapped, turning my back on her. Whatever. If she wanted to condemn me for being who and what I was, then that was all her deal.

But was she condemning me?

I snarled at that little inner voice that pointed out not once since coming back from destroying those Demons had she tried to reprimand me; not once had she tried to school me in better ways to punish my Demons.

"Cole," Nova tried again.

Growling under my breath, I stormed away from him, away from Mika and out of my realm. I heard the door open behind me and knew Nova had followed me out.

"She is trying to punish me."

"For?"

"For being a fucking Demon. She knew what I was, but when she sees me acting on it, she condemns me for it," I argued.

Nova didn't reply straight away, and the small look of confusion on his face was almost enough to make me want to lash out.

"What the hell did you do?" he demanded. I turned my glare on him and stiffened.

"What?"

"You heard me. What the fuck did you do? I've spent time with Mika, I know her pretty damn well, and it's not like her to be so quiet, so... submissive. She fights, she swears, she gets fired up. And being around you two the last two weeks has been like watching fireworks. A whole lot of tension and things I didn't particularly want to be around. And the last few days? Nothing. She's ice cold and you're ready to punch anyone that looks at you the wrong way," Nova argued.

So he could see it too. I'd heard of women using the silent treatment before as a kind of punishment, but I'd never experienced it myself. Honestly, I hadn't thought silence from a woman could possibly be conceived as a punishment. I know, boo me, right? But fuck. There was a time and place for being mouthy, and most women I knew just didn't know how to differentiate.

But this wasn't just the silent treatment. She would reply if I asked her a question, she would talk to Nova if he called out to her. She was polite. But there was no... light. There was no fire, nothing. All emotion seemed to have disappeared, and *that* was what was making me so uncomfortable. That fire in her was a big part of the reason I'd been drawn to her in the first place. And now it was gone, and I hated it. What was worse, I was pretty sure I'd been the one to put those flames out.

"I don't know," I finally answered, waving my hand to create a chair before flopping down onto it. The truth was, I hated seeing her so down. I hated seeing her fire gone, her attitude, that sassy mouth and raw defiance. What the fuck had happened to me? I was a King of Hell—why the hell did I care what one woman thought of me? Why did I care if she was happy?

"This is priceless," Nova laughed, and I glared. Throwing my hand out, I tossed power his way in retaliation, knocking him back several steps.

"Fuck off," I growled. "You know, if that prophecy is right, then your day is coming. And I'm going to relish in your misery when you find yourself suckered by your woman."

Nova's face sobered slightly, and his dark eyes considered me carefully. "Is that how you see her now? As your woman?"

I shrugged and looked past him to stare at the wall.

"It's not a bad thing to… feel," Nova started, looking as uncomfortable as I was with the direction of this conversation. "I know we don't really do that. But maybe it's okay, this one time, to feel that way."

"Nova—"

"Look, the two of you are bound now. For better or worse, your lives are now intertwined, and there's no undoing it. You gotta find some middle ground. And by the looks of it, her misery is yours, and I suspect it works the other way around too. Work together, not separately. Maybe you'll find a compromise?"

I clenched my jaw and continued to glare at the wall.

Me, compromise? The word wasn't one I was all that familiar with. I knew what it meant, of course, but having never been in this situation before, I hadn't had much cause to… compromise. Nova was right, her misery did appear to affect me, even though I tried not to let it. Was this how it would always be? Was this another side effect of The Mark? Was this how it made sure to keep us together and constantly looking out for each other's health, happiness and wellbeing for as long as we both lived? How long would that be? Mika was a mortal. Witches had a lot of power, but an extended life was not a part of that. So, what happened to me when she died of old age? Our souls were bound. Would I die when she died? Would she maybe live longer if she wasn't mortally wounded? And would she age where I would forever stay the same? There was so much we didn't know.

But what we did know was simple and I needed to get a handle on it.

I had to find a way to meet her in the middle. Because I wasn't sure how much longer I could take seeing her look so desolate and... empty. It wasn't right.

"Compromise," I murmured aloud, tasting the word.

"It won't be so bad," Nova assured. I sent him a look of disbelief and he grinned. "I'm going back to my realm. Make it up with your mate, brother," he added as he strode away.

My mate. I guess that was what she was. My soulmate. Life-mate. Beloved. Other half. Companion. Life partner.

However you wanted to phrase it, that was what she was. Our souls, mind and body were bound. Despite heart still being left out—at least for now, I grudgingly admitted—we were irrefutably stuck with each other. And seeing her hurting caused me a pain I had not known existed. I was a Demon King—pain was kind of my forte. I thought I knew it all, but apparently even after all these years, I still had a thing or two to learn.

Steeling myself, I stood and waved away the chair I'd created. I needed to make things right with my mate.

~

"What are we doing here?" Mika asked as we stood outside her house on the surface a few hours later.

I shifted uncomfortably, needing to make things right, but unsure on how.

"I uh... I thought you might have some things here you missed. I thought we'd collect them and bring them back... home," I answered, stumbling over the word *home*. It had been mine for as long as I could remember. I'd never thought to share it with anyone. Mika looked up at me with dark, questioning eyes, and I tried to force a smile and immediately regretted it. I wasn't that guy, and this scraping at her feet to get her to smile at me again was uncomfortable.

"You must have some things here you want?" I continued.

"Yes," she answered after a small hesitation.

"Right, well, let's go get them," I repeated, taking her hand, and pulling her up the walkway to her home. I was scanning the area constantly, making sure no one had found her home yet. While Krae and the Angels had seen her and now had confirmation that she existed, I doubted they knew where she lived yet, and so I figured this a relatively safe excursion to take her on.

With a wave of my hand, I unlocked her doors and we entered. We hadn't been back here since the morning I'd taken her to Hell with me. Everything was still, nothing had been disturbed. Mika waved her hands and said something under her breath, and the windows in the house opened, letting in the gentle breeze outside. I watched in awe as the plants in her home that had been drooping suddenly came to life in her presence, and I felt a small knot in my stomach dissipate at the tiny smile on her face as she felt the plants welcoming her home.

I knew all there was to know about Witches, and yet somehow, I had managed to temporarily forget that nature was their calling. Greenery was what soothed her, and nature responded to her. Letting a plant die that was in her care had to hurt her in a way.

"How are we going to get my things back?" she asked.

"I'm a King of Hell. I can send them to our realm with a wave of my hand."

I watched her freeze slightly at my use of the words "our realm" and her jade eyes considered me carefully. I surveyed her without giving away my thoughts, wondering what she was thinking, desperate to invade her mind and find out for myself. But I refrained—barely. She needed space; she made that clear. She needed to be seen and heard. And fuck it all if listening to myself didn't want to make me kick my own wussy ass.

But this woman.

This fucking pain in the ass Witch had me in knots. I didn't like it and I needed her to go back to fighting with me so that I could stop feeling so out of my depth. I didn't feel inadequate often—ever—but Mika had managed to tip me on my head, and I had no idea how to navigate these waters.

With a nod and a small smile in my direction, Mika began packing her things and putting them into the center of the room. There wasn't a lot. A few books and bits and pieces. She had a single bag of clothes, and the rest was mostly plants. I shouldn't have been surprised at that. It didn't take her long at all, and by the end of the process, she stared around her home with wide eyes, looking small and vulnerable. I couldn't stand the sight, and so I edged slowly up behind her, gently gripping her upper arms and brushed her mind with mine.

She was sad.

Fuck it all, she was sad, and I had no idea how to make it right.

"Tomika, I wish that I could apologize for taking you from your life and mean it," I began, pressing my lips to her hair, frantically searching for the right words. "But I stand by what I have always said and thought, Little Witch. Your freedom was always on a ticking clock. If not me, then another would have found you and bound you to them, and you would be where you are now. Maybe you would have preferred someone else, but I am grateful that I was the one to find you. I do not know how you would have been treated by the others. The thought of you at their mercy has me thinking up new tortures," I told her honestly.

"It's not just that," she whispered after a moment, her voice a little husky. My heart lurched at the sight of her tears as she turned to face me. Her usually warm green eyes were glistening, and I had to refrain from pulling her into my arms.

"Then what is it?"

She drew in a few steadying breaths and flicked a look around her apartment.

"This is my life. In this small pile is anything that is even remotely important to me. I don't have photo albums to take with me. I thought for a moment that I should let someone know that I'm not missing, I'm just not living here anymore. But then I realized, I have no one to tell. No one would come looking for me ever, no one would even notice that I'm gone. I've been alone in this world for so long, and I'm tired of feeling lonely," she whispered brokenly, and a tear tracked down her cheek as she glanced away. I couldn't keep my distance now. I stepped in close to her and wrapped her in my arms, surprised and relieved when she sank against me, letting me hold her. I didn't say anything to her. I had no idea what to say that would make her feel better. It was a blessing for me that I had no one to convince that she was in safe hands, but I still wished she had someone important in her life to miss her, to need to know where she was now. I hated that she felt so alone and unloved.

With a wave of my hand and a murmured command, I sent her belongings to our realm and tried to think of the right words to calm her, to soothe her despite the fact I wasn't sure there were any.

I pulled her back slightly and tipped her face up to me. Her eyelashes were spiked with tears, and I brushed the wetness from her face, my heart cracking at the sight. There was a deep, unrelenting need in me to fix this, to make her smile again, to take away all the hurt and all the despair and make her happy again.

"I know it doesn't make up for how you're feeling. And I know there is a lot left to work on. We're probably going to fight a lot more. You're going to want to throw things at me, maybe even use my own blades on me," I began, and I saw her eyes light for a moment with amusement.

"I know I'm not easy to be with, and I find it hard to change. And I'm sorry, but you'll never find me willingly putting you in a dangerous situation where I am not confident that I can keep you safe—no matter what you want or who else is at risk. I have found that your safety matters a good deal to me," I continued.

"Because I'm a Witch," she murmured with a half-hearted smile. I sighed heavily and groaned before I shook my head and stepped away from her.

"I really wish I could say that it's because you're a Witch that your safety matters to me," I began, scrubbing a hand over my head quickly. I peered down at her wide eyes and inwardly cursed. She was going to make me say it. More than that, I got the impression that she needed me to say it.

Steeling myself, I summoned all my courage and ignored the taunting voice in the back of my head telling me I was a pussy.

"I find myself drawn to you, Mika. I care about you. I hate it when you're numb; I want your fire back. I want you angry at me, yelling and fighting and throwing around your attitude. I'll happily take pulling my hair out over you being miserable. I will change the layout of our realm; we'll add in whatever you need to feel at home and happy there. We'll go places, see things, do things. I'll try whatever I can to make you happy, Mika. I will. Just don't ask me to put your safety in jeopardy, because it won't happen," I continued. I was in for it now, but it was better I get this out of the way so that we could set things right.

"Cole?" she whispered, hopefulness and reservation warring within her.

I stepped forward again and framed her face with my hands, staring down at her intensely.

"I know that I can't offer you everything. I can never go back and unbind us, nor at this point, selfishly, do I think I would want to. And I won't promise to allow you to accompany me to places where I feel like your safety would be in jeopardy. I am a King of Hell. I am not the hero, nor will I ever be. I am a villain in every story, and I won't change that, not even for you. I have been running my circle of hell for eons, and there is a way that things are done. You may not like it or agree with it, but you have to trust that I know what works for Demons and what does not," I continued, trying to think of everything that had pissed her off this last week.

"Cole," she prompted with a small smile when I continued to ramble on, and I felt a grin tug at my lips as her eyes sparkled.

"What I am saying, Mika… is that while there are some things you do not have and some things I can never give you," I continued, drawing in a deep breath as I looked at her seriously. "You will always have me."

Mika swallowed hard, her green eyes wide and studying. I

watched her soft lips part and heard her breath hitch as she considered what I said, what I was trying to say without saying the words. Because right now, I wasn't sure I was capable of saying them, even if I meant them. I'd never said those words to anyone before, I'd rarely even thought them, if at all. I was already showing her that she was my biggest vulnerability, I was letting her see me where no other had. I just couldn't put those words out there right now. Not yet. Maybe someday when things between us were solid and good again, and I was feeling more confident in how she felt about me.

When she didn't say anything, I began to feel foolish and scrambled for something to say.

"I know it's not much, and I know maybe I'm not who you envisioned spending your life with. I have flaws, I am not perfect, and I'm going to piss you off more often than not," I started, and some part of me realized that I was babbling. I never babbled— ever. I was never at a loss for words, and I never felt nervous like this.

"Mika—" I began but didn't get to finish.

Mika launched herself at me, her arms and legs wrapped around me, her lips pressing down on mine. It took me a second or two to realize what was happening before I folded my arms around her and kissed her back.

Like a tidal wave, I felt her emotions unlock and wash over me. Fire, passion, laughter, joy—she was all there. I was sure there was more, emotions that were not so positive, but for now I wanted to see the good.

I slid a hand through her dark hair as I spun us around and walked us down the hall to her bedroom. Relief was still coursing through me, but it was quickly being overshadowed by more primal needs.

Mika kissed me harder, deeper, her hips grinding against me. I staggered into her room and fell with her on the bed, grinning when she laughed in surprise.

Our kiss turned heated, rough, demanding. I yanked her clothes from her while her fingers pulled at mine. I was aware that we could have wished our clothes away, but there was something about stripping the clothes from the person you wanted to devour. As every delectable inch of her creamy white skin appeared, I grew harder. As soon as we were both free, I slid my hands between us to find her already wet. I needed her—now. I couldn't make this slow and memorable. My body was raging at me, demanding that I take her, that I feel her again after days apart, and I was helpless to stop. After slipping first one finger and then a second inside her to make sure she was ready, I removed them and gripped my cock, pressing myself to her entrance.

"Please," she begged, and I thrust forward.

Mika cried out in pleasure, her back arching and her nails digging into my biceps. Her body was my heaven, and I strived to make her feel the same way as I moved inside her, bringing us both to a world-rocking orgasm. I wasn't sure if it was in my head or actually happening, but it was as if small, invisible strings had begun to weave us together. I could feel our heartbeats syncing, my breath was hers, our pleasure intermingled so that I didn't know who was feeling what, only that it was growing bigger and better than ever. Fuck, she was perfect. Every inch of her somehow felt made for me.

"Harder," Mika pleaded, and I groaned and stopped holding back. I watched her face as she bit her lower lip and threw her head back, her cheeks flushed pink and her breathing labored. I felt her getting closer, her body tightening on mine.

"Fuck, your pussy is so tight," I panted as she edged closer and closer to climax. Mika slid her hands up my chest and she tugged my face down to meet her mouth. I kissed her hard, her teeth nipped at my lips and her hands slid into my hair where she tugged hard enough to make it sting.

"Fuck," I gritted out and thrust faster, harder, feeling her tighten until she tore her mouth from mine and screamed my name. I swore again and came with her, emptying myself until I was totally boneless. Gasping for air, I took a moment to fill my lungs before I propped myself up with my elbows on either side of her head. Mika's lashes fluttered and then lifted, her green eyes dark with satisfaction.

I felt the warmth in her, the happiness, the way her heart seemed to flutter when she looked at me, and I knew my grin was one of satisfaction.

"For whatever it's worth," Mika whispered unevenly, raising a hand to brush a thumb over my lower lip.

"You'll always have me, too."

I felt those invisible strings tighten and tug, as if binding us closer, and I leaned down to kiss her again, unable to speak or properly process what I was feeling. It was all too much. It all felt too real and like I was too exposed. The villain never got the girl, not truly. And I wasn't going to even attempt to convince anyone that I was a hero when I was most certainly the bad guy. I'd never wanted a woman for myself for the long run, had never fantasized about having a life-mate or spending eternity with someone. The thought was preposterous. If I had ever wished for it, I probably would have worried about not being worthy of her. I mean, what kind of woman would accept a King of Hell if she had the choice? Mika was with me now, yes, but I didn't delude myself into thinking that she would have chosen me if she'd been given another option. She was making the best of a bad situation and I was the one reaping the benefits. But I would try.

For her, I would be the best that I could be.

Only for her.

I pulled back sharply when I suddenly felt danger near and pulled away from her.

"Cole?"

I waved my hand, and I was dressed before I stood up, ready for action. I wished like hell I had more than the one blade on me.

"Get up, you need to get out of here. We're surrounded," I whispered in her mind, unwilling to say the words out loud and alert our enemy that we knew they were here.

"Angels?"

"Yes. Rogue Demon's too—traitors."

How the fuck had they found us? How did they know where she lived and how had they known that we were here now? I had told no one. Not a single damn soul had known that we were coming here. Mika had been hidden up until now when she… I closed my eyes in dismay, mentally kicking my own ass.

Witches left behind a signature when they used magic. The second we'd walked in the door, she'd opened the windows using her magic, she'd packed her bags and given the plants a boost. Now that the Angels knew a Witch existed, they would have been scouring the surface, looking for the smallest sign that there was a Witch nearby. And I had led them right to her. Clenching my jaw, I checked the window at the end of the hall, watching as an Angel strode arrogantly up to the front door. Mika was pulling on her pants when I turned back to her.

"We need to go. Now," I growled.

I was reaching out for her when there was a *whoosh* and an Angel appeared beside her. I yanked hard on her arm, pulling her away from him and to my other side while at the same time reaching for my blade. I dodged the Angel blade aimed at my gut and struck out with my own.

"Cole!" Mika shouted and I turned to see her throw some of her own magic, but she missed, and a second Angel reached for her. "No!" I bellowed, moving quickly, but I was too late, I knew it. His hand gripped her upper arm and before I could get close enough, they were gone.

"Fuck!"

CHAPTER FIFTEEN
MIKA

"Let me go!" I shouted, yanking hard, stumbling as we arrived in some new place.

I looked around wildly at all the grey. Grey walls, floors, even the ceiling was grey. Talk about depressing. I backed up and glared at the Angel who'd taken me. He smiled, and he was beautiful to look at.

Ethereal.

"You're safe now," he explained, his voice soft and calming.

"Safe?" I repeated, confused.

"Yes. You are no longer in the clutches of the Demon King; you are with the Angels, now," he repeated. I blinked rapidly, trying to understand what he was saying. Did he honestly think that he had just saved me? I mean, ordinarily I could understand that.

"And if I don't want to be with the Angels, either?"

He smiled indulgently, like I was a child who had said something funny. I gritted my teeth against the indignation.

"Of course you want to be with us. There is no chance of you being on your own now that your existence is known. And if you're not safe with us, then you'll be in the clutches of a Demon," he explained.

I swallowed hard and watched him carefully. He was tall and strong looking. He was dressed all in black, and his golden hair stood out in stark contrast. His eyes were crystal blue, and his face could have been carved from stone. He was certainly handsome, but there was something about him that rubbed me the wrong way. Where Cole had drawn me to him at once, I wanted to get away from this Angel.

"What's your name?" I asked, keeping my distance. The Angel smirked as though proud that I seemed to have come to the same conclusion as him.

"Alastair," he replied with a small bow.

"Cole?" I reached out through our mind link, hoping he could hear me, but there was nothing but silence. For the first time, I grasped that I could no longer feel him. The void in my mind now felt massive. I couldn't sense him there, and it wasn't until that point that I realized just how much I'd gotten used to his presence.

Fear began to tug at me. Was Cole dead? Was that why I could no longer sense him? Surely not. I'd seen him in action, and he hadn't even been trying them. And our souls were bound. I would have felt it if he died... right? It was then that I noticed the odd, almost transparent symbols on the walls. They were strange, something I'd never seen before, and they seemed to be moving ever so slowly. Was this some kind of Ward? Was it blocking Cole from reaching me, and from me reaching him?

"Cole!" I tried again, getting desperate. How the hell was I going to get out of here?

"Where am I?" I asked Alastair. He once again gave me that indulgent smile and looked around.

"We're not in Heaven yet. I'll await the rest of my garrison once they're done dispatching of the Demon King. But we'll be safe here," he assured.

Not in Heaven, so... I should be able to leave on my own, right? And Cole wasn't dead, or the rest of his group would have shown up. Why couldn't I talk to him then?

I nodded as if I understood and slowly began to wander around the room, wrapping my arms around myself as I began to draw power from my core in preparation for my escape.

No, I hadn't been happy being kept captive by Cole, but we'd *just* come to an understanding. Cole knew me now, and I was pretty certain I knew him. I'd seen a part of him I was sure he hadn't shown anyone else. This Angel? Well... he looked and sounded like a condescending fuck. I was beginning to realize that there was no good or evil here, just the celestials and the rest of us. It was their war, their wager, their fight, and us mortals were just caught in the middle of it.

"How have you remained undiscovered, Witch?" Alastair asked. I noted how he didn't bother to ask me my name. Of course not; I was a tool to use. Why get to know the help?

"I didn't know what I was, exactly, until a couple of weeks ago," I answered slowly.

"How could you not know?" he demanded, his tone conversational, but I could feel the undercurrent of authority and scrutiny.

I shrugged. "I was adopted. No one I knew could do what I could, and so I kept it hidden. The celestials I have healed over the years were unconscious when I reached them, and I made sure to get out before they woke up," I explained, being as honest as I could. That part, at least, was the truth.

"And the Demon King? How did he discover you?"

I ducked my head and considered this. Was there anything I could say that would make things worse? I couldn't imagine so; they all seemed pretty hell-bent on killing each other no matter what.

"I healed him... he was awake. He understood what I was and took me to his realm with him," I explained with a shrug.

"So you've been a captive of the King all this time, not a consort?" he asked, edging closer. I turned to look at him to see his eyes roaming over me slowly. I frowned, feeling somewhat vulnerable.

"What's it to you what my relationship with him was?" I asked.

"It shows your character, and if you can be trusted," Alastair answered, moving closer. I was backed up against a wall now and I didn't like the look on his face or the sinister feeling I was getting from him. I continued to drag in energy, hoping to feel out a way to get out of here. I'd need to move quickly, I felt like my window of opportunity was closing.

Alastair leaned in close to me and I watched him close his eyes and drag in a breath. Frowning, I tried to back up but found myself against a wall. What the hell?

His crystal blue eyes snapped open, and he sneered at me in disgust.

"You reek of the Demon. You've been in his bed. You've let him defile your body," he spat. He couldn't have looked more disgusted had he tried.

I cocked an eyebrow.

"You sound jealous," I quipped. He scoffed.

"That Demon knows nothing of pleasure. But you, Witch, have proven your loyalties are to him and not to the soldiers of Heaven. You cannot be trusted. You will be confined to a cell in Heaven, and you *will* use your healing talents to heal those of us when we need it. Your days of consorting with the enemy are done," Alastair snapped, grabbing my upper arm in a bruising grip.

Now.

I unleashed the concentrated ball of power from within me and shot it through my hands. It hit him hard in the chest, sending him flying backwards until he slammed into the opposite wall. Pain hit me for a second as it ricocheted through him, but then it died off as he lost consciousness. Without waiting to see how badly he was hurt, I closed my eyes and reached for the elusive corner of my mind. I'd been in Cole's head plenty when he traveled by shadow. I could open his door when no other could. I could merge with his mind in a way no other ever had. We were bound as one. Why shouldn't I be able to travel this way too?

Not knowing how to work it, I grabbed that little bit of shadow I could see from the corner of my eye and wrapped it around myself and thought of Cole. I thought of the first time we met, of the way he touched me, kissed me.

Cole.

I thought his name and felt that familiar gut-churning feeling I got whenever he took me traveling by shadow. I clung to the image of Cole in that first meeting and when I felt the world stop moving, I opened my eyes. I staggered, my stomach heaved, and I fell to my hands and knees. I dry heaved for a second as the dark spots in front of my eyes lingered and then cleared. When I was sure I was done, I pushed myself up on unsteady legs and looked around.

I was in that warehouse where I'd first met Cole.

"Cole!" I called for him through our mind-link, desperate to see him, hear him, to know that he was alive.

"Mika! Where are you?" Cole demanded.

Relief inundated me and I almost collapsed again. Instead, I sent him a mental image of where I was and concentrated on him. I could feel his injuries, his worry, and his fury.

A second later there was that tell-tail *whoosh* and I spun to see Cole striding towards me.

Almost at the same time, two more figures appeared beside me. Angels.

I started for Cole, but they restrained me. My frantic gaze met Cole's glittering black eyes, and he never stopped moving, never changed pace. He pulled two daggers from his belt and without making a sound or hesitating, without even missing a step, he threw one at the Angel to my left and threw the other at the Angel on my right. Both Angels fell to the ground, the blades protruding from their heads.

Pain hit me hard, and my knees almost buckled, but Cole was there to catch me.

"Are you okay? Did he hurt you?" Cole asked, looking me over. I glanced up at his worried gaze and shook my head, the sudden urge to cry making me mad. I wasn't a crier. And I was no one's damsel.

"No, He was going to lock me away. He said he could smell you on me, and that it proved I had chosen a side. I wasn't to be trusted," I answered.

Cole nodded as if this was what he expected and then he pulled me forward so that I was wrapped in his arms. I closed my eyes and held onto him tightly. Was this what it was going to be like now? Was I really going to be stuck in Hell for the entirety of my life or risk being picked up by the Angels? Surely there had to be something I could do, some kind of magic that would cloak me? Cole pulled back to look at me, and I felt him in my mind, checking over my memories. Ordinarily, I would have been annoyed and accused him of calling me a liar. But I could feel his worry, feel his horror at the thought of the Angels having me and hurting me. He was making sure that nothing had happened that he needed to know about. We'd talk about this later, right now I was going to let him satisfy his worry.

"I'm proud of you," he whispered. I blinked and then smiled.

"Hey, I traveled by shadow," I remembered. He grinned then and nodded.

"Apparently being bound to me gives you that ability," he answered with a shrug. I smiled and then he pulled me forward for a kiss. I kissed him quickly, my heart still trying to climb up my throat. Today had been too close.

I felt them then, the Angels. I could feel their numbers, their power. I pulled back from Cole to see his expression turning grim.

We were surrounded, and the numbers around us were way more than what had surrounded my house.

"Cole," I whispered, wanting to leave but already knowing he had other plans.

"They're never going to stop coming for you," he told me, brushing a thumb over my cheek.

"We can go, right now," I pleaded, tugging on his hand. He shook his head.

"Then call your brothers, get help," I demanded. Cole stilled and his expression blanked for a moment before he shook his head.

"They uh... I don't know what was on the blade they nicked me with. But I can't hear my brothers, I can't reach out to them," Cole explained softly, his expression torn.

"Release the Witch!" a voice bellowed.

I spun to see an Angel approach; this one was somehow... *more* than the others. He was dressed the same, was tall and deadly looking. He had dark hair and eyes, but radiated power.

"Uriel," Cole murmured with a small, mocking incline of his head.

"Release her, Demon filth," Uriel demanded again.

"Not on your life, you flying fucker," Cole replied, his grin meant to antagonize.

"You forfeit your life then," Uriel snarled as more Angels joined him. Five, then eight, and within a few seconds, the room was filled with them.

"Cole," I urged, clinging to his hand. We needed to leave. Now.

"I won't rest easy while there is still such a threat to you," he answered, squeezing my hand in response.

"You can't take out every Angel there is. Even I know their numbers are too great."

"Listen to the Witch, Cole. You will die here today," Uriel called again, his voice commanding.

"Fuck off, dick-bag," Cole snapped.

"Just—"

"My liege," another voice called, this one closer. I spun, gasping at the sight of Krae standing not three feet away.

"Traitor," Cole snarled, a low rumble in his chest.

"Cole!" I tried again. His dark eyes met mine, full of swirling emotions.

"Do me this one favor, and this time, do as I ask. Stay in our realm where you're safe," Cole urged.

I opened my mouth to argue, but he planted a hard kiss on my mouth, and then shoved me hard.

I found myself tumbling into darkness.

I was suddenly standing in the library of our realm, panting, my heart hammering. I spun around, looking for Cole, hoping that he had come with me even when deep down, I knew he hadn't. No.

There were too many Angels. Too many for him to fight alone. I had to do something.

Okay, so I wouldn't be of much use to him there. Hurting them hurt me. Being around any of them while they were hurt, hurt me. But Cole had brothers…

I was running for the door before I finished that thought and ripped it open as I stormed into the entrance hall. I was about to go bashing on the doors in the hall when I saw Nova standing in the arrival room with two of his brothers. He caught sight of me and paused, his expression going from amused to worried

"Mika, what's wrong?" he asked.

"It's Cole. We were on the surface, and we were ambushed. He's surrounded, and there are far too many Angels for him to fight alone, one of them is named Uriel and he was seriously scary. Some of the rogue Demons have teamed up with them as well. He sent me back but didn't come with me," I spouted quickly, panicked.

"Cole can survive a great deal—" Malik began, and I cut him a glare.

"You said Uriel was there?" Nova clenched out, his blue eyes suddenly burning like a flame.

"Yes," I replied uncertainly.

"Why isn't he answering me when I reach out? I can sense him there but it's like... it's like..." Adrik asked, at a loss for words.

"Cole said one of them nicked him with their blade and since then he hasn't been able to reach any of you. They poisoned him somehow, left him vulnerable," I explained quickly, the urgency in me rising with every passing second that Cole was on his own.

"Where is he?" Nova demanded. I quickly told them where Cole was, and they said they knew the place.

Two of the brothers nodded and jogged towards the doors to their realms, probably to arm themselves against the oncoming fight. I turned to look at Nova and he was dragging in steady breaths before he looked back to me, studying me curiously.

"You're in love with him," he stated. I swallowed hard and let out a long breath.

"I need him safe," I replied rather than confirming his statement. Nova nodded slowly and then his blue eyes warmed.

"You're good for him," he added.

"Only if he survives. Go, please," I urged.

Nova nodded, and with a small squeeze of my shoulder he left. A moment later, they were wrapped in shadow and then gone. I stood in the empty entrance room and wrapped my arms around myself.

Please, please be okay.

CHAPTER SIXTEEN
COLE

Slash. Counter strike. Lunge. Axe-kick.
I dodged the lethal Angel Blade aimed at my chest and sent a stream of fire from my hand directly at the Angel who'd almost stabbed me. His shrieks of pain filled the air as I spun around, fire hitting those closest to me. I dropped the fire and sent a wall of power towards four of the Angels crowding close. Their bodies flew through the air to hit the wall opposite me, and I caught sight of their figures crumbling motionless to the floor.
Another spurt of fire, another slash with my blade and an elbow to the face of another.
Knuckles grazed my chin and a boot hit my thigh hard enough to send me toppling to the ground. I was up in less than a second, my blade slashing and driving deep into the stomach of yet another Angel.
I had to have killed at least three of those bastards and four Demons, but they kept coming. I noticed that Krae and Uriel were sitting back, letting their minions wear me down before they took me out.
And they would.
I was alone in this fight with no way to contact my brothers. Maybe Mika had told them, but even if she had, it was likely they wouldn't get here in time.
I found myself being backed up against a wall and gritted my teeth. Fuckers, they wouldn't even fight fair. But what did I expect from pretentious Angels? I summoned the hellfire again as I aimed it at the group of Angels getting closer, and my gaze fell on the small band of Demons still here. Power flooded me; rage at being defied and betrayed. Raising my right hand while

keeping the Angels at bay with the left, I concentrated on every lesser Demon in the room. When I had their locations mapped out in my mind, I encircled their life-forces in my mind and then closed my fist, dragging it from them. As a rule, my brothers and I had decided not to use this ability unless it was needed. We generally liked our Demons, but these fuckers were deserters, betrayers, not worth the courtesy of a kind end. Their deaths would fuel my power instead.

I opened my eyes to see them staggering, stumbling, struggling to breathe, to move. Krae stiffened, his face awash with anger, and I silently willed him closer. If nothing else, I was taking that fucker with me. I continued to drain the lives of the Demons around me until they were nothing but lifeless husks. I channeled the power from their life force into the hellfire I was shooting at the Angels, and it roared into a wall between us, keeping them at bay. Two more Angels shrieked and backed away, covered in flames. Hellfire wasn't like ordinary fire. One could not put it out with water.

"What's your angle?" Uriel demanded after another Angel fell back, screaming in agony. I shot him a questioning look, knowing that I appeared as relaxed as ever, as if holding up a wall of hellfire was nothing. It wasn't nothing. It was draining, but I was stalling, trying to figure out how to survive.

To get back to Mika.

"You saved the Witch, but not yourself," Uriel clarified. I shrugged my shoulders. Krae began to laugh, and I glared, focusing all my anger on him.

"He is in love with her."

"Love? Demons do not feel such a thing," Uriel pointed out, a glint of malice in his eyes.

"And Angels do?" I countered, grabbing the metal pole beside me and fashioned it into a blade before I threw it at an Angel who was more concerned with getting too close to the flames. He fell back, groaning. It wouldn't kill him, neither would the fire, but it would hurt like a bitch.

"You saved her life and will die in her place. But you will never keep her safe. We will get our hands on her, and your death will serve no purpose," Uriel goaded.

"I see you're feeling safer on the surface now that you're surrounded by your garrison. Are you finally ready to face Donovan for what you did?" I returned, knowing that despite what the Angel said, he was scared of my brother.

The smile on his face dimmed and he glowered.

"I was never afraid of that Demon trash," he snarled.

I grinned. Being a King of Hell gave me insight into people's fears and insecurities, and Uriel was most definitely eager to avoid my brother.

"Enough of this! Krae, go and get the girl," Alastair suddenly demanded from the other side of my flames. He was being kept back as well. Him too, I decided. I would take him and Krae with me before the night was done. If I was going to die, then they'd go with me. No one touched my woman and lived, no one threatened her and continued to breathe free air.

I may have been reluctant going into this when Mika and I had first discovered our connection, but now that we had given in to almost every part of the binding, I found I didn't care. Even if I never admitted to loving her, I couldn't imagine being any less angry or hurt if something happened to her. She was it now, she was my weakness, my vulnerability–but she was also my strength. She gave me a reason to fight and to come out of the fight when it was all said and done.

I glanced back at Alastair, at the Angel who had threatened my Witch with life in a cell and ground my teeth together. I realized he was sick of being lower-level, that he was tired of following orders and constantly thought of as less-than. He wanted power. He wanted prestige. Alastair wanted what Uriel had.

"No matter how many Witches you take for yourself, Alastair, you will never be an Archangel. You will never measure up to Uriel or the others," I tormented, knowing the Angel would hate my words.

His face flushed with fury, and I grinned again.

"Krae, I will not repeat myself a third time. Go find the Witch. You're the only one who can get around down there," Uriel commanded.

Krae hesitated, his eyes flickering with fear.

"You should be scared," I told him, playing on his fear. "You are the most wanted Demon in Hell at the moment. There won't be a single Demon not looking for you."

"Krae," Uriel snapped again. Krae swallowed and tried desperately to hide his fear. He was a moron. Only idiots worked with the Angels against their own kind. Uriel was using him for his own gain, and then he'd destroy the Demon. Somehow, Krae thought he'd survive this little alliance.

In that case, he was a special kind of stupid.

"I want that Witch!" Uriel shouted, his voice booming like thunder inside the warehouse, rattling the window and walls.

"Temper, temper," I murmured, still grinning.

"Shut up, Demon filth," he snarled.

"Make me."

"I will end your miserable existence before this night is out, mark my words," Uriel snarled, his eyes burning with rage.

"Don't make promises you can't keep," I taunted in a sing-song voice, feeling my energy begin to wane. I refused to show it though, and refused to let them know that I was running out of time.

"I will reach down your throat and pull your intestines out of your mouth," Uriel threatened with a growl.

"You say the sweetest things," a new voice interjected.

I flicked my gaze to the corner to see Adrik step out of the shadows, a small smile on his face, but his green eyes were alight with danger.

"While I'm sure it would improve my brothers looks a good deal, I think we'll forgo that experience," Malik added, stepping from the other corner.

Relief hit me hard for a moment and then a new voice spoke.

"I told you centuries ago that your death sentence had been written," Nova announced, appearing seemingly out of nowhere, his voice deep and carrying. Uriel's attention locked immediately on my brother whose face was impassive, belying the utter fury burning in his eyes, and the sudden surge of power in the room. "Nova," Uriel said his name evenly, no waver, no emotion. But we tortured souls for a living. We knew how to smell fear, and Uriel's was so strong now I could taste it.

"I told you that day on the battlefield after you kept me bound and forced me to witness the death of my friend and her entire family that your days were numbered. Weeks, months, centuries even. But you would die at my hand," Nova continued as he stepped closer, his eyes on the archangel.

My gaze skittered to Adrik and I wished more than ever that our connection was there, but it was still numb. He caught my eye and noticed my flames dimming and the Angels inching closer. He nodded to me, and I released the flames as soon as he took over.

I struggled to refrain from gasping, to refrain from showing the toll holding hellfire up for so long took. If these assholes knew that I was weaker now, it would definitely result in my death.

"Still not over your little Witch bitch?" Uriel goaded; his bravado painfully fake.

"I do not make idle threats. If I say I am going to do something, I will. And it is long past time that I deliver on my promise," Nova said with a soft whip of contempt in his voice, but the impact could not have been greater had he shouted it. I could feel the fury and disdain coming from my brother, and it was then that I realized our connection had been restored. I inwardly sighed. I wasn't sure what had happened, maybe whatever poison I'd been injected with had finally faded. Having been cut off from them, brothers who I had been connected to since we were born, had been an incredibly uncomfortable and empty feeling.

"We attack at the same time," Malik announced, and I realized he'd slowly edged around the group so that he was now standing behind the group of Angels trying to get around the hellfire. *"Together,"* I agreed with a nod.

Nova watched Uriel for a moment longer before we all moved at once.

I leapt for Krae as Malik and Adrik ran for the group of Angels. Nova's eyes were only for Uriel, and it was an unspoken agreement that the Archangel would answer to Donovan.

Chaos reigned, and I reveled in the fight, in the feeling of my blood singing as I swung my blade, at having my brothers at my back as we fought. At the thought that I might actually have a chance to get back to Mika. And fuck it all, when I did, I was making sure there were no doubts in her mind as to what we were to each other. I was finishing this binding so thoroughly that there would be no doubt about our bond being completed.

I'd detested It in the beginning, fought it and everything it represented. But the thought of ever losing Mika left me feeling empty and hopeless. I had to make sure there was no possibility of ever losing her.

Krae's black eyes found mine and for a moment, he looked at me in terror before anger and a fierce determination to survive took him over.

Our swords clashed with an almighty sound, and the battle between Angels and Demons resumed once again.

~

MIKA

I was going out of my mind.

Cole hadn't blocked me from his mind, not that I was sure that he totally could any way, but I was able to get impressions of the fight through his mind and it was bloody.

Scary. Powerful. Full-on.

Blood and death were everywhere. I could feel Cole's injuries. They were minor compared to some of the other's he's had in the past, but it still made me wince every time a new one was added to the collection.

I had to do something to help him. But what? Any time I was around that kind of violence I could feel the pain being inflicted. I'd be a distraction.

My neck burned and itched for the millionth time, and I tried to ignore it. It was The Mark. It was telling me that he was in danger. I knew he was, but there was nothing I could do without being a distraction.

I spun to look at the books.

There had to be something in there, something that would shield me from feeling all the pain around me. I started pulling books from the shelves, but I was still connected to Cole, and I was feeling an urgency to be there riding on me.

"Fuck!" I hissed, tossing a book at a shelf. I needed to be there, I had to be. I ran my hands through my hair and bunched them there as I tried to figure out a faster way to do this. More of Cole's pain hit me, something bigger this time and I bit back a shaky sob.

Wait. I was a goddamn Witch. I dropped my hands from my side and looked over the shelves more carefully. Dragging in a deep breath, I closed my eyes and held out my hand, visualizing the bookcase in my mind. I kept my intention in the forefront of my mind, knowing that above all else, intent was a major factor for any casting. I needed a book that would help me keep the pain around me at a distance so that I could be there and not feel it all. I felt a surge of power and when I opened my eyes, a book was floating in the air in front of me.

Startled, I stepped back a moment, releasing my power. The book began to fall, and I quickly grabbed it. I gaped. I just summoned a book to me.

Shaking my head, I moved to the couch. I could celebrate that part later. Right now, I needed to find a way to block my ability to feel others' pain. I needed to be there to heal Cole and his brothers, and I needed to find a way to protect them without crumbling in pain.

I powered through the book, my eyes scanning for anything that could help. I stopped suddenly when I came across a shield incantation. It would only be temporary, but hopefully enough to protect me so that I could help. Reading it carefully, I made sure it was what I was looking for and that I could pronounce every word clearly and correctly. Trying to memorise the words, I repeated the words in my head a few times, worried I'd say it wrong.

But when another stab of pain went through me, strong enough to steal my breath, I decided I'd practiced enough. I murmured the incantation, imagining an invisible, impenetrable wall going up between the world and that part of me that could feel the pain of others. When I was sure I'd done it right, I grabbed two blades from Cole's stash, sucked in a deep breath, and closed my eyes. Time to go.

When I opened my eyes, the world spun, and I still felt sick and dizzy. I bent over for a moment, my hands on my thighs as I struggled to draw in a breath without being sick. The sounds of battle were raging around me, but I noted with a weak smile that I couldn't feel a damn thing. I could still feel Cole and his injuries, but I had to assume that was because we were bound.

I straightened when the world stopped spinning and took note of what was going on. Several small fires were burning in random spaces; broken glass, wood and metal were scattered everywhere.

Uriel and Nova were locked in an intense battle, both injured but neither badly hurt. Malik was fighting three angels at once, but he was moving with such gracefulness and ease that he didn't appear to need any assistance. Adrik staggered for a moment, and I watched as an Angel lifted his blade.

"No!" I shouted and threw power around him, my intent to shield him. I wasn't sure if my magic would be enough to shield him from an Angel blade, but I was grateful when it did.

Adrik glanced at me for a moment, a mix of gratefulness, annoyance and frustration crossed his face. I watched as he edged closer to me as he fought off the Angel before striking a final blow. I winced as his blade sunk deep into the Angel's chest and was so grateful I didn't feel it.

"What the hell are you doing here?" Adrik snapped.

"Helping, and saving your ass, apparently," I replied.

"Cole will be pissed," he reminded.

"But you're alive," I shot back.

"Every Angel in this place will try to get to you," Adrik added, throwing a ball of energy out to knock down one of the Angel's fighting Malik.

"Then I guess you'd better stay close," I answered.

Adrik looked momentarily amused before we entered the fray. I searched through the mass of bodies, tried to listen through the deafening clang of steel on steel, but I finally found him.

He was battling Krae and Alastair, his face lined with concentration and fury. I paused for a moment, stunned at the raw beauty of him. He moved with ease and grace; a dancer in his finest hour. He threw power and fire like it was nothing, while simultaneously fighting with a sword. He was injured, I already knew that, but nothing life-threatening. And by the way he moved, I doubted anyone else could tell that he was hurt either.

Adrik fought off another Angel as we made our way through the mess, his actions delivered swiftly and with deadly precision. I kept my eyes peeled, throwing out power where I could, hoping to give Cole's brothers time to get rid of their opponents.

As I was scanning the crowd to see how the others were faring, my gaze caught on Nova who was locked in a furious battle with Uriel. The two were lightning quick, their strikes meant to kill. My breath caught as everything seemed to happen in slow motion. I started running in his direction before I could fully comprehend why. I watched as Nova was kicked so viciously that he was thrown backwards. Uriel advanced on him; his blade gripped tightly as Nova struggled to get to his feet. I was running faster, faster, but I knew I was going to be too late. I was summoning my power, building it deep inside me as I hurried. Uriel gripped Nova using a fistful of his shirt and yanked him close. His smile was victorious, mocking. He said something to Nova I couldn't hear, and then as I was throwing my power out at him, Uriel drove the blade home just beneath Nova's ribs. Nova's face blanked in shock, and I screamed in denial as the force of my power hit Uriel, sending him flying through the air to smash through a window. He disappeared out of sight, and I skidded to a stop as Nova fell to the ground.

I registered Cole's alarm; knew I had unintentionally distracted him from his fight when I screamed, but I had to focus on Nova now. Blood seeped from between his lips and his breath rattled when I propped his head onto my knees.

"Hang on, I've got you," I assured, ripping open his shirt to reveal the nasty wound that was gaping and gushing with blood.

"Need... you... safe..." Nova whispered, gripping my arm to prevent me from healing him.

"Shut up and let me do what I'm meant to do," I snapped, fear for the Demon King who had become my friend overriding any concerns I might have had at being in this warehouse in the middle of a celestial fight.

"Little Witch?" Cole's voice brushed across my mind. I held off healing Nova for a second.

"I am here. I am fine. Nova was stabbed with an Angel blade, I'm healing him," I answered as I blocked out the fight raging around me and instead focused on the wound before me.

I closed my eyes and rested my hands just over Nova's wound before I felt that energy within me ignite. Like magic from a tree root buried deep inside me, I felt it build and build within my body, filling me up until my hands grew white-hot and I sent the healing energy pouring into Nova. Everything else around me dimmed and muted as I focused all my attention and energy on healing the being before me. I followed the extent of his damage from the inside out, cauterizing it, mending what was broken and torn, setting a soothing balm over it as I went.

Consciousness was tugging at me, and I slowly began to become aware of what was around me. A sharp, painful, searing pain that was so white-hot it was icy, shot through me. My breath left me in a gasp, and I stiffened, my eyes snapping open as I tried to figure out what had happened.

"Mika?" Nova cried, and for a moment, the anguish in his voice, the panic, had me confused.

"Tomika!" Cole's echoing cry in my head had dread coursing through me, thinking he'd been injured and needed me. I struggled, trying to get to my feet, but I couldn't feel my legs. Pain rolled over me, and then increased ten-fold. I opened my

mouth, maybe intending to scream, I don't know, but no sound came out. I could taste copper in my mouth and a burning in my gut.

Nova roared in outrage, his fury almost enough to knock me back as he lunged behind me. I blinked rapidly as my vision flickered for a moment and slowly looked down. I frowned, not quite able to fully understand what I was seeing. Was that a sword?

A sword tip was sticking out of my abdomen. I could see the blood, dark and thick, running down my stomach to pool on the floor beneath me. The icy-hot pain suddenly increased more, and I grasped what had happened.

"Mika!" Cole's voice bellowed, the volume of it deafening, overpowering every other noise in the room. I glanced up as he appeared in the crowd of celestials, his black eyes locking on me, his eyes widening in horror and fury.

It was laughable that, as he ran towards me all I could think was how devastatingly beautiful he was. He was completely masculine, muscular, dominating and fearsome. But that look of terror on his face was for me. The hopelessness and the fear shining at me through his dark eyes was all for me.

I did that to him. This previously untarnished, untouchable Demon King was tearing through a room full of celestials with that kind of fear in his eyes, all for me.

Pain shot through me again and I inhaled sharply, a whimper pushing through my lips. Trying to move did no good, my lower half was numb, and I was pretty sure that was not a good thing even though I was grateful not to feel the full extent of my injury. Cole reached me, but he didn't stop at my side as I expected him to. His expression morphed into one of a deadly fury and he actually looked scary to me for a moment. He raised the bloody sword in his hands and swung. Blood spurted beside me, and there was a dull thud. I could guess what had happened, but it all seemed so unimportant right now. Cole appeared suddenly beside me, and he dropped to the ground, his hands touching me as if he were afraid he'd break me.

"What do I do? Tell me, how do I save you?" he demanded. But instead of answering, I just smiled. I couldn't speak, could barely breathe. And all I could think was—I really wished I'd gathered up the courage to tell this overbearing King of Hell that I loved him.

"Love... that's what this is. This must be what it feels like. I love you. At least I got to feel what it was like before I died. I'm glad that it was with you," I whispered, not sure if the words actually found their way inside his mind or not. Because at that moment, pain washed over me, pulled me under. My vision dimmed and my head swam. I could feel Cole's hands gripping my arms and his voice shouting at me, but it was distant, fading... gone.

~

COLE

Hearing her voice scream in that warzone almost got me killed. The Angel I'd been fighting missed taking my head off by a hair's breadth. However, knowing she was here was enough to spur me into faster action, destroying the Angel before me.

"Little Witch?" I called, looking for her, trying to get a sense of where she was and how she'd gotten here and just what the fuck she thought she was doing coming to this place. She was a Witch, she'd be feeling every ounce of pain inflicted here.

"I am here. I am fine. Nova was stabbed with an Angel blade, I'm healing him," she answered before she faded from my mind. I realized then that she was already healing my brother. Gratitude at her presence filled me as the thought of losing a brother left me feeling cold, but fear was still paramount in my mind. I hated the feel of it, the taste of it on my tongue. The idea that she was here, amongst all this bloodshed and danger spurred me on through the crowd. I kept tabs on her as she healed and I swung my sword, trying to get to her.

I touched Nova's mind. He was in pain; he was angry, and he was planning Uriel's death. He didn't like that Mika was here anymore than I did, but he accepted that she was and clung to his need for revenge.

I caught sight of her through the jostling crowd. She was kneeling with Nova's head propped up on her knees, her eyes closed and her whole being focused on what she was doing. I lost sight of her as another Angel tried to stab at me. I fought back, every stroke deadly in its precision. I was done playing.

Mika was in danger; I had to get to her.

I had just taken the head off the Angel I'd been fighting when, through my connection to Mika, I felt a white-hot pain lance through my back and abdomen. It sucked the breath from my lungs, and I staggered.

"Tomika!" I cried, knowing she'd just been injured. I could feel her confusion, the numbness, and her worry for me and for Nova. She didn't seem to realize yet that she'd just been gravely injured.

I heard Nova's roar of fury and hoped my brother was taking care of the danger to my woman. I shoved aside two Angels, lashing out with my sword as I sliced through one and took the arm off another. I rounded the crowd when I stopped suddenly at the sight of her. She was still kneeling, her black hair falling around her shoulders and blocking her face as she looked down at the blade protruding from her abdomen. She'd been run clean through, the sword still in her back.

"Mika!" her name was pulled from deep within me. I thought I knew fear, I thought I knew despair. I thought I knew the true meaning of it all up till that moment. Until then, I appreciated I had never truly known.

I raced for her, but as I got closer, I saw Nova fighting with Alastair. That fucking weasel had wormed his way away from me the moment the fight had started, putting Angel after Angel between us to save his own ass. And he had fucking stabbed my woman.

Rage boiled over and I roared my anger, stepping up beside Mika as Nova backed him up towards me. Alastair turned in time to see me, sword raised above my head, arcing down towards him. His eyes widened in fear, and he had no time to do more than gape as I took his head clear off his neck. Blood splattered around us, some of it landing on me. His head rolled onto the ground; the expression of terror still frozen on his face. A second later, his body crumpled to the ground beside his dismembered head, and I turned away, back to Mika.

I dropped to my knees beside her, my sword on the floor between us.

"What do I do? Tell me, how do I save you?" I demanded, careful where I touched her. I could feel her pain, but she didn't seem to be able to feel it herself. She was in shock, her mind unable to digest what had happened, blood was gushing from her body at an alarming rate.

Fuck! She was losing too much blood too quickly; not even Witches could heal from everything.

Instead of answering, she just smiled at me. It was gentle and small, her eyes going in and out of focus. She opened her mouth as if to speak, but no sound came out. And then I heard her in my head, her voice soft and so full of warmth.

"Love... that's what this is. This must be what it feels like. I love you. At least I got to feel what it was like before I died. I'm glad that it was with you," she whispered.

I bit back the roar that wanted to tear from my throat, and I cupped her face.

"Mika... Mika, listen. Stay with me, baby. I'm right here. Hold on, tell me what to do," I begged, pleaded. But she was slipping away; I could feel her warmth disappearing, her light fading. My mind splintered as she slowly slipped away, the strings that I'd felt weave themselves between our hearts shriveled and weakened.

"No!" I shouted, and a sudden and overwhelming coldness crept over me, something I felt right in my core... my soul.

Mika's eyes fluttered briefly before she slumped forward.

"Tomika!" I shouted again, desperately gripping her arms. She went limp and I shouted. I pulled the sword from her body and pulled her in close, and I felt it as the last bits of her lifeforce flickered and then went out.

Pain. Isolation. Anguish.

I knew the meaning of these words, but nothing, *nothing*, came close to how it felt to actually experience them. I held Mika close to me, held her tightly as if the warmth from my body would keep her here, as if by keeping her close, my heart would beat for hers, my lungs would breathe her air. I was the other part of her soul; I had bound us. She wasn't supposed to go yet.

"Cole," Nova's voice was emotionless and soft beside me. I sucked in a breath and looked around us at the battle going on, at the number of Angels that kept pouring in no matter how many of the fucking assholes we slayed.

They did this.

It was because of them that Tomika was dragged into this. One of theirs had run her through with a sword, and they would *all* pay for that crime.

No one harmed my Witch and lived to tell of it.

No one.

CHAPTER SEVENTEEN
COLE

"Nova," I said my brother's name softly as I slowly stood with Mika in my arms. I glanced down at her pale, lifeless face and a fury unlike anything I'd felt before began to build inside me. "Take her," I told Nova softly.

"Cole," he began, but when I slowly dragged my gaze to his, he swallowed and nodded, his jaw clenching. His sorrowful expression rested on Mika, and he took her limp body from me. I caught sight of the two Demon Blades Mika had strapped to her waist and I pulled them free.

"Malik, Adrik, leave now," I demanded, and I was sure they could feel the command in my voice. I was telling them, not asking. I allowed the anger in me to build and build, allowed it to fill every cell, every iota of my body.

My brothers confirmed that they were leaving, and I watched as every Angel turned to look at me as their other rivals wrapped themselves in shadows and left.

The Angels stepped closer, sure, and confident as they approached. Glancing down at my hands, I looked at the blood that drenched them, that smeared up my arms and across my chest from where I'd held Mika's lifeless body. She was gone. Dead. The light of my life, the other fucking half of my soul... was dead.

I was holding onto my fury by my fingernails, just waiting... waiting...

Now.

With an almighty roar that was torn from the very depths of my being, one filled with all the anguish, fear, regret, and fury I was feeling, I sent out a wave of power and hellfire that encompassed everyone and everything around us. The warehouse we were in and two others around us went up in an almighty *boom!* Angels shrieked and cried out for help, and as they attempted to put out the flames, I moved among them, driving my blades deep into their chests over and over and over.

The memory of Mika's pain, of her fear, of the way she looked kneeling with a blade through her body kept my anger boiling and the flames around me constant. I slammed wave after wave of power down onto the Angels, keeping them down as I tore through them like they were nothing.

Mika was gone.

Mika was dead.

These fucking holier-than-thou fuckers were the reason she was gone, and I was done playing their game. I was done with this war, done with their pretentious attitudes.

I don't know how long I was there. Blood sprayed onto me, around me. The sounds of shrieks and cries of agony was music to my ears. Pain, terror, and fear were heavy in the air around me, and I reveled in it. Nothing would ever bring me joy or light again like Mika had. I hadn't wanted her in the beginning, not the way she had come to be in the end, but I did now. I had only just admitted it to myself. We hadn't even really had a chance to just be. They had taken her from me, and now they would all pay.

When no other Angel moved or showed signs of life, only then did I pull back my power and watch as the flames died down around me. The entire warehouse was littered with charred and dismembered remains. There was the odd Demon one here and there, but mostly they were Angels. There had to be close to one hundred Angels here, and yet, my thirst for blood was nowhere near quenched.

"Mika," I reached out to her automatically, and my mind touched nothing. There was a void where Mika used to be, and the anguish of losing her hit me all over again.

I dropped to my knees and let out another roar. I shouted until my voice was raw and my lungs burned. Slamming my fists into the blood-soaked cement over and over, I bellowed my denial, my voice shaking the walls and shattering the windows. The feeling of having her torn from me was pure hell. I had never managed to deal out this level of pain to any soul before—I hadn't known it was possible.

I fell back onto my ass and drew my knees up. I rested my forearms on my knees and then dropped my head into my hands. She was gone.

Love... that's what this is. This must be what it feels like. I love you. At least I got to feel what it was like before I died. I'm glad that it was with you.

Her last words replayed themselves in my head and I felt my heart shatter. A drop of moisture hit my hands, and I touched my cheeks, realizing I was crying. Fuck.

I wasn't sure I'd ever cried a day in my life. But the agony of losing her, of playing those words in my head had me at my weakest ever.

She had loved me. With the last of her strength, she'd told me that she loved me.

Me. A fucking no-good evil son of a bitch. She was purity and light, she was attitude and sass, but she was everything good in the world. And she had loved me.

Me, a King of Hell.

I'd never said the words to her. I hadn't been able to. Back at her home, I was certain that I loved her, but the words had felt too hard to say. They'd left me feeling weak and vulnerable, and so I'd buried them, refusing to say them.

She never heard me say it. She never truly knew that I loved her too.

Hours passed. I watched the shadows stretch around me as night approached and the sun disappeared from the sky. And still I stayed where I was, my eyes unseeing as I stared at the blood-spattered wall in front of me.

At last, I was blessedly numb. Cold. Empty.

I could live with this. It was better than the all-consuming rage and despair that had filled me hours ago.

"Cole."

I closed my eyes at the sound of Nova's voice in the dead silence. I didn't respond, but then again, I didn't think he really expected me to.

"Let's go, brother," he suggested, his voice closer now. "Our brothers are going to check to see if anyone escaped, let's get you back home," he added, and I felt his hand rest on my shoulder. I didn't say anything; the energy to do so was too much. I closed my eyes and sucked in a breath as Nova wrapped us in shadow and then we were traveling back to Hell.

When we arrived in the marble hall, I looked around slowly. I could still see her here. The way she'd spent ages trying to find an opening or a way out of here when I'd first taken her. She'd been so stubborn, so hot-headed and sassy, I'd wanted her from the moment she'd woken up after taking on my Angel Blade wound.

How had she survived that wound, but not this one?

"Come, brother. You're clean now, let's get you to your realm," Nova suggested. I looked down at myself and noted with mild surprise that I was clean of all the sweat, gore, and smoke.

"Where is she?" I whispered; my voice broken.

"She's in my realm at the moment. We were waiting for you to see what you wanted to do," Nova answered, and I could hear the pain in his voice, the guilt, but I couldn't be bothered to do anything about it.

"Bring her," I ordered as I climbed painfully to my feet. I was uninjured physically— it was more the weight of knowing that Mika was gone that made me move slowly, painfully.

Nova left my side, and I walked blindly into my realm, leaving the door open for him to enter when he was ready. I looked around, and things already felt different. I caught sight of the pile of boxes and plants in a neat stack and sucked in a breath. Mika's things had been transported here earlier. Had that only been earlier today?

I felt Nova approach, but I couldn't turn to look at him, I couldn't watch him carry her lifeless body in.

"Where…" Nova started, and I pointed at the bed.

Without another word, Nova carried her inside while I

steadfastly avoided watching. I scanned my eyes over the
bookshelves and caught sight of a book on the couch. I picked it
up and found it opened to a shield spell. My eyes burned as I
looked down at it. Mika had found a way to shield herself from
feeling the pain around her so that she could come and help.

"Cole..." Nova trailed off, and I knew he wanted to say
something to help me, but there was really nothing he could do
or say.

"Goodnight, Nova," I whispered, my voice rough.

Nova hesitated before he slowly left, closing my door behind
him.

I turned to the fireplace and stood, watching the flames for
hours. I couldn't move, I couldn't do anything. I had to figure
out a way to move forward from here, but the prospect of doing
so made me want to be sick.

I had been so against feeling anything real for Mika, that I hadn't
quite noticed when it had happened. She'd worked her way
beneath my skin, found her way into my bloodstream, into my
very core. The Mark had bound us together in such a way, that
even in such a short amount of time it felt as though she'd been
there forever. Or maybe she had always meant to be there. Mika
had found that prophecy, but none of us had really given it
another look over since then. Like me, they were all probably
too resistant to the thought of ever opening themselves up to
someone, that the very idea had us all trying to pretend it wasn't
a possibility.

But it was possible. And now I wasn't sure how to move
forward. Her mind, her body, her soul, and her heart had all,
even for a small amount of time, been connected to mine. We
had become one entity, one being. And to feel her gone now, to
feel the gaping void where she had once been, was both painful
and achingly empty.

I'd been perfectly happy in my life before meeting her. Well,
maybe happy wasn't the right word. Content was more how I'd
felt, and it had been enough. Yes, I'd been getting tired of the
monotony, but it had been a living I'd been able to enjoy before.

But now... I couldn't imagine spending eternity in this life, knowing what I could have had... having had a taste of it, and knowing that it would never be a possibility again.

I shook my head and clenched my jaw.

I'd thought Nova was overreacting when he'd blown apart that battlefield all those years ago after watching his Witch friend burn. None of us had understood his friendship with her. But if Nova had felt for Tabitha, anything close to what I felt for Mika, I did not blame my brother in the least for the vendetta he had against Uriel and every other Angel in existence. Nova had spent close to one hundred years in his realm after Tabitha's death. All of us had been worried about him, not sure what he would do next or if losing his friend like that would be the thing to send him into insanity.

I was too numb right now, too tired, too lost to feel anything else. I wondered if I'd ever feel the heat of anger and fury again; if I'd ever feel alive when fighting. The idea didn't hold much appeal right now. I wanted to stay here, in this cold, unfeeling place and never be forced to feel anything for anyone ever again. What was the point, anyway?

Was this what the prophecy had been talking about? *From the first to the last, the Brothers Nine will fall...* maybe this is what it was referring to. Maybe we'd all lose our hearts and souls to the women we were destined for, only to lose them and ourselves along the way. If so, then I truly hoped that my brothers never found the women they were meant to find. I wouldn't wish this pain on any of them.

"Tomika." I whispered her name, reached out and once again felt like I'd been kicked in the gut when there was a gaping *nothing* there. My mind was constantly reaching for hers, but there was never anything there. Would I go insane? Was this how my ending would come about?

I swallowed hard and closed my eyes. I wanted to see her. But I also wanted never to lay eyes on her again. What would be the point? But my body refused to obey as I turned towards the bed and slowly raised my gaze to her prone figure.

I sucked in a sharp breath and started towards my bed. She was so tiny lying there. Somehow, she looked smaller than usual. I edged closer; my eyes glued to her figure now that I'd started making my way towards her.

Her face was pale, her black hair fanned around her in silky strands. Had she always been so small? Had she always looked so fragile? She was covered in blood and grime, and I swallowed hard before I waved my hand and she was clean once again, her clothes new, her skin clear and her hair brushed.

She looked like she was just sleeping now, and I wasn't sure if that was worse or not. It was like she could open her glittering jade eyes at any moment and spout some sassy comment that would make me want to both shake her and kiss her senseless at the same time.

But she would never do that again.

I conjured up a chair and fell backwards into it, my eyes glued to her face. Without looking, I summoned a bottle of scotch and leaned back before taking a healthy swig. My eyes burned as the liquid heated me up from the inside out, but I knew it wouldn't last. I would stay cold inside forever now, and there was nothing I could do to fix it.

~

Two days passed much the same. That was how long it had taken her to heal from the Angel Blade wound she had taken on from me when we first met. But when more days came and went, I knew she was never getting back up.

By the fifth day, I hadn't moved from my seat. I just sat staring at her, sometimes seeing her, other times unable to see anything. I stared until I fell asleep out of pure exhaustion. Then when I woke, I drank and did it all over again. My brothers had reached out to me, all of them, even Devlin and Corvin, but I hadn't bothered to respond. What was there to say? She was still dead, and I was attempting to see how many bottles of scotch it took for a King of Hell to get alcohol poisoning. So far at fifteen bottles, I hadn't hit my limit.

I had been staring at her for days, drinking. But at least I could say one thing. The feeling of loss had started to dissipate, finally lulled into numbness by my excessive intake of alcohol. My heart didn't ache quite so bad. My mind was blinded and was no longer hitting a wall of nothingness whenever it unconsciously reached out for her. The burning in my soul had faded so that it was little more than a twinge.

I figured as long as I lived my life at the bottom of several bottles, I could probably continue on in life.

I was raising the bottle to my mouth when for a second, I thought I saw her hand twitch. I froze and waited, but it didn't happen again. My fucking eyes were playing tricks on me. A combination of exhaustion and alcohol was making me see things. Again, I raised the bottle to my lips and froze when I could have *sworn* I saw her chest rise and fall gently. I watched, waited, holding my breath. Had I imagined that too?

It happened again!

I leaped up from my chair, letting the bottle crash to the ground as I staggered closer to her, my alcohol-soaked brain suddenly feeling crystal clear.

"Tomika?" I whispered, my voice cracking from under-use. Hope sparked within me, and I waited again, holding my breath.

"Please, baby. Are you there?" I reached out, desperate. And for the first time in almost a week, there was something there to connect to. A wordless cry tore from my lips and I took her hand in mine, wanting to shake her but worried I'd hurt her.

I watched with burning eyes as her chest moved up and down again and then began a constant rhythm.

She was alive!

CHAPTER EIGHTEEN
MIKA

Dying hurt.

Coming back hurt more.

I felt like I'd been floating in a sea of nonsensical voices, tones, and whispered pleas. Pain was there, as was confusion and desperation. A deep longing, a hopelessness and agony unlike anything I'd felt before were all constant companions, and I had to wonder what the hell was going on.

"It's time to start coming back, Witch," a smooth voice encouraged.

It hurt too much to come back, but it seemed hopeless to try and resist the allure in that velvet voice.

Where was I?

I remembered healing Nova, I remembered the battle raging on around us, the violence and bloodshed. I'd been healing Nova when there'd been a white-hot pain in my back and gut, something that made me go numb from the waist down, and yet somehow allowed me to feel an icy pain all over my body.

I'd been stabbed!

I mean, I guess I already knew that. But now that I was remembering it again, I was really pissed off about it. Some asshole Angel had stabbed me in the back while I'd been healing. What the hell?

There was no up or down here, no sense of direction. There was no ground, no sky—just an everlasting empty blackness all around me. I couldn't even see myself, but I was here, I had a consciousness.

Where the hell was I? Had I died? Had that sword killed me? And if I was dead, then where *was* here? And who had that voice belonged to?

"Come on, Witch. He's waiting for you, and I have other things to be doing," that velvet voice whispered again. I turned, even though I didn't see my body. There were no landmarks, so I have no idea how I know I turned, but I did.

Finally my gaze landed on a figure. He was tall, startling good-looking and dressed in a dark trench coat. His dark hair was tied back, his face classically handsome, almost aristocratic.

"You need to go back now," the man told me.

"Reaper."

I simply thought the word, my voice refused to work, and yet he seemed to hear me.

I remembered him now. He had been in that house, standing over the dead woman.

He smiled gently, and I was once again struck by the old-world elegance he seemed to personify.

"Where am I?" I asked with my thoughts again, trying to ignore the odd feeling of not using my mouth to speak to someone who was not Cole. The Reaper shrugged, a graceful move that somehow did not look out of place on him.

"Neither here nor there. You're somewhere in the in-between. But you need to go back now," he explained.

"How am I not dead? I was stabbed," I reminded. Again, he gave that gentle, indulgent smile. Unlike with the Angels, his smile didn't feel condescending.

"As I told you when we first met, a Mark like the one you and the Demon King share are rare and very powerful. It ties you together. He still lives, and so shall you."

"You mean… I'll be immortal, like him?" I asked, needing clarification.

"*Tomika.*"

Another voice sounded, far away, really far, and yet it seemed to echo all around me in this empty space.

Cole.

Just thinking his name had me feeling a shiver and my soul cried out.

Cole—my Demon King.

He had been there in the fight; he'd killed whoever had stabbed me and he'd reached me just in time. I could still see the pain on his face, the denial, and the plea from him on how to help me. But I'd been unable to speak, unable to move.

I'd told him I loved him. Well, I'd tried. I wasn't so sure if he'd heard the words or not, but I hoped he had. I wasn't sure where I was now or how to get out of here, but I'd needed Cole to know at least once, that someone besides his brothers loved him.

Was Cole trying to reach me? I wanted to reach out and touch him, to say his name, but my voice didn't seem to want to work. There was nothing for me to hit to make noise, I wasn't even an actual physical being, so I had no idea how to reach out to him.

"He needs you. You must go back now. Your spirit is strong enough now," the Reaper explained, jolting me out of my memories.

"My spirit?" I repeated, feeling dazed.

"I must go now. But follow him, go to him. He needs you, and it's time for you to go back," the Reaper explained softly, once again not expanding on his answers.

"Wait," I called, but with an eloquent bow that somehow did not look strange on him at all, the Reaper disappeared, leaving me alone in the giant empty space.

"Please, baby. Are you there?"

This time, Cole's voice was louder, closer, much more intimate. Despite having no physical form, I could feel tears sting my eyes and relief hit me. He was real, he was there, and I could feel the pathway reforge in my mind as if it had never disappeared.

"Cole?" I whispered, trying with all my might to reach him.

Suddenly I felt heavy. My initial reaction was to go back, to get away from that heavy feeling, but when I did, I found myself somehow deeper in this cold, dark place. I didn't want to be here, I wanted to be with Cole. I reached again and tried to force myself to feel my body, to take control of it again.

Heaviness.

It was hard to breathe, my heartbeat felt too hard, too loud, too harsh. It felt as though it took far too much strength to get my lungs to draw in air, but I forced myself to do it. I wanted to open my eyes, I wanted to touch Cole, I wanted to speak to him and tell him out loud that I loved him.

"I'm here, Little Witch. I can hear your heartbeat, I can see you breathe. I'm right here," Cole's voice was soft, and I wanted to cry out in joy at hearing him so close, so real. But the effort to even move my eyes beneath my lids was tremendous, and so I waited.

"Cole?" I whispered, hoping to hear his voice.

Joy and relief burst over me, and I knew it was from him.

"I am here, Tomika," he answered gently, and I could hear the hoarseness in his voice, the strain.

"Am I alive?"

"You weren't. You have not taken a breath in five days," he replied, and I was stunned into silence. The Reaper had said I was in the in-between, but I couldn't imagine how that had to have appeared to Cole.

"I was dead?"

"Yes," Cole replied, and in that single word, I could hear every ounce of pain, fear, and hopelessness he'd been suffering. At least that explained why I'd woken up in such a strange place.

"For five days?"

"Six, actually. You started breathing yesterday," he answered.

"The Reaper."

"The Reaper?" Cole's voice was angry, scared. *"Mika; don't go with him. Stay with me,"* he pleaded.

"I'm not going anywhere, Cole. He was here. He told me I was in the in-between, not dead but not alive. Apparently, my body was *dead though,"* I explained. Cole's relief was instantaneous and overwhelming.

"I believe it has something to do with The Mark. Being a Witch, maybe it helped you to heal from your wounds. I told Nova that you are alive, and he came and saw you for himself. He is almost as relieved as I am. He has decided to research The Mark and the prophecy more thoroughly while you come back to us," Cole answered.

I gave the mental impression of a nod and felt Cole's arms wrap around me, tight and warm. I held him back, wishing I could actually move enough to touch him, to open my eyes and see him. But this would do for now. I had been dead, and not just for a few seconds or minutes like some people had experienced. That was going to take some time to wrap my head around.

I felt the heaviness weigh on me again, and I struggled to stay conscious. I wanted to stay here with him, hold him, wake up and see him, but I was being dragged under again and before I could say anything more, I was gone.

~

I pried my eyes open slowly, relieved to find that it took no more effort than when I'd had a rough night. I blinked a few times and let everything come into focus. Slowly, I raised my hands, again grateful that the effort it took was the normal amount. Frowning, I did a mental check over myself. I couldn't feel any pain, no stiffness or aches. I moved my arms and legs carefully, ran my hands down my stomach. But there was no sign I had ever been hurt, much less dead. I turned slowly in the bed, knowing before I saw him that Cole would be there.

He was asleep, his dark lashes like crescents on his cheeks, his lips parted slightly in sleep. I was struck hard with the knowledge of how beautiful he was and how powerful he could be.

I rolled over and slowly reached my hand out to take his. He stirred slightly. I smiled and brushed my mind against his.

"Cole."

I watched as he frowned slightly and then his eyes flew open. Those dark eyes pinned me with a look so mixed with emotion I couldn't tell one from the other. His hand gripped mine tightly and he rolled until I was tucked beneath him, his gaze moving over my face.

"You're awake," he whispered, his voice almost choked.

"You're here."

Cole shook his head and brushed my hair away from my face. "I haven't left your side."

Tears burned my eyes and I leaned up to kiss him. Cole didn't hesitate to kiss me back, and I slid my hands up his chest to link at the back of his neck. He sank against me, and I reveled in the way my body came to life immediately. This kiss was far different from any we'd shared before. It was deep, passionate, slow. There was so much emotion being poured into it, so many words unspoken that when we finally pulled away, I was breathless.

"Don't you ever fucking do that to me again," he ground out, and I caught sight of the sheen of tears in his eyes. I shook my head and framed his face with my hands.

"I'll try," I replied. He cracked a tremulous small smile and then kissed me again, harder this time. I pulled him closer, moving against him, unable to get him close enough. My body burned, my mind melded with his so that I could feel everything he was feeling.

"More," I pleaded.

Cole waved his hand and I found us both naked and hot, his hips wedging themselves between my thighs. This wasn't a desire; this wasn't a want. It was a need, pure and simple. I needed him, needed to feel him as close as I could get him, and I could feel that same demand in him.

He was hard between my legs, ready to go, and I was ready for him. This wasn't going to be long and drawn out. He wasn't going to drive me to insanity with pleasure. This was going to be hard and fast.

Without breaking the kiss, Cole pressed against me and then thrust hard.

I cried out against his lips, and he raised his head from mine. I gasped as he surged forward again, sinking further inside. Over and over, he drove inside me, and I could do nothing more than hold on. He was overtaken with this need to share my skin, have us be one again. I could see into his mind, feel what it had been like for him these last few days. I could see how desperately alone he'd felt with my sudden absence.

We'd almost been lost. This connection had been temporarily numbed and I hated that he had gone through that, that he had suffered so much.

His eyes were dark with anger and lust and something else I

dared not name in case I was wrong. I moved with him, feeling his pace quicken and his cock begin to swell. I was well on my way to a screaming orgasm, and I moaned his name, clawed at his back in an insane attempt to get him closer.

"Come, Mika," Cole demanded through gritted teeth, and as if my body had been conditioned to obey him, I came with a cry. Cole came a second later, his roar of release still ringing in my ears as he thrust hard and fast inside me.

I panted, and Cole tucked his face into the crook of my neck as he struggled to get his own breath back. We just stayed like that for the longest time in silence. I knew he was mad at me. He was mad that I'd gone to the warehouse, mad that I'd gotten in the middle of it all, and mad that I'd been hurt... that I'd died.

I could tell him my reasoning, explain to him my desperation to be at his side and to help. Maybe he would understand. I was sure he could file through my mind right now and see it all, but for now, he had every right to be mad at me.

It didn't matter that I hadn't really died. The Reaper had said we were tied together, and that meant I had dwelled in the in-between until my spirit was strong enough to go back. I didn't understand it really, but I didn't much care right now. I was alive, I was back in Cole's arms. I could look into it all later. The point was, Cole wasn't going to forgive or forget this anytime soon. Not that I could blame him. I could feel him still reeling from losing me and then getting me back. Touching his mind to feel what he'd been through in the last week was beyond painful.

"You suck," Cole finally mumbled against me. The words sounded so foreign on his lips that for a moment I frowned.

"What?"

"You heard me," he muttered and then lifted his head to glare down at me. "You suck. The torture I've been through in the last few days has taught me that I, as a King of Hell, know *nothing* about real pain. The Hell I've been in was so fucked up, Mika, that I don't even know how to describe it."

I opened my mouth to respond, and he pulled away from me, rolling to sit up with his head in his hands. I scrambled into a sitting position and put my hand on his shoulder.

"Tell me what to say," I begged. "I know that anything I say will sound inexcusable and not worth what you've been through. I felt your pain. So just tell me. What do you need to hear from me to make things better?" I asked because I knew in large part, this was my doing. But in my defense, after seeing the fight they were in, I was pretty sure Cole would have died in that battle. And where would I have been?

"There is nothing," he muttered and scrubbed his hands over his head. "Honestly, it's my own fucking fault."

He muttered under his breath and stood up. I was momentarily distracted by the droolworthy shape of him that I zoned out for a second.

"Mika!" Cole shouted. I dragged my gaze back up to his face and he grinned with exasperation.

"Normally I wouldn't mind you checking me out like that, and I will definitely see to it that your desires are filled in a moment, but it would be nice if you were actually listening the first time I tell a woman that I'm in love with her," he added.

I sat back in shock for a moment, wondering if I heard him correctly or if I'd zoned out again.

"Sorry, can you repeat that?"

Cole grinned and sat on the edge of the bed. He gripped my hips and pulled me onto his lap so that I sat with my legs either side of him. He cupped my cheek and slid a hand through my hair before he brushed a gentle kiss across my lips.

"Tomika Johnson," he began and sighed. "The first time I saw you, I almost killed you. You were a human with knowledge of the celestials, that is against the rules. And when I discovered you were a Witch, I had to have you."

I frowned. As far as declarations of love went, we weren't off to a great start.

"Perhaps we started out the wrong way. I sought to use you as a tool for my purposes and didn't much care that you were a living, breathing, being with opinions and needs. But you expressed your opinions... loudly," he added, and I smiled.

"Somewhere along the line, Mika, despite my attempts to keep space between us… I fell in love with you," Cole explained, his dark eyes staring into mine. I felt my heart stutter and leap, butterflies let loose in my stomach.

Cole—King of the First Circle of Hell—loved me?

"Well?" he muttered uncertainly when I didn't say anything.

"I died, didn't I?"

Cole frowned. "Yes," he replied hesitantly.

"And I stayed dead… didn't I? I haven't actually come back to the land of the living," I added, still shocked.

A slow grin spread over Cole's face, and I felt warmth spread across my chest at that smile.

"Did you really think I'd never feel this way about you?" he asked.

"Well… I'm not sure. But don't think I didn't notice that it took my dying for you to admit it," I quipped.

Cole laughed and brought his open palm down over my backside. I yelped and he grinned, something a lot more heated making its way into his eyes.

"Don't forget that it took you dying to say it to me," he reminded me. I grinned and tugged sharply on his hair.

"I guess that makes us pretty well matched then, huh?" I whispered, brushing my lips over his.

"Fucking perfect," he murmured, chasing my lips, but I leaned back, purposely making him work for it. His dark eyes glittered knowingly, and I smiled.

"Hey Cole," I whispered, framing his face and kissing him gently.

"Mmm?" he murmured, his gaze unfocused.

"I love you too."

He stilled, and I felt the air in his lungs freeze as he stared at me, something new brightening in his eyes. He smiled again, slowly, and I shrieked when he spanked me again.

"Don't think saying pretty words is going to get you out of your punishment," he replied.

"I died, don't you think that was punishment enough?" I asked, wiggling to get out of his grasp which only made him hold on tighter.

"No, and it's time you learned your lesson," he laughed and tossed me onto the bed. I tried to get up, but he was on me in a second, pushing me down onto the mattress so that I was lying on my stomach. He straddled my legs and stroked across my backside with gentle fingers

"Cole!" I protested.

Slap.

The sting of his palm against my backside made me yelp.

"This is seriously not necessary," I tried again.

Slap.

"Cole!"

Slap. Slap. Slap.

Between every open-palmed slap, he stroked his fingers across the same spot, soothing, and I shivered and shuddered, feeling my body respond in a way I had not expected.

"In the future when I tell you to stay in our realm, are you going to listen to me?"

"Probably not," I answered quickly. That earned me another three spanks and I shrieked, still struggling to get away.

"The next time I tell you to do something for your own safety, are you going to obey?" he pressed on.

"Not if you could die," I answered without hesitation. Three more spanks. My cheeks were getting sensitive now and between my legs was damp.

"When I give you an order, you are going to obey," he demanded, his voice rough.

"Cole?" He waited. "I love you too."

He moved and flipped me over before straddling me once more, his dark eyes clinging to mine.

"Say it again."

I swallowed and leaned up onto my elbows, raising a hand to trace his face.

"I love you. And I'm sorry you went through so much pain," I whispered, meaning every word of it.

I watched Cole as he swallowed hard, the motion of his throat catching my attention before I looked back up at his eyes.

"Never again, Little Witch," he replied hoarsely, sliding his fingers into my hair where he gripped tightly, bunching my hair and tipping my head back. "I do not want to go through that ever again."

I nodded, as much as his grip would allow, and I waited as he slowly dipped his head to mine. His tongue flicked out, catching my lips for a second before he tugged gently at my lower lip with his teeth. I opened my mouth, and he immediately swept inside, claiming me with a single kiss.

Heart, soul, body, and mind. I could feel each one fusing together, tying tighter than ever before as he kissed me hard. I laid back down as he pressed me into the mattress and parted my thighs as he slid his hand between my legs. I whimpered as he slid first one finger, and then another inside me, playing with me, bringing me closer and closer to the edge.

"Fuck, I love you. I love how your body responds to me, how wet you get for me," he groaned, and I nodded, breathing heavily.

Cole gripped one of my legs and brought it up over his shoulder, and as he met my gaze again, he slammed all the way inside me. My back arched as I almost sobbed his name, my hands fisting in the blankets beneath us. Pleasure bordering on pain, and it was exquisite.

"Yes! I love your pussy, baby," Cole murmured, and I moaned, trying to move with him, but unable to keep up with the brutal, punishing pace he was setting.

"Yes, Cole," I panted, not at all surprised at how close to coming I already was. I was wired to respond to him, my body craved his and I loved it. I loved how easily he could turn me on, how well he already knew my body and how willing he was to learn more, to try more, to push my boundaries to discover new things I liked.

I felt every stroke of his long, hard cock as it worked in and out of me, reveled in every moan and muttered curse as he found himself getting closer to climax. I loved that I could make him lose control like that.

I wrapped my legs around him and tried to turn us so that I was on top, but Cole shoved me back into the mattress, his hand at the base of my neck.

"Not now, not this time," he growled. I inhaled sharply at the rough and dominant action, my body tightening around his and his eyes lit with understanding and knowing. Slowly, he slid his hand up around my throat where he applied pressure. My eyes had to have rolled back in my head as pleasure increased and I moaned again, rocking against him, clawing at the bedspread.

"Oh, I thought you'd like that. Good girl," he practically purred, and I cried out when he tightened his grip a little more, his thrusts becoming more frantic, harder. I freaking *loved* it when he called me a good girl. I was getting closer, closer, my entire body tightening and tensing until...

"Yes!" I screamed, my throat raw and my lungs burning. Rolling waves of bliss rocked through me and I felt him thrust twice more before he roared my name and emptied himself inside me. My orgasm lasted forever, on and on until I wasn't sure I could handle it anymore.

Cole slowly released his grip on my throat, and I gasped, panted, my hair sticking to my face from sweat, my gaze slightly fuzzy and ears blocked by what felt like cotton wool.

"Mine," Cole growled, panting, his dark eyes drilling into mine.

"Yours," I conceded.

CHAPTER NINETEEN
COLE

Two days.

We'd been fucking like rabbits for two days.

My brothers, Nova in particular, but also Malik and Adrik were requesting to see her, but I wasn't willing to give up my time with her yet. I was still struggling to believe that she was back, that she'd somehow survived. Every time I thought about it, which was all the time, I had to reach out and touch her to make sure she was really here. And that inevitably led to more touching and more fucking, which led to us falling asleep from exhaustion just to start it all over again when we woke up. It was a vicious circle, but one I was happy to be stuck in for now. Every time we fucked, I made her say it, made her say the words that still hadn't sunk in yet. The impossibility that someone loved me like that had seemed permanent. But here she was, my Little Witch, in love with me. I knew it was real because I spent a lot of time in her mind lately, just as she did with me. It was hard to accept the truth, even when it was staring me in the face.

I trailed my fingers over the curve of her hip, her waist, up her ribs to rub her breast as she slept. Mika frowned and groaned.

"Cole... I need a break."

I laughed softly and kissed her neck, closing my eyes at the simple act of having her here in my arms.

"How about we go and soak in the pool?" I suggested. Her eyes shot open, and she looked at me suspiciously.

"Are you going to try and have sex with me once we're in the pool?"

Again, I laughed, and she grinned. "Only if you want me to."

"That's the problem," she complained, but her lips were curling into a smile. "I'll always want you to, but my body just can't handle it right now."

"Then we'll simply take a bath," I answered. Mika nodded slowly, and I could feel her exhaustion. Grinning, I slid out of bed and picked her up before I walked us over to the hot springs pool I had built. As we sunk into the hot water, she groaned and closed her eyes.

"You're not helping my resolve not to fuck you," I cautioned. She cracked an eye open and smirked.

"It's good for you to try and learn something new. At your age, keeping an active mind is important," she answered with a grin. I grabbed her hands that were clasped around my neck and forced them apart. With a shriek, she fell into the water and came sputtering to the surface a moment later, pushing the hair back from her face.

"Now, now, Little Witch. You had best be respecting your elders. Or have you forgotten your lesson already?" I teased. She laughed and splashed some water at me, but I caught her hand and tugged her closer. She sighed and rested her head on my chest for a moment and I waved my hand towards the natural soaps Mika had in her belongings. A small amount of it appeared in my hands and I ran them down her back, her arms, kneading it into her sore and tired muscles. Her sighs of pleasure and moans of delight did nothing to help my hard dick pressed between us, but I was happy to forego sex if it meant she had time to heal. I did this to her legs and feet after sitting her on a ledge. I ran my hands over every inch of her, even those tender sensitive spots before I began rubbing shampoo into her hair. Mika almost fell asleep and I grinned as I helped her wash it out.

"Your turn?" she asked, half-asleep.

"Next time, baby," I answered and exhaled in exasperation when I felt Nova tug at my mind for the hundredth time.

"What?"

"Nova has been nagging me since you woke up to talk," I answered.

"Then let's talk to him. I would like to see him too, to be

honest," she answered. I glowered and she laughed, patting my cheek. "Not like that, you moron."

"You say the sweetest things. No wonder I love you," I murmured.

Mika laughed as she exited the steaming pools, and I watched as she closed her eyes. After a few moments, she was dried and fully dressed, her hair brushed and drying in damp strands.

I gave Nova the okay and allowed him entrance into our realm. Our realm.

That was a surprisingly easy term to get used to. I watched as Mika waved her hand towards the bed and it was made, fresh and clean. I grinned. I guessed she didn't want our guest to see any evidence of our last two days. I followed her and got dried and dressed just as Nova entered the room.

His gaze moved until it landed on Mika, and he smiled, relief on his face. Mika's lips curved happily, and she hurried over to hug him.

"You're alive," he murmured, closing his eyes for a second as he hugged her.

"And so are you," she replied with a small, choked laugh.

"Thanks to you," Nova recalled, pulling back to look down at her. Guilt shadowed his features and Mika shook her head.

"I was doing what I do best. Don't you dare feel guilty about it," Mika scolded before hugging him again.

"Okay, that's enough. One hug was plenty," I snapped, not liking all the touching.

Nova's blue gaze met mine and he smiled before pulling away. "You look better, brother," he noted. I nodded, uncomfortable with how he'd seen me last time. But thankfully, he didn't continue talking about it.

"What happened to Uriel?" Mika asked after a moment. Nova clenched his jaw and ducked his head a moment.

"He got away," he answered, his voice low and angry.

"For now," I added.

Nova glanced up at me and slowly nodded. I'd help my brother get that motherfucker. If Nova had felt anything near what I'd gone through over the last few days when they'd killed Tabitha, then I would help him hunt down that asshole one day, and then he could tear him apart.

"I actually have another reason for visiting other than to see you both," he explained after a moment, nodding towards the couch. Mika reached for me, and I took her hand, pulling her onto my lap as we sat. Nova sat opposite us and pulled out a book. One we were both familiar with.

"The book with the prophecy?" I asked. He nodded.

"There was a lot more in here for us to know about The Mark," Nova explained. Mika sat up, but I was glad to see there was no more interest in finding a way out of it, just curiosity.

"What does it say?" she asked.

"Well... basically, this Mark is unique to our kind—the Kings of Hell. Once you bind your souls, the other bindings—body, heart and mind—are like dominoes waiting to fall. There's no escaping any of them. Once the soul-binding is complete, you Mika, became immortal like us. You can die, temporarily, but you'll come back," Nova explained.

Fuck. I wish I'd known that a week ago. Mika looked at me and I could tell she was thinking the same thing.

"What else?" she asked.

"You can conceive," he threw out quickly. Mika stilled on my lap, and I gripped her thighs. I hadn't given children a thought. None of us could have kids, we'd always known that. So how...

"Because Mika was mortal when you were bound, she can bring that ability over with her. However, you can only conceive once every fifty years or so. Think of it as nature's birth control," Nova added with a grin.

"How will we know when I can get pregnant?" Mika asked softly, and I caught the tail-end of the worry in her mind. We hadn't once used any form of contraception. I hadn't thought it was necessary. Witches, like Demons, could not contract diseases like humans. And Demons didn't have the ability to have children.

"I guess you'll just know. It mentions something about a cycle and that your body will let you know," Nova explained with a shrug.

Mika sagged slightly against me, and I laughed at the relief. I wasn't ready for kids yet either. The idea of it was going to take a while to get used to. I'd always known we couldn't have kids, so I'd never considered what life could be like with them.

"Your offspring will be a Demon-Witch hybrid. Not sure I've seen one, so it'll be interesting to see how that turns out," Nova threw in. Mika nodded slowly, and I could still feel her shock.

"Was that all of it?" I asked. Nova shook his head and sighed.

"It seems, when you Marked Mika, you set in motion a chain of events that we're going to be helpless to stop. One by one, each of us brothers will fall. From the first to the last. Now I don't know if they will all be Witches, but it looks like you have started us all off to finding our mates," Nova explained.

"Uh... sorry?" I answered uncertainly. Nova grinned and shook his head.

"You guys were fated, the information regarding the prophecy was very clear. We each have *one* mate out there, and she has already been chosen for us. We'll know it when we find her, and we'll feel that unstoppable desire to Mark her like you did with Mika," Nova explained.

Mika had gone very still, and I looked up at her with a frown. Her mind was closed to me again, the way it sometimes did when she was trying not to think of whatever it was that she was hiding. I squeezed her thigh to get her attention.

"Mika... just tell me already."

She looked down at me with wide eyes, and I raised an eyebrow.

"Nova and I have known since your first day here that you've been holding something back. Surely you know you can trust us by now," I encouraged.

Mika bit down on her lower lip and considered my words, guilt eating at her, but also a desperate need to tell us. She raised her eyes slowly to look at Nova whose face was impassive.

"I think you already know," she barely whispered. He didn't move for a moment, and then slowly nodded.

"Know what?" I demanded, frustrated at being the only one who didn't know.

"You're a twin," Nova announced. I felt my eyes widen and I turned to look at her.

"Really?"

Mika nodded and sighed, her shoulders slumping as she got to her feet.

"My twin and I were together until we were seven, then we were separated. I wanted to keep her a secret from you at first because I didn't want her forced into a life like this, where she would be a prisoner and used like she was some kind of tool against your enemies," Mika began. I didn't say anything to that, completely understanding.

"But then you told me how Witches are rare and will be hunted. And I began to worry about her, about how safe she really was out there. While I don't want her held anywhere against her will, I don't want her caught by the Angels either," Mika added, her gaze on Nova. Why was she telling him? And then I realized... she was only telling him because she wanted him to be the one to find her.

"Only you, Nova," Mika whispered her eyes hard and determined. "I only trust *you* to find her," she added.

"I swore to your ancestor, Tabitha, that she and her family would be safe," Nova began softly. "I failed when she was alive. And when you came back, I thought that was my second chance to redeem myself. Your family always produces female twins. I thought you had to have a sister out there, unless something happened to her," Nova explained softly.

"Will you find her? Keep her safe?" Mika asked softly, but there was a desperation to her. She had held onto this secret longer than anything else in order to protect her sister.

"You have my word, Mika. I will find her and protect her with my life," Nova answered solemnly.

"She will not be a prisoner," Mika added with a glare. Nova grinned and shook his head.

"If she is anything like you, like your ancestors, that would be impossible," he answered. Mika considered him carefully for several long moments before she released a pent-up breath and her shoulders sagged.

"Thank you, Nova. I know she'll be safe with you."

After a moment, Nova turned to look at me. "I will head out to look for her in the next couple of days. In the meantime... We found Krae. He's in my realm," Nova announced.

"You found the traitorous bastard?" I growled.

"I thought you might like to be a part of the interrogation," he answered. I looked over at Mika, trying to gauge her reaction and she shrugged.

"I won't get in the way of your Demon business," she promised.

I turned back to Nova and grinned. "Let's go pay him a visit."

~

I left Mika to get some rest and followed my brother into his realm. Nova preferred to have a castle setting in his realm lately. Stone walls, brass chandeliers that held candles, iron holders for live-flame torches. We walked straight for a balcony, and I followed Nova down the spiraling stairs. We entered the sixth circle of Hell and I nodded to a few Knights who stopped to stand at attention as we walked on by. We passed The Pit, and I took a moment to see how things were progressing. I had neglected my duties as King for the last few weeks, and I needed to get back to it soon. But for now, my attention was all for one Knight.

I followed Nova into his dungeons, and we walked past several cells until we came to one at the back. We paused outside the door and Nova turned to look at me.

This asshole had betrayed my brother. He had intended to have him murdered in order to take his throne. Krae had then almost killed me and would have succeeded had Mika not happened by. He turned to our enemies and attempted yet again to kill us. He was the reason Mika had died. Krae may not have been the one to stab her, but he'd been the reason we were there, why there was a fight, why the Angels now knew about Mika.

"Let's go."

We entered the dungeon and my gaze moved immediately to the former Knight of Hell who was chained to the stone wall. He was already pretty roughed up, bleeding and swelling.

"The other Knight who found him took a personal affront to his betrayal and delivered a little warm-up punishment," Nova explained when I continued to study Krae. I nodded and looked the Demon over. He didn't bother to raise his eyes, just kept his head hung low.

He was pathetic. I almost wanted to walk out and just let others deal with him, but then I remembered the last few days I'd spent in my own personal Hell. I remembered his smirking face, his audacity to work with the Angels and the Rogue Demons. No, this fucker needed a little personal vengeance delivered before he suffered through mundane pain.

"Do not touch my mind until I reach for you, Little Witch. I do not wish for you to see this," I warned. I felt a flutter of warmth and acceptance.

Turning around, I grabbed the edge of the dungeon door and slowly closed it, carefully disconnecting my mind from Mika's, allowing every murderous thought I'd had about this Knight over the last several weeks to flood my mind and feed my anger.

"Let's get started," I said softly to Nova.

Hours later, I shook my head at the sobbing, bleeding mess of what remained of the ex-Knight and wished myself clean and fresh again. I was done. I had handed out my pain, but I just didn't care for him anymore. I had a woman to get back to, and this sorry excuse for a Knight had taken enough of our time away from us.

"Time to hand him over to Corvin?" Nova asked. Krae whimpered at the sound of our brother's name. And so he should. Corvin was in the ninth circle of hell, and he dealt with the true evil in the world. The level of torture he and his Knights delivered on a daily basis was truly something for all Demons to fear.

"Yeah, I've had enough of this waste of space taking up my time," I answered.

"Please, no. I'm sorry," Krae sobbed, trying to reach us but the chains didn't allow him.

We ignored him and headed for the door where Nova called for two of his Knights. He gave them instructions as to what to do with Krae, and then together we left the dungeons.

I allowed my mind to touch Mika's again and found her just waking up from a nap. Her warmth enveloped me at once and I let go of every dark and ugly thing down here. I had something amazing waiting for me in my home, and Krae had taken up the last of my time that I'd allow.

EPILOGUE
MIKA

"Fuck off, Cole," I snapped, throwing a pillow at him.

"No," he returned.

"Seriously, go away. You're annoying me," I repeated, flinging another pillow at him.

"I'm so glad you two are beyond this point," Adrik sighed, watching in amusement as Cole and I argued. It wasn't an odd occurrence to watch us fight. Despite the fact that we were in love and that we were bound together for all time, we still fought like crazy. Admittedly, it usually resulted in mind-blowing make-up sex, but I was beginning to tire of his constant supervision.

"I refuse to leave you alone," Cole reminded.

"I noticed. But I'm not alone. I'm practicing my magic and healing with your brothers. Do you really think I would betray you with one of them, or that they would even consider betraying you with me?" I demanded.

Cole glowered and crossed his arms.

"Well?"

"I don't think that."

"Right. Well then, you need to loosen up the reins and go take care of your circle. I'm fine here, go," I demanded.

Cole usually only got this antsy when I was outside of our realm. In there, I had full power to toss anyone out with a single command. Our realm answered to us, and so when someone was in it who didn't belong, I had the power to throw them out and keep them out, therefore keeping me safe. Cole hated when I insisted on working in the arrival room because any of the Demons or his brothers could bump into me there. While I didn't trust all of the Knights or other Demons, I trusted Cole's brothers not to try and run away with me.

"Fine," Cole grumbled. "Nova reached out earlier anyway. He thinks that he found your sister's last address, but she's moved on again. So, he'll keep us updated as he goes."

My heart clenched at the thought of my sister. I knew she was alive, I'd known all this time, but I needed to know that she was okay. And the fact that she moved so frequently had me worried. She was obviously on the run. Nova was yet to find a place where she'd stayed longer than a month, and almost always with a different name. Who was she running from? Was it someone who was human, or did she know Angels and Demons were looking for her?

I felt the warmth of Cole's arms around me at once, despite the fact that he was on the other side of the room. I closed my eyes and drew on his strength. I knew looking for my sister would be hard, but I never counted on feeling so helpless and worried. Somehow, when I hadn't looked for her, I'd managed to convince myself that she was living this amazing, safe life. I should have known better. If I could not deny my need to heal, then she wouldn't be able to either.

I looked down at the star birthmark on my arm and recalled one of the few memories I had of her. We were six and called each other Star Sisters. We thought our stars gave us special powers. We weren't far off, it turned out.

I had spent the last several weeks learning everything I could about my family, or what there was to learn anyway. And I had been experimenting with my power, building on it, working at using it longer and more intensely without getting tired. It was like any workout; the more I trained, the better I got. I was learning to remember spells and other incantations that I had no previous knowledge of. I was thriving as a Witch, finally happy to know *what* I was.

But, it had been a long day already, and now thinking of my sister, I was exhausted. I just wanted to know that she was safe, and that Nova was able to get her somewhere where she'd be out of danger. Maybe we could see each other again? We hadn't seen each other in forever, but I missed her so much.

"Come on, let's call it a day," Cole suggested. I huffed my displeasure but nodded. He was right, I wouldn't be able to concentrate now anyway.

"Thanks, Adrik. Same time tomorrow?" I asked.

"Sure."

"But in our realm," Cole demanded. I glared and rolled my eyes. It had been two months since I'd gone and died on him. I knew he wasn't likely to get over it any time soon, but it had been *two months*! Was he ever going to let up even a little?

"Not where your safety is concerned, Little Witch. Never then," Cole whispered.

I smiled gently and leaned into him as he wrapped an arm around me as we walked into our realm. If someone had told me when Cole had first come into my life that I would be this happy this early on, I'd have laughed in their face.

Turns out. Fate really does know what it's doing.

~

COLE

I grinned as Mika sank against me, and I reveled in that trust. She was mine, totally and completely, and I was hers. I had no doubt about it, and honestly, I didn't care who knew. My brothers gave me shit about it, but that was okay. None of them knew what they were missing out on and how everything we went through, everything I compromised on, was well worth it in the end. I had realized early on that her happiness was a vital part of my peace of mind. However, it was a balancing act when her happiness compromised her safety. And her safety, above all else, even her happiness, was paramount.

Thankfully, for the most part, Mika knew and understood this. She fought back—hard—and I loved it. But when it came down to it, she let me keep her safe. If she was feeling petty, she'd make me feel bad about it later, but then I punished her and our make-up sex was off the charts hot.

My little minx was insatiable and I was more than up for the challenge.

Our realm had more greenery in it than it used to have, and I'd gotten used to Mika talking to the plants. It was amusing to see that the plants actually responded. They grew thick and lush, and seemed to lean towards her whenever she walked by them, as if eager for her touch. And she never let them down, always reaching out to stroke a leaf or a flower. It was different, but also soothing to have so much life inside the cave.

Another obstacle we'd faced, and this argument had lasted a week, was whether or not Mika could go on the surface without me. I said no, she said yes. We fought, and it got ugly. Eventually we compromised on her *always* being accompanied by my most trusted Knight, Niro. He was the first Knight I ever promoted and had never once swayed in his loyalties from me. I was worried at first, still smarting from the betrayal of Krae, to put one in charge of looking after my mate. But all the Knights had been taken down to Corvin's realm and watched what happened to any Knight or Demon who betrayed us. The demonstration was long, bloody, and brutal. I felt secure that Niro would not betray me before the demonstration, but I was certain now.

Niro kept in contact with me constantly when he took Mika to the surface, and she had agreed to wear a magically enhanced ring that allowed for me to track her. She had seen the truth in my mind when I explained that this was not to keep tabs on her, but to have the chance to find her if an Angel or Rogue got the jump on her and took her away. I was a little worried that whatever the Angel's had done last time to prevent us from communicating would affect us again, despite the ring. I had plans to test it sometime later using myself and another Demon. Mika knew I was telling the truth in my reasons to have her wear the ring and allowed it. I had one made up for myself and told her that we were as good as married. That statement had earned me a slap on the back of my head. Apparently, being bound mind, body, soul, and heart didn't count and that if I wanted to marry her, I'd have to ask, and we'd have a wedding. I rolled my eyes. I was not interested in it, but I could see into her mind and saw that it was important to her, to be asked this time and feel like she had a choice.

It was more important to her than she even let herself know. And she said she wanted to be married before we had children. Children.

That was still a mind-fuck for me, but I had begun to warm up to the idea. I didn't want to start anytime soon, but the idea of having a kid was growing on me.

I pulled Mika inside our realm and slammed the door, spinning her around and pressing her against it. She grinned and didn't resist as I kissed her. It was a long, slow kiss that went on and on until we were both breathless. I ran my hands down her back, to her backside where I squeezed and then lifted her up. She wrapped her legs around my hips immediately and I kissed her again, determined to wipe away that shadow of sadness and worry in her mind now that the subject of her sister had been brought up.

Fuck, she was it for me. She was beyond anything I could have dreamed up, anything I could have wished for. She was sassy and sexy, vulnerable, and strong.

She was everything.

And she was *mine*.

THE END

THANK YOU FOR READING

KINGS OF HELL
COLE

If you loved Cole's & Mika's story, then come find me on Facebook or Instagram to stay in touch.
There will be many more Kings of Hell books, as well as a multitude of other paranormal romances by Alexis Maree!

The Kings of Hell – Adrik (Book Two)
IS AVAILABLE NOW!

Thanks again for reading, be sure to come find me so you don't miss out!

DID YOU KNOW...
I HAVE TWO OTHER PEN NAMES?

I know that seems like overkill, but there is a method to my madness.

Books under the name **Alexis Maree** are for paranormal romances. Not everyone likes to read this genre, so I like to keep them separate.

Likewise, not everyone likes contemporary romances, so I have another pen name for those...**T. Maree.**

Then last, but certainly not least, are my sinfully sexy romances, the ones that border on the line of "*should she really put that down in print?*"
Some people don't like those kinds of spicy scenes, and so I decided to keep those separate from the rest under the name **Luna Maree.**

So, if you'd like to check out what else I've written, go onto my website.

Happy reading!

Alexis | Luna | T.